Zeppelin Tales

AIRSHIP 27 PRODUCTIONS

Zeppelin Tales Volume One
Death Seeds the Clouds © 2013 Jim Beard
Airship 27 © 2013 I.A. Watson

Published by Airship 27 Productions
www.airship27.com
www.airship27hangar.com

Interior illustrations © 2013 Pedro Cruz
Cover illustration © 2013 Mike Fyles

Editor: Ron Fortier
Associate Editor: Gordon Dymoswski
Production and design by Rob Davis
Promotions and marketing by Michael Vance

ISBN-13: 978-0615915548
ISBN-10: 061591554X

Printed in the United States of America

10 9 8 7 6 5 4 3 2 1

Zeppelin Tales

TABLE OF CONTENTS

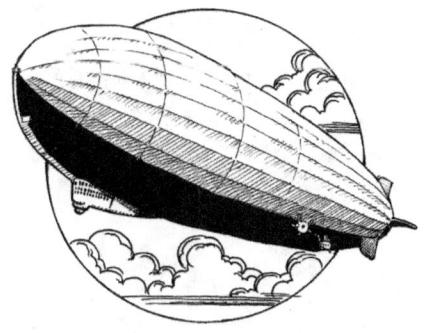

Death Seeds the Clouds

By Jim Beard

O n his sixteenth birthday Tracer Talbot's father presented him with an airplane. By way of gratitude, the very next day Tracer ran away to become an itinerant air courier. Since then, he and his old man had become the best of friends.

Tracer's father had proclaimed his son a "real barnstormer" at the tender age of twelve, and the animals of the family farm had learned to recognize the sound of the old Beardmore W.B. III the young lad practiced in—and get out of its way. Tracer was born with feathers in his blood.

His birthday 'plane was a Vickers Vimy, typically used as an army ambulance—Tracer never knew exactly where his father acquired her and he had never asked. He called it Anna Lynne and told people she spoke with a British accent. Anna Lynne was a fat old thing but served Tracer well.

Together, they worked their way up and down the Canadian border, hauling freight and sometimes people and making very little money. Tracer had never been happier in his entire life.

Anna Lynne was several years old now and the countless miles that Tracer had put on her in that time had begun to take a toll. That and his almost constant lack of funds to keep her in good health, of course. The life of an itinerant air courier had been an exciting career for a young man such as Tracer but it didn't exactly break the bank. He'd eaten a lot of crackers and missed a lot of servicing for his Anna Lynne, but his current gig promised a hefty enough sum that he figured he could treat the old girl to a visit to the airplane doctor.

That current gig, now riding in the hold, came in the form of a stunning female beauty with a tiny waist and nice legs. Dressed in stylish yet sensible clothes, she'd arrived perfumed and pretty at Tracer's temporary quarters in upstate New York and asked to be flown to Nova Scotia. She offered two-thousand dollars for the ride. Tracer almost choked on his crackers.

The young woman introduced herself as "Miss Smith" but he was pretty sure that wasn't really her name. Tracer, possessing what most folks called a good-natured disposition, didn't ask a lot of questions of his new boss, just when she needed to arrive at her destination and when she'd be ready to leave. Simple as that. Miss Smith opened her satchel, pulled out a wad of bills and paid the young man half in advance. He liked her already.

Somewhere over Canada Tracer Talbot coaxed more power out of Anna Lynne's twin Napier Lion engines and together they ascended to 12,000 feet. He was tempting fate, that he knew all too well, but he wanted to get above the clouds and felt sure the old girl could handle it—at least for a little while.

Breaking through the clouds then, he saw the giant airship.

To be more accurate, he didn't just see it—he almost ran into it. Tracer had come up right underneath the immense crate and far too close for his or Anna Lynne's comfort.

So, the young pilot had little time, then, for the incredible sight to register on his hazel eyes, for the turbulence created by the giant's own motors hit his Anna Lynne like a boulder dropped on a feather bed. He clutched at the controls and did what he did best—flew. While he tried to settle the craft, Tracer looked up at the source of his current troubles.

He guessed the Zeppelin—if it *was* a Zeppelin—to be at least a thousand feet long and covered in a silvery, reflective coating of a sort. He also counted at least ten monstrous engines along its unimaginable length. It was big, a monster. Tracer had never heard of an airship that big and he wondered who could have built such a whopper—and why.

But, at that moment, it was fixing to upset his Anna Lynne.

Tracer pushed the stick down, tried to keep Anna Lynne's nose from pointing at the airship, but the winds buffeting them threatened to rip the wings right off her fuselage. Fighting the stick was like trying to rein in a bucking bronco. Maybe worse. The giant Zeppelin seemed to pay them no mind and Tracer decided that no matter how fantastic a sight the airship was he didn't care much for it trying to throw him out of the sky.

Somebody's unreasonably large balloon had cast a long shadow over them. It didn't sit well with Tracer Talbot, or his air wagon for that matter. They got along pretty well and he didn't want to break up the partnership just yet.

A light touch of a hand on Tracer's shoulder reminded him just then that he had a passenger onboard.

"Everything's jake," he shouted good-naturedly to the girl over the nigh-deafening drone of the great airship's engines. "Go back and belt yourself in! It may be a bit bumpy from here on out!"

Then, Tracer did something pretty strange; he started singing.

He was born Oliver Jenkins Talbot but his father took to calling him "Tracer." The elder Talbot had designed a new kind of tracer bullet that was used heavily by Allied forces in the war. When his young son's penchant for singing at every occasion, sad or happy, began to manifest the old man used to say he could always trace his boy high and low through his singing. Rain or shine, Tracer Talbot sang.

While trying to keep Anna Lynne from kissing that airship, he belted out "Loch Lomond."

Miss Smith rolled her eyes and clicked her tongue. The quality of Tracer's voice was not all that abhorrent, but, as a music teacher he had once ferried to Green Bay, Wisconsin once told him, he had "questionable pitch."

He and Miss Smith had said very little to each other before takeoff and with Anna Lynne's tiny open-air cockpit all but separated from the rest of her bulk there'd been scant few words since. Tracer had thanked Heaven for that; he didn't need the distraction of Miss Smith's legs while flying. Unfortunately, in the heat of the current crisis, the young woman stood her ground and refused to return to her perch in the hold.

Regardless, Tracer Talbot had a few other things to worry about.

Even above the din of the airship's motors, he could hear the gunshot-pop from Anna Lynne's left engine. Looking over at it and fearing for the pistons, Tracer saw a bright flash, then tongues of fire and smoke soon after. Dark, black-as-pitch smoke. The entire aircraft shuddered and the stick jumped in his hand as if it had gained a life of its own.

The young pilot did not curse, though no one could blame him if at the moment he did. Tracer instead broke into "You're the Top." He knew it was one of Anna Lynne's favorites.

They skirted quite close to the flat underbelly of the great airship and Tracer caught flashes of its immense, sleek gondola as they passed. Then, up ahead, he saw something dropping down from the ship.

It looked for all the world like a circus trapeze.

A memory floated up from the depths of Tracer's recollect. He'd read somewhere that some Zeppelins were what they called "flying aircraft carriers." To wit, they had hangars for small, one-seater planes. The scaffolding extending in front of him had to be that which held the planes in the airship and also released them. Two and two sidled up to each other in Tracer's brain and lo, the number four presented itself.

He pointed Anna Lynne at the steel trapeze. The smoke and flame from her busted engine were becoming even thicker and her response was sluggish at best. Tracer sang louder.

"What are you doing, sir?" shouted Miss Smith behind him. Tracer thought her voice carried an accent of some sort—probably Eastern European. He couldn't pinpoint it.

"Go back," he bellowed. "And plant yourself in front of the side hatch! Don't open it until I tell you! Okay?"

"Open it?" she queried. "What do you mean? Why should I open it?"

Tracer ignored her and concentrated on keeping Anna Lynne's nose up. He matched the speed of the great airship and brought his old girl as close up to the trapeze as he could without connecting with it.

Close, but no cigar—not quite yet, he mused.

He looked up and into a darkened t-shaped opening in the belly of the airship. He saw immediately it was definitely made for a small fighter plane, not for the girth and length of a Vickers Vimy. Tracer stole a glance behind him, through the small opening between the cockpit and the hold. To her credit, Miss Smith had positioned herself in front of the hatch, hands planted firmly on its latch but not trying to open it. She looked up at him. Miss Smith appeared calm, for the most part.

He winked at her.

Still fighting the stick and flying with only one engine, Tracer urged Anna Lynne forward and settled her with the trapeze arrangement just outside her side hatch. Cole Porter's observation of the weight of Garbo's salary sprung from his lips. It was now or never.

Tracer swiveled his head back to his passenger. "Now! Open it!"

Back in Chillicothe, Ohio, the young man had never been mistaken for a daredevil or a show-off by the locals. In fact, there were times when the elder Talbot was complimented by his neighbors for raising such a level-headed boy; Tracer entered into crisis in a thoughtful manner—most times. Such an attitude, an outlook on the world and its love affair with fate, had gotten him through not a few scrapes since he had left the little town.

He fervently hoped this attitude would see him through the present conflagration.

Tracer heard the hatch thrown open behind him and felt the rush of wind through it. Stealing yet another glance to check his aim, he spied Miss Smith gripping the hatch frame and braving the force of the wind. The onrushing gale tore at her small yet appealing figure and whipped her skirts up to reveal strong thighs above shapely calves. With heels firmly planted on the deck and her chestnut brown hair dancing like a dervish around her head, she looked virtually Amazonian.

"Shove off!" yelled Tracer, and without missing a beat the girl disappeared through the hatch. Anna Lynne lurched.

Because of the airplane's ponderous design, the pilot had no real idea if Miss Smith had made it onto the trapeze. For all he knew, she'd missed and fallen to her death. Wasting no time and trying desperately to shove the image of the girl's legs into a locker far at the back of his thoughts, Tracer put on the air brakes and watched as Anna Lynne seemingly jolted backwards.

He got right up underneath what he hoped was his ticket out—the steel trapeze. It was all so seat-of-the-pants. The thought disquieted him for some reason.

Miss Smith and her wonderful legs hovered into view, incredibly holding onto the trapeze for dear life. Still, she was not frantic. Tracer wondered what kind of a person she was to be able to hang from an arrangement of welded metal piping roughly 12,000 feet above the earth and not scream in terror.

Mentally, he shrugged; it obviously didn't matter much at the moment.

The girl's perch hung directly over him now. Tracer deftly unclipped his pilot's harness. Reaching up he grabbed a steel pipe and realized he was looking right up Miss Smith's skirts.

Anna Lynne's other engine popped its cork. Tracer pulled himself up. Anna Lynne dropped. The two parted ways.

Now engulfed in fire and smoke, the Vickers Vimy plummeted earthward. Tracer Talbot watched as his Anna Lynne, his sixteenth birthday present, began to break up as she shrank out of view. First a wing, then the other, then the entire fuselage cracked in two. Finally, she was gone.

Miss Smith tried to pull the young man up to where she held onto the trapeze but her efforts were, understandably under the circumstances, feeble. The wind was too strong.

Tracer pulled himself up, somehow. Some inner reserve of strength lent him the sheer muscle to lift his body higher and to a relatively more secure place on the steel arrangement. His head swam. Looking at Miss Smith's concerned face, she seemed to go in and out of focus. Tracer wrapped his arms and legs more tightly around the steel tubing.

He felt a hand on his cheek, soft and timid. "The Daring Young Man on the Flying Trapeze" sprang into his head, but he thought better of allowing its release.

Once inside the giant airship, Tracer Talbot and Miss Smith were taken in hand by two steel-faced men dressed in silvery garb. The clothes resembled the outer coating of the airship itself. Tracer wondered at that.

He also afforded himself a look around the hangar into which he and the young woman had ascended. It was devoid of aircraft; Tracer could only surmise the presumed plane was out on patrol.

He also noticed Miss Smith was a wreck.

Disheveled and wind-blown, she still looked very lovely to Tracer but he could tell she herself wasn't too thrilled with her present condition—her outfit was torn in several places, though she still held tight to her satchel. Miss Smith asked their handlers if there was an area that she might use to "freshen up."

A polite-yet-tight smile appeared on the face of one of the men and he asked both Tracer and the girl to follow along, please.

Together, they exited the hangar and entered a long corridor. Tracer guessed that they were inside the airship proper and not its gondola. He knew that in such rigid-construction craft—as opposed to glorified balloons—cargo and crew were often housed internally. My, what a big airship this one was, he thought.

The corridor's floor felt springy, almost as if padded somehow. So too did its walls. Tracer mused that the ship might be a loony-bin of some sort. He started singing "My Old Kentucky Home."

The group stopped at a cross corridor and one of the men lightly touched Miss Smith's elbow. Tracer noted that her arm jerked minutely. If the man also noted it, he paid it no mind.

"If the young lady would follow me," he said. "I will show her to a cabin." He gestured down the new corridor. Miss Smith nodded curtly.

They started down the hallway and Tracer likewise, but the other man caught the pilot's arm. "This way, sir." He made a motion in the opposite direction. "The captain would like a word with you, please."

Amazed at his surroundings, Tracer Talbot also noticed he didn't feel like he was in an airborne craft. If not for the constant drone of its engines, he would have imagined he was still on the ground - quite a difference from Anna Lynne.

The thought of his old girl brought him up short, but he belted out a new stanza of "Old Kentucky Home" and motioned for his guide to lead the way.

The corridor they traversed—Tracer guessed they were now headed toward the fore of the ship—soon opened up into a wider passageway. At that point, the young man realized they were passing by the airship's hold. The massiveness of the area took Tracer's breath away. Here there were more of the crew, all dressed in the same silvery uniforms, and all of them focused on squaring away huge crates, drums and other containers.

Tracer read off the stenciling on the crates: wheat, corn, salt, sugar, and other similar foodstuffs.

"Need a lot of food for a large crew, I imagine," he said to his guide. "How many do you have at any given time?"

The man in silver only smiled slightly and gestured for Tracer to keep moving.

Eventually, they came to a large hatchway. Tracer's guide spun the hatch wheel and turned the latch. The hatch swung open soundlessly, revealing a darkened room beyond. The man bowed ever so slightly and motioned for Tracer to step inside.

Tracer Talbot good-naturedly entered the room, figuring he had little choice at the moment. He'd meet the captain of this monumental airship and tell him his sorry tale. Perhaps they'd have a drink over it and a friendly laugh.

The hatch swung closed behind him and the young pilot was utterly swallowed up by the inky darkness. The room had an antiseptic odor about it.

Standing silently for a moment, listening and hearing nothing, Tracer began to hum "My Country 'Tis of Thee."

Presently, a soft glow began to appear on the opposite side of the room. It grew brighter and in the middle of it Tracer could make out the silhouette of what appeared to be a very large man sitting in a chair. There was a certain strange bulkiness about him, but Tracer guessed it wasn't that the man was fat but rather that he was cloaked in either heavy garments or perhaps even armor of a sort.

He could also discern a dripping or bubbling sound that periodically grew louder and then ebbed away. Tracer could now also make out the edges of an immense porthole with louvered shutters—closed—behind the shadowy figure.

"Captain Nemo, I presume?" said Tracer.

Came a light wheezing noise, almost a chuckle. "Well," said the man. "I am certainly glad to know that our young people of today are well-read."

"But no resemblance that you see?" asked Tracer.

"No," answered the man. "No, Verne's captain was more, shall we say, *erudite* than myself. I am a bit more rough-around-the-edges, sir."

The mystery man's accent was difficult to place, not unlike Miss Smith's, thought Tracer.

"Why can't I be allowed to see you?"

The man sighed. "My sincere apologies for that, my young friend. Let us just say that you would not care much for what you would see. Put it down to shyness on my part, if you wish. But do allow me to introduce myself - you may call me Captain Dusk. And you are…?"

"O.J. Talbot," the pilot responded. "My friends call me Tracer. This is an incredible airship. Is it a Zeppelin?"

"Right to the point," chuckled-wheezed the man. "I like that. Technically, I suppose in some ways it *is* a Zeppelin, but it is also a one-of-a-kind creation. A fact you may already have discerned. I have moved far past Count von Zeppelin in his day. The *Silver Cloud* is one of the marvels of the modern world—and I say that without an ounce of ego or bluster.

"Now, you say your name is Talbot? Would you be in any way related to Wellington Talbot, the inventor of the Talbot Tracer?"

"My turn to be impressed with you, I guess," Tracer replied. "Yep, he's my old man."

The man shifted his great bulk in his chair and the dripping-bubbling sound increased momentarily and then fell away again. Once settled, he spoke anew.

"Excellent. Your father is a great man. His service to the war effort cannot be understated. Yes, a great man. He cared for the common soldier in the trenches. He stood for something.

"What do *you* stand for, young Tracer?"

Tracer found himself in a mood to ignore the line of questioning. He wanted to know more about the craft in which he was apparently now stranded. But there was one other thing he needed to say.

"Thank you for saving us. It was good of you to bring us aboard."

"Yes," said the man. "I'm afraid that as well as our object-detection apparatus operates, you came in a bit too fast and a bit too low for us to avoid you completely. My apologies again."

Tracer furrowed his brow. "Object-detection…?"

"Ah, perhaps you are unfamiliar with the recent work of Girardeau and Kühnhold? The device works with radio waves to detect the—"

"You mean what Tesla was working on?" interjected Tracer. "I lost track of that. Didn't realize it had advanced that far."

"It has its, well, blind spots, but my own innovations with the technology have put us ahead of everyone else. It is not a perfect system, of course, but I stake the *Silver Cloud*'s safety on it, young man."

Tracer found his even keel beginning to slip away. He decided to dispense with the pleasantries.

"Who built this airship? And why? And who are you, exactly? You say 'everyone else' - what country do you represent?"

"All good and rightfully pertinent questions, sir," said the man. "You and your companion have been through a horrible ordeal and I suspect you would appreciate time to rest and recuperate from it. Let us say—"

Tracer cut him off. "I lost an airplane, my livelihood, because of this monstrosity. Yes, you did save us, in a fashion, but you have to admit this is all together an odd situation…" He waved impotently at the ceiling, the floor and walls, trying to take in the immensity of it all.

The man sighed again. "I am not accustomed to being questioned. *I* built this airship. It is of my own design and constructed under my exacting specifications. I represent no single nation, not any more…but, in a way, I represent *all* nations.

"There is much I am not willing to tell you, Tracer. My crew and I are in almost constant danger of exposure and we are in almost constant motion to stay out of said danger. We have many enemies, those that would both stop us from our work and capture this craft for their own. I cannot allow either of those to transpire. There are many, many people who depend upon us."

Tracer chewed on that, rolled it over and took it apart. It didn't seem to make much sense to him.

"What work?" he asked. "You're referring to all that food in your hold? How could the world not already know of this gigantic ship? It isn't exactly the kind of thing that'd be easy to hide! And the fuel to power it and the helium you'd need to fill it…"

"A hydrogen-helium mixture, to be exact," noted the man. "I can see by your face that you know that to be an impossibility, but suffice to say that I have discovered that the addition of a certain other element to the mix solves the inherent problems with the utilization of both of the gases in question. The new combination is light, inexpensive to produce and, most important, completely non-flammable.

"This ship—*my* ship—will not be another *Hindenburg*."

The young man felt he wasn't really getting anywhere with his host. Maybe he was coming on too strong, but wasn't *he* the one put-upon here? Didn't he have the right to pose a few questions instead of fielding them?

"May I ask where you were going, you and your passenger, when our fates intertwined, Mr. Talbot? And what can you tell me of the young lady?"

"You'll have to ask her for her particulars, Captain," barked Tracer. "She hired me to fly her up to Nova Scotia—I suppose that's out of the question now—otherwise, I don't know a scrap about her. Sorry!"

The shadowy man seemed to lean forward a bit, despite his bulk, and Tracer heard a rustling of cloth and something else. Something he couldn't quite put his finger on.

"Hmm, I will have her brought here to me, then. Know that I cannot be too careful with those we come into contact with, my young friend. As I said, there are adversaries who would stand in my way. Stop what I do."

"And again I ask you—what *is* that?" queried Tracer. Good-naturedness only went so far, as his old man always said.

"We bring comfort and aid to those around the globe who need it, Mr.. Talbot. Those oppressed and those distressed and those whose fortunes put them on the bottom of the pecking order. This ship is an *angel of mercy*, if you will. It provides sustenance and, well, hope. Or at least I'd like to think so.

"War is coming, Mr. Talbot. Another world war. Oh, there are certain nations who'd like to believe it isn't, who'd like to hide their heads in the sand, but a new global conflict is inevitable given the current atmosphere. The aggressors and the invaders are already lining up their soldiers and

"The shadowy man seemed to lean forward."

their butchers to have at it with the weaker, peace-loving nations of the world."

Tracer controlled his voice, to hide the cold feeling that had just washed over him.

"And you think *you* can play a role in the fight?"

"No!" bellowed the man. "It's not a stage play! It's *war*, sir, and this ship, this vessel that took me twenty-five years to build with my own money, will hover above it and bring light to those who are torn apart by that war. I was once a man of war myself, decorated and feted, but those things pale after a while. *Peace* is the only pursuit in my…my second chance at life. A life of peace, yes."

The man went silent and all that Tracer heard for some long minutes was a slight wheezing. He felt he dared not speak.

"I regret the unfortunate loss of your aircraft, Mr. Talbot," said the man, finally. "I regret the necessity of bringing you into my orbit. Very few people on this planet know of the existence of this airship. I intend to keep it that way. It makes it easier to slip in and out of certain areas in the world that have need of what I can provide. I hope you understand."

"I understand that this is the most cockamamie deal I've ever seen," said Tracer. "Just do me a favor and spare me any more of your spiel. Drop me and my passenger off at the nearest airfield and you can go on about your business…whatever it is."

He turned toward the hatch and placed his hands on it.

"It seems I must apologize again, sir," the man said. "The situation is an unusual one, to be sure, but I cannot allow it to extend beyond my control. For the time being, you and your young lady must stay here on the *Silver Cloud*. As my guests, of course."

Tracer wheeled around on his host. "What?" he shouted. "You have no right to keep us here! How dare—"

The hatch opened suddenly and crewmen jumped in. Securing Tracer's arms behind his back they hauled him from the darkened chamber in swift fashion. The young pilot barely got out another squawk before he found himself back in the lighted passageway.

Shrugging the silver-clad men off of him, he affixed a smile to his face and started to sing. This time it was "London Bridge."

He was shown down the passageway and back to where he had been separated from Miss Smith. There, he was told that his cabin was the third on the left and that he should relax there until he was called to the mess.

The crewmembers turned on their heel and departed back down the corridor.

"Well, that's a fine how-do-you-do," murmured Tracer.

The young man stood in the passageway for some minutes, soaking up the ever-present drone of the great airship's engines and pondering his luck. The captain's words played over and over in his brain. A part of Tracer said that he was lucky to be alive. Another part of him felt sure he'd have to refund Miss Smith's thousand dollars—and that he wouldn't see so much as a fin from her in the future.

More disgusted then he ever remembered feeling before in his young life, Tracer made up his mind to wash his face and hands, comb his hair and then go and find Miss Smith for a pow-wow.

He whistled a bit more of "London Bridge" as he approached his cabin door. Tracer then turned the latch and stepped inside.

It took him only a split-second to realize he wouldn't have to go looking for Miss Smith. She was right there in his cabin, wearing nothing but a pair of step-ins and a smile.

"I believe you are in the wrong cabin," said Miss Smith.

A little voice in Tracer's head said that he should turn around. He ignored it. He also ignored the impulse to start singing "You Must Have Been a Beautiful Baby."

"Ah, I was just, ah, going to, um, go looking for you," said Tracer, finally.

"I would say that you have found me, yes?" asked Miss Smith as she slowly covered her nakedness with her hands. The bemused smile on her face was still present.

Tracer somehow managed to unglue his eyes from her lithe form and point them at the floor. It was then he noticed that the young woman still wore her shoes, her skirt lay crumpled around them and her blouse was flung in a heap on the floor behind.

Something about the situation nagged at him, despite the more obvious pleasurable aspects of it. Tracer marveled at the sheer coincidence of walking in on Miss Smith at the very moment she was undressing. And, apparently, hastily so.

"Mr. Talbot, won't you please turn your back for a moment?" asked the girl. Tracer hurriedly swiveled around, red-faced that he had ignored his original intention to do just that.

He heard her shuffle about behind his back, moving things around. She then told him it was fine to turn around again.

Tracer did so and found her dressed in a simple robe and sitting in one of the cabin's chairs, her feet now bare. He noticed her toenails were lacquered. The young woman urged him to take a chair himself and tell her where he had been and what was going on. He talked.

First, Tracer apologized for barging into what he now knew to be her cabin; recent events had obviously swirled his brain around. His cabin was, he remembered, on the *left*. Then, he regaled her about meeting Captain Dusk and everything the enigmatic man had said. He also told her that they were, more-or-less, prisoners on the airship.

Miss Smith contemplated that news for a moment. Tracer realized that this was the longest conversation they had had since she walked into his makeshift office back in New York. Heaven only knew where they were now.

"You say this Captain Dusk is a…philanthropist of sorts?" she queried. "It seems almost like a story out of book. Could he really travel the world in this ship, helping people in different nations? Do I understand that correctly?"

"Well, I guess you have as much a lock on it as I do," replied Tracer. "Sure, it seems pretty crazy, but…well, he seems sincere. And crazy."

Miss Smith pursed her lips. Tracer noted that she had a dimple. "He is heading north, so I do not see why he cannot simply deliver us to an airfield or some similar sort of place…"

The young pilot felt as if there was nothing much to be gained by going over it again with the girl and told her so. They were stuck like flies and until something changed, they had to cool their heels on the greatest airship ever known to mankind.

He stood up, gave her a little bow, recommended that she be prepared for her own interview with Dusk and bid her ta-ta for now. He had to clear his head. Miss Smith, he sensed, was calm enough and in control of her emotions to be left alone, at least for a little while. The male in him said "stay" but the pilot in him said "fly."

Tracer exited the cabin post haste.

Outside Miss Smith's room, the young man stood a moment, looked left and then right—and then felt eyes upon him. He looked in the direction of the disturbance.

A crewman stood at the end of the hall. He looked for all the world indistinguishable from the rest of his brethren save for a face that some people might have described as "cruel." Tracer was pretty sure he didn't like the fellow.

The two stared at each other. Neither of them budged. It was almost a kind of contest. Then, the crewmember turned and walked off down the corridor.

"Now, what was *that* all about?' asked Tracer of no one in particular.

He'd already made up his mind to go and try to see as much of the giant airship, this *nouveau* Zeppelin, as possible. That is, if the crew didn't stop him. After that little incident, Tracer wasn't so sure they wouldn't.

With the rumble of the *Silver Cloud*'s engines always cloaking him with their cacophony, Tracer Talbot made his way through the ship. At first hesitantly, almost stealthily, but he soon found that the crew he encountered didn't seem to pay him much mind. Maybe they were just tolerating him, he thought, or maybe it was simply that they'd been ordered to allow him to wander—within reason, of course.

He *was* a prisoner, after all.

Tracer discovered a few things about the airship's crew: there were a lot of them, there were both male and female and there were representatives from all the races and many nationalities.

Every single one of them was exceedingly diligent in their work.

The pilot saw no goldbrickers, no ne'er-do-wells, no goof-offs. Everyone went about their business not robotically but absolutely methodically. Watching them, observing them in action around the ship, Tracer found himself growing prideful of the crew even though, he remembered, he had no connection with them. They were just that good.

He visited the great hold again and saw the storing and inventorying of the foodstuffs. He observed the area of the ship that held a kind of sickbay and was impressed by the modern array of medical tools. In the galley, Tracer discovered that the *Silver Cloud*'s crew did not pass out all the good food to down-on-there-luck principalities but saved some of it for the world-class chef the ship harbored.

Tracer also ran into his cruel-faced friend again.

Outside the galley and with the smells of some sort of soufflé or ragout stuck in his nostrils, he pulled up short when he once again felt eyes boring down on him. With a feeling of déjà vu, Tracer looked up to find the crewman once again staring at him.

Quelling an urge to punch the voyeur in the face, he turned on his heel and caught the elbow of a comely crewperson who passed nearby. She happened to be female.

"Say, sister," said Tracer in what he believed to be a friendly, pleasant voice. "Pardon me, but any chance of copping a few cigs up here?"

"I'm sorry, Mr. Talbot," cooed the girl. "But regulations prohibit smoking while on-board. Though much of the ship is non-incendiary, we still take every precaution to prevent fires. You understand, I'm sure,"

Tracer was about to ask how she knew his name and perhaps, if he felt the wind was blowing in the right direction, what she was doing that evening but when he looked up to see if Cruel-Face was still glomming onto him and then turned back to her, she was gone.

"Another fine *voh-dee-doh-doh*," he rumbled.

He chose a direction and singing "*La donna è mobile*" he continued with his inspection of the troops.

A feeling that Captain Dusk and his crew operated with a sense of purpose and altruism began to sweep through Tracer. He wanted to hold a grudge against the man for holding him here and for steeping everything in mystery, but he had to admit it appeared Dusk was telling the truth about the *Silver Cloud*'s mission.

One thing that Tracer had not come across yet was an armory or any sort of weapons. Surely the ship and its crew would need to defend themselves at times. He'd seen a hangar for some sort of aircraft, of course, and the reminder of that sent him searching for more information on the great airship's defenses—and why it might need them.

As well as he could, the young man traced his steps back to the hangar where he and Miss Smith first arrived onboard. Then, feeling a bit lost, Tracer asked a silver-clad crewman for directions.

"Sorry, sir," said the crewman, politely. "But the hangars are off-limits to all non-crewmembers."

Tracer smiled. "I suppose it'd be a great imposition to ask about armaments, too, Crewman...?"

The crewman returned the smile. "Yessir, 'fraid so, sir. And it's Brake, sir."

"Say," began the pilot. "Perhaps you can throw me a bone and tell me about these silver togs you all sport—what's the story on them?"

"Well," Crewman Brake said. "It's not exactly against regulations, I suppose. They're made from an incredible new process the Captain invented; all hush-hush and everything. Virtually bulletproof."

Tracer could hardly believe his ears and said so. "What? You're joking! Come off it!"

"No, sir. I wouldn't kid you. The captain calls it his 'silver lining'—whole ship's covered with it, too. They say it can even stand up to a blast from a shot gun! Never seen a situation yet where we had to test that, but we've been in some mighty tight scrapes and…"

The man trailed off, obviously realizing what we was saying and sensing some disloyalty in it. Tracer was chagrinned, but his good nature didn't allow him to be too harsh on his new friend for being so circumspect.

What his even-headedness didn't allow for was the stare from Cruel-Face. The man was once again dogging Tracer's heels, standing just around a corner but still within sight—and earshot.

"Say," said Tracer. "Who's that man? The one there that's so rudely eavesdropping on our friendly conversation?"

Brake turned and looked in the direction of the pilot's inquiry. "Oh, him? New fellow, came aboard about, what? Two months ago or so? Nice enough, I suppose."

"Nice enough for a punch in the snoot, I think," replied Tracer, watching as Cruel-Face slipped away again. "He's really beginning to step a bit too hard on my good-natured soul."

His new friend chuckled ruefully. "Listen, it may just be nerves—we're all a tiny piece of shaky right now. Every since the alert went out."

"Alert?"

"Yes," said Brake. "I, uh, probably shouldn't tell you this but with you and your girlfriend aboard, I suppose you have a right to know. Captain issued a ship-wide alert not long before you arrived. We're all to be in tip-top shape and Bristol fashion and ready for anything—have no idea why. But, the Captain's not a nervy one, not him. If he sees the need for us to be on alert, something must be up. You can bank on it."

Tracer digested that and pondered it. What could it mean? It couldn't be about he and Miss Smith; the man plainly said the alert came down *before* they'd arrived. Tracer and the girl were innocent players in all this. He didn't want to be here as much as everyone else didn't want him to be here.

"You all have great admiration for Captain Dusk, don't you?"

"Oh, yes, sir," enthused the crewman. "We'd follow him into the mouth of Hell itself."

Tracer clapped the man on the shoulder. "Well, let's hope it doesn't come to *that*, eh?"

The padded deck of the *Silver Cloud* resisted any attempt by Tracer Talbot to stomp back to his cabin. Good nature be damned, he thought, some times a man just wants to hit something.

He stopped short of his cabin door and lingered in the passageway to once again collect his thoughts.

What would his father say if he were present? Tracer knew that his old man would most likely have pressed a bit harder with his questions, demanded a bit more satisfaction. He was a man who, with the exception of his wayward son, didn't let things around him get out of control.

Tracer sighed and counted off his problems. One, lost an airplane. Two, stranded on a massive Zeppelin. Three, no idea of current heading. Four...

Miss Smith. Why did he keep forgetting about Miss Smith? In some ways, Tracer was responsible for her. She was his passenger. And he kept abandoning her.

He made up his mind there and then that they needed to stick together to stick it out through this situation.

The young man turned toward the young lady's cabin, a plan forming in his head. He'd regale Miss Smith with the sights he'd seen on the *Silver Cloud* and solicit her to lockstep with him as a unified force against all malignant forces. He might even go so far as to ask her what her first name was.

The girl's amused smile from before filled his thoughts as Tracer walked up to her door and prepared to politely knock upon it. He whistled a few bars of "In the Year of Jubilo."

Then, someone clocked him on the head from behind—hard.

Dizzy from the pain of the cowardly blow, Tracer Talbot was in some ways glad that it had happened; finally here was a situation that he could actually do something about. Or at least he would try.

There had been many fights in his childhood. A happy-go-lucky boy is a magnet for bullies and thugs, and Tracer being a bit happier perhaps than most he attracted his fair share of disgruntled playmates. He learned to scrap, though to his recollection he had never started a fracas himself.

On the *Silver Cloud*, Tracer felt something warm run down his head and into his eyes. Blood. *His* blood. He wiped at it. It resisted his attempt at clearing it. Seemed there was more of it by the second.

Something hit him in the stomach and Tracer sat down hard on the floor. He looked up to see Miss Smith's door open and the lady herself appear. With a small yelp of surprise, she fled back into her room and slammed the door.

Good, thought Tracer. She'd be out of danger. Now all he had to do was get the elephant in the corridor to stop head-butting him.

Rough hands grabbed at him, hauled him to his knees. Somebody was shouting. Tracer's head refused to cooperate and allow his ears to operate at peak efficiency but he could tell it was a man and that the man was big. He also seemed to speaking with an accent—Tracer felt sure he could identify the nationality but he couldn't be certain with his head pounding as it was.

Then man then kneed Tracer in the face. It didn't help his sense of balance at all. But it did point his eyes up at the man's head, enough that the pilot could see that it was Cruel-Face.

The next thing he knew he was wobbling on his own two feet and Cruel-Face was now shouting directly into Tracer's ears. This helped to clear them somewhat.

"...does that feel, boy? Eh?" queried his opponent. "There is more with that came from!"

Tracer wanted to refuse the offer, but the man bundled him up with his neck locked down tight under the man's arm and they were suddenly marching down the corridor together.

Where was the airship's crew, thought the young man? Surely the noise was enough to bring them to investigate.

Cruel-Face seemed to read Tracer's mind. "My fellow crewmates have been barricaded from this part of the ship," he explained helpfully. "There will be no one to help you, boy."

The pilot was seeing a bit clearly now, something of a miracle considering the blood was being kept from his brain by his assailant's chokehold. Perhaps that was it, he thought - no more blood running in his eyes.

They rounded a corner and the man slammed Tracer's head into the bulkhead near a door. The stars came out. Tracer stumbled and fell.

He had had just about enough of this particular square dance.

While Cruel-Face worked the latch, Tracer pulled open a reserve locker of strength and pulled himself to his feet. The man was a split-second too late to react and Tracer hit him in the kidneys with everything he had. Cruel-Face grunted like a pig and flopped against the wall.

Something fell from the man's hand and thumped onto the floor. Tracer saw it was a mechanical device of some kind. Squat and tubular, he also saw it was covered with blood and bits of hair and skin.

Now he knew what Cruel-Face had used to bash him in the skull. But what was it? Tracer didn't recognize the object, but it looked like it was a part of some larger unit.

The pilot took a terrific blow to the chin for his leisurely observation of his foe's makeshift cudgel. Cruel-Face had come back swinging and was making up for lost time. He grabbed Tracer's shirt and winging him around then threw him at the door. Tracer hit the portal and went sailing through it. Cruel-Face followed hurriedly and slammed the door shut behind them and locked it.

"So you have been giving yourself a tour of this magnificent craft, eh?" said the man. "Well, allow me to show you around the hangar bay—but please, be very careful, my friend. As you can see, the drop is a very long one."

Still lying on the floor, Tracer took in his surroundings. It seemed to be the same hangar that he and Miss Smith arrived at and still sans airplane. He also noticed that someone had been working on a project off to one side of the area; it looked to Tracer's eye like a large radio transmitter of some sort.

Things fell into place then for Tracer Talbot like eggs in basket. This man was most likely not a real member of the crew, but an infiltrator. He probably represented one of the enemy forces that Captain Dusk had mentioned, one of the ones who wished to halt the captain's march of altruism across the globe.

The transmitter was to tell Cruel-Face's fellows exactly where the *Silver Cloud* was—and bring them to its location.

Tracer sprung up and dived at Cruel-Face. He hit him, soundly. First a left, then a right, then a roundhouse that almost tore the man's head off. Wild-eyed from the attack, Cruel-Face shook off the blows and grabbed a large wrench from a pile of tools near the transmitter. He whirled it back and forth like a scimitar.

Trancer, still in his flight togs, face bruised up. In foreground is huge opening in floor ....seeing clouds below.

"You are a dead man!" screamed his foe. "Your usefulness is at its end!

"He whirled it back and forth like a scimitar."

The signal has been sent and everyone onboard this airship is only minutes away from a fiery conclusion!"

Tracer realized the man had been repairing the transmitter, fixing it after...what? A part had failed? It didn't matter much now; if he was telling the truth then the *Silver Cloud* was in a heap of trouble. If Tracer Talbot, itinerant air courier was going to doing anything, anything at all about the situation, it was now or never.

He leaped into the fray.

The heavy drone of the craft's powerful engines throbbed through the pilot, setting up a sympathetic vibration throughout his body. He felt energized, despite the blow to his head, the blood in his eyes and the ache in his gut. Tracer remembered fights he had as a kid and the look his father gave him as he returned from the battles; chagrined but proud. Proud that his boy had stood up for himself. Stood up for something.

Tracer whooped a war-cry and charged at Cruel-Face, head down and fists swinging. He caught the wrench with one hand and tore it out of his opponents grasp, amazed at the luck. The monstrous tool went skittering across the hangar and out the opening. It fell, far, far away.

The two men fought. They tore at each other like wild beasts. Any semblance of humanity quickly disappeared after the first few blows and they faced off as two elemental forces. The hangar was not a very open space but they wove between struts and girders to land punches and kicks on each other. Soon they were both bloodied.

Far off, Tracer heard pounding at the door to the space. Then, yelling came to his ears. The crew had finally caught on to what was happening— maybe they had even figured out that the great airship's location was now compromised. He hoped they'd break in soon. He was tiring.

Cruel-Face had at least four inches and most likely twenty pounds on him. His knuckles punished Tracer's body brutally. He hurt all over but the pain had begun to seep away into an all-consuming numbness. He fought on.

Then, Tracer stumbled. It might have been a patch of oil or it might have been Cruel-Face's cunning ability to fight like the greatest of welterweight; regardless, the pilot skidded and fell and his enemy was on him in a flash.

"Ach, I have you now, boy," said Cruel-Face, almost solemnly. "Your death is overdue. Come, let us finish this."

And his hands flashed out and wrapped around Tracer's neck, tightly. The young man was prone, hanging over the open bay doors with nothing but air at his back. Twelve-thousand feet down was Mother Earth, calling to him like Jason's sirens.

He made up his mind not to die like that.

It sounded simple when Tracer looked back on it, but it was the clarity of mind that came to him in times of crisis that he never took for granted. He had plainly made a decision that this was not going to be his time.

With a surge of energy, he drove his palm up into the man's nose. It popped like a dry twig and blood spurted out. Cruel-Face's death-hold on Tracer's neck loosened, ever so slightly, giving him the impetus to push out first with his knees and then with his feet.

The larger man flipped up like a wooden board and then flopped down and through the open bay doors. His body caught on the trapeze arrangement and for a split-second he looked more like a piece of rag caught on a barbed-wire fence than a human being. Presently, he fell.

Tracer caught himself from following his foe. Hanging on to the support structure, he watched as the man tumbled end over end, a thin stream of blood trailing him like a crimson scarf. Soon, he disappeared from view. Tracer was reminded of Anna Lynne.

He lay there for what seemed like an eternity, and then hands grabbed at him and pulled him away and out from the hangar.

Crewman Brake's face swam into focus before him. The roaring wind and the sounds of the airship's engines were silenced as if someone closed the door to the hangar. Brake sat Tracer up in the outer corridor, propping him against a wall.

"What happened in there?" asked Brake. "This entire part of the ship was shut down—we couldn't get in! Where's Machen?"

Tracer presumed the crewman was referring to his sparring partner. "He's gone. Out the booby hatch. It was him or me. I chose me."

Brake nodded silently, as if he understood. "He attacked you? Whatever for?"

The young man tried to sit up a bit more but found it ever so painful to do so. "He...I'm not sure. He was repairing a...transmitter of a sort. Hit me from behind with the...broken bit? Whatever it was, I think he activated it. Sent a signal to, well, someone."

The crewman looked grave. He shook his head ruefully. "We always keep our presence, our exact location a secret. Captain Dusk always flies silently. If our enemies know where we are...how could something like this have happened?"

Tracer wasn't sure and did not feel like offering any theories or opinions at the moment. He was too busy trying to find one single spot on this body that did not scream out with pain.

"Here's someone who'd like to see you," said Brake. "I have to help secure the hangar and dissemble that transmitter. Captain's already been briefed. We're trying to sort through this and figure out just how bad it all is."

Miss Smith appeared then and without warning she flew into Tracer's arms. Her face was wet. She hugged him until his frame could take no more and it protested from the attention.

Tracer looked at the young woman's face and saw there a mixture of shock and horror. He wondered if Machen had been menacing her before he'd shown up at her cabin. Tears flowed down her soft cheeks.

"I am so glad you are alive!" she said. "I thought that...that brute had killed you in front of my door at first, and then I heard you making sounds as he dragged you away. Oh, Tracer! I was so very frightened for you!"

Crewman Brake chose that inopportune moment to return, this time with a medic for Tracer's injuries.

"As I said, the captain's been filled in on everything," reported Brake while bandages were wound around Tracer's head. "Machen was assigned to that hangar—we'd been having some trouble with its launching mechanism—and it appears he's been building that transmitter for the entire time he's been with us! He'd recently replaced a part and apparently gotten it working. It was transmitting when we got to it."

Tracer looked steadily at him. "Not a very good catch, was he?"

"Well," said the crewman. "His credentials were impeccable, I'm to understand. He was a quiet thing but we had no trouble with him. No trouble at all. I can't fathom it. I mean, it was him that lowered the trapeze to catch you both up..."

The medic, having attended to the young pilot's head, was now checking him for broken bones. Tracer grunted as the man felt along his limbs.

"I suppose he was just following orders then, eh?" He glanced over at Miss Smith, to gauge her current status. She looked a bit haunted, thought Tracer. Deep in thought, distracted, but she glanced at Tracer on occasion with concern on her face as she knelt by his side.

"Say," said Tracer. "We just changed direction, didn't we?"

Crewman Brake looked a bit sheepish then. He reached up and smoothed back his tousled hair. "Well, seems I'm telling you everything that's supposed to be confidential, but yeah, very good. The ship has changed direction. We were heading north—now we're heading east. How did you know?"

Tracer smiled, painfully. "Something I just felt in my, ahh, aching bones. Where exactly are we headed now? Or is that confidential, too?"

"Well," began Brake. "I…hold on a moment."

He walked over to a telephone arrangement that had begun buzzing. Picking up the receiver, he identified himself, listened for a few seconds and replied quietly. Then, he looked up at Tracer.

"Captain wants to speak to you."

The *Silver Cloud*'s mighty engines revved at that moment. Nothing subtle about it; everyone onboard could tell that the incredible airship had just increased its speed. An electric current of anticipation seemed to leap from person to person then.

Tracer shifted, grunted and then tried to push himself up and away from the wall. So distracted was Miss Smith that she did not lend a hand to help him.

Moving over to Brake, the young man accepted the 'phone in the crewman's outstretched hand as if he was being handed a venomous snake. One of the last people on Earth—or above it—he wanted to talk to at the moment was Captain Dusk.

"Hello, Mr. Talbot," came the wheezing voice over the 'phone. "It seems as if I'm always apologizing to you but please accept my sincere condolences for your troubles."

"Yeah, about that," said Tracer through gritted teeth. "Listen, no trouble at all. Happy to give my life for you and your gallant crew."

"Sarcasm ill becomes you," said Dusk. "But it's interesting that you should say that. We are now under an unfortunate state of siege, young man. I need to ask you a very serious question.

"Are you willing to fight?"

Tracer Talbot had reached a few crossroads in his life, young as it was, and he knew one when he'd reached it. The decision to run away from home, to choose the life of a pilot and to be a vagabond one at that were all choices he made with much thought. He was proud of those choices. He made them and then didn't look back.

Instinctively, he felt he knew what the enigmatic commander of perhaps the greatest airship ever constructed was asking him. Despite losing his own airplane and the inconvenience of being held a prisoner, Tracer had begun to understand what it was that the crew of the *Silver Cloud* faced every single day of their lives. And he knew he wanted to be part of it.

"How?" he asked.

"Good," replied Dusk. "I can tell we understand each other. I can feel your father's spirit in you. That need for excitement, yes, but also that unquenchable desire to be of use, to aid those who are in need themselves."

Tracer closed his eyes. "Yes."

"Crewman Brake will show you to another hangar. This ship is equipped with a small fleet of one-man fighters, the very best that money can buy. We use them for our own protection, and to protect others if need be. At this moment, and thanks to our departed friend Machen, our location has been transmitted to our enemies."

"But you're trying to move away from them?"

"Yes," wheezed Dusk. "But we cannot outrun the inevitable. They will come and try to destroy this ship. She is nigh-impervious to bullets, but if they drop a bomb on her, well, I'm afraid that would be more than we could handle and survive. We will have to engage them one-on-one. Alas, I am short a few good pilots at this time…"

"Show me to an airplane," said Tracer. "I'll fight. We'll give 'em what-for. I have a score to settle."

"Excellent, young Tracer. I am placing in inordinate amount of trust in you, but not unfounded I feel. Your father would be proud of you, I'm sure."

The young pilot chuckled. "I'm not. He'd probably just tell me I was being stupid."

He hung the 'phone back in its cradle and turned to Brake and Miss Smith. The wind had changed and a course correction made. He smiled, though it was still painful to do so.

"Let's get crackin', Mr. Brake," he said to the crewman. "Lead me to my 'plane."

"Yessir, sir!" yelped Brake as he mock-saluted. "Right away, sir!"

Tracer turned to follow him but found his arm caught by Miss Smith. He looked into her eyes. They were particularly gorgeous, he noticed.

An alarm began to peel throughout the airship. It served to cover the heavy beating of Tracer's heart. The girl moved in closer, lips parted and inviting.

Then, she slapped him.

Surprised, Tracer wheeled back and stared at Miss Smith with questioning eyes. He searched her face for an explanation as he rubbed his reddening cheek but she was an enigma.

Brake stuck his head back around the corner. "C'mon, Mr. Talbot! Our incoming enemies aren't going to wait around for you to join us before they begin their attack!"

Tracer looked at him and then again at Miss Smith as she was shuffled out of the hangar. She looked beautiful. But he couldn't glean the thoughts behind the mask of her face.

"Women," he said simply, and turned to go.

Brake led the way through the *Silver Cloud* with Tracer nipping at his heels. The crewman tried to fill him in as they approached another hangar.

"I was just informed that our detection system picked up a handful of blips heading in from the west. Looks like small fighters. I wish I knew where they were being launched from..."

They pulled up in front of a hatch. Brake turned to his shadow.

"American or British?" he inquired.

"Huh?" said Tracer, confused. "I'm not sure what you—"

Brake clamped a hand on the young man's shoulder and looked him straight in the eye. "American or British aircraft. Which would you prefer?"

Tracer almost laughed. "You mean, you have *both*?"

"Sure," said the crewman, matter-of-factly. "Doesn't everyone?"

"American, of course!" yelled Tracer, itching to get on with the show.

Brake thumped him on the back, forgetting Tracer's injuries. "Good! That's what I guessed a good Yank like you would say! Right this way, flyboy!"

They stepped into the hangar bay. The space was almost filled by a gleaming, deadly-looking airplane unadorned with identifying markers. Tracer nodded in approval, made happy humming sounds.

"A P-36A," cooed Tracer, admiring the lines of the small single-seat fighter. It gleamed as if new. A few other crewmen crawled over it, preparing it for flight. One of them noticed the two men's arrival and hopped over to them, waving clipboard.

"Captain called and told us to expect a new man, Brake," he called. "We'll get you suited up in a few seconds, Mr. Talbot."

"Almost looks like she's never been flown before," said Tracer, his eyes flowing over the 'plane lustily. He couldn't wait to get his hands on her and see what she could do.

Brake nodded. "Almost, but not quite. Captain got them last year, when the Americans put in their order for them—biggest order of fighters in almost twenty years. War is in the air, I guess."

Tracer turned to the crewman with the clipboard. The others had started the P-36 and begun to open the bay doors below it. He had to yell to be heard above the din.

"What's she packing?" he bellowed.

"Two .3in Brownings, one in each wing. I know it doesn't sound like much, but she makes up for it in stability," he replied.

"And the engine's a—"

"Yes," said the man. "A Pratt & Whitney. One thousand and fifty horses. She'll do you just fine."

Tracer was already suiting up and adjusting his cap. He slammed his goggled into place, gave Brake a cheery flip of a salute and leaped into the cockpit of the Hawk. Captain Dusk insisted war wasn't a game, but Tracer Talbot felt just like he did when he was eight-years-old and playing fighter pilot in an old wooden crate. Maybe the stakes were a bit higher now, but the exhilaration was the same.

To be perfectly honest, he was ready to whale the tar out of someone.

The sun was setting in the west and the sky was growing dark. The clouds took on all shades—pinks and yellows and browns. Tracer was glad to be out and about, no longer stuck inside the windbag.

Once released from the hangar bay he swung the Hawk up from underneath the *Silver Cloud* and attempted to get his bearings. The 'plane handled well though she felt a world of difference from Anna Lynne. Tracer knew he needed to have all his wits about him at all times—it had been a few years since he'd last flown a single-engine loop-de-looper.

He ascended and got above the airship. Looking down on her, he marveled once again at her size. She was easily a thousand feet long if not more. Tracer also caught sight of his fellow fighters and the radio began to crackle and hiss with voices.

There were twelve of them in all, a mixture of P-36s and British Gladiators. Tracer discovered he was tagged as "Cloud 9." He got on the channel and began to sing.

Farewell and adieu to you, Spanish Ladies
Farewell and adieu to you, ladies of Spain
For we've received orders for to sail for old England
But we hope in a short time to see you again

In return he received a barrage of raspberries and catcalls, some of them in other languages. It all seemed good-natured. Tracer felt a stirring of pride in their little fleet.

The good feeling ended when Cloud 1 broke through the chatter to announce, "Incoming! From the northwest! Mind the sun in your eyes, boyos!"

Tracer looked up—carefully, for the setting sun was torturous - to see a wave of enemy airplanes break through the clouds. Before they knew it, they were under attack.

The incoming aircraft—at least twelve to match their twelve - sported the marking and colors of a certain nation whose recent aggressive incursions on other countries had rankled the global community. Tracer bit his lip and shot bullets at the airplanes with his eyes. This was a chance to score an early victory in the world war that was sure to come. He was glad for the opportunity.

The pilots of the *Silver Cloud* had a simple mission: keep the enemy from getting above the great airship and dropping a bomb on it. If in fulfilling that singular command enemy aircraft must be destroyed, so be it. Lives were at stake, and not just onboard the airship.

Tracer picked out a 'plane and threw his Hawk into a dive. The air erupted around him as hot slugs swarmed like angry hornets from metal nests. The young pilot sang out again as he let loose with his own torrent of bullets.

We'll rant and we'll roar like true British sailors
We'll rant and we'll roar all on the salt sea
Until we strike soundings in the channel of old England
From Ushant to Scilly is thirty-five leagues

He kept his opponent in his crosshairs and his finger on the trigger, all the while pushing his Hawk to greater speed. The enemy's fuselage sprouted barbs of fire. He could see the pilot react to the barrage, screaming and then gone.

It was Tracer Talbot's first kill as a pilot. He blinked and in a heartbeat it was all over.

The debris from the other 'plane plink-plinked against his canopy as he thrust through the fiery destruction. Before he knew it, he had one on his own tail. Tracer didn't care for the feeling.

He jinked to the left, then to the right, then in a half-roll that almost plastered him against the side of the great airship. Somewhere in the back of Tracer's otherwise-occupied grey matter a little voice reminded him he was supposed to be preventing enemy craft from getting up over the *Silver Cloud*. He prayed his fellows were up to the task—he needed to keep the hook out of his own mouth.

His foe sprayed bullets like fireflies in snaky patterns around Tracer's Hawk. With a grin of irony, Tracer realized the tracers were probably his father's.

Yanking back on the joy-stick, Tracer brought his nose up and gained a higher perspective on things. His shadow stayed right with him and the young pilot silently complimented his unseen foe on a neat bit of flying. But he didn't intend on passing out any more kudos. It was time to end it.

Executing another half-roll, Tracer smoothly followed with an s-turn in which he damn near almost wrecked himself—but the other pilot wasn't so lucky. Tracer half-stalled, got right behind the enemy 'plane and let loose with his own barrage of lead. A pretty flower of fire blossomed and again the young man mentally notched his gun belt.

Ignoring a queer noise that was now coming from his engine, Tracer throttled it and brought himself up and over the airship. He wanted to get a higher view of the situation. He noted the *Silver Cloud* taking rounds to its sides but the strange silver material which covered it seemed to be taking the punishment well. Chalk one up to Captain Dusk, he mused.

Tracer's radio crackled with chatter. His sense of the battle was that his side was holding its own. Another enemy plane blew by him with one of his fellows hot on its tail, guns chattering. Tracer's head started to whirl like a dervish and he fought back an onrush of panic. Why start getting jittery *now*? he thought. Have a shaking fit when it was all over and he was back onboard and safe, he chided himself.

Out of the corner of his eye he caught a flash of metal and suddenly an enemy craft was up and over the *Silver Cloud*—Tracer could see the bomb strapped to its belly. Senses not only alert but screaming bloody blue murder, he jammed the stick and drove headlong towards the other 'plane.

The enemy got into position and Tracer Talbot knew in his gut he had only one, small, practically tiny chance of correcting the situation. He let loose tracers, trying desperately to find his mark in the blanketing fall of

"...he jammed the stick and drove headlong towards the other plane."

night, seeking for the other 'plane and its bomb. Dad, he thought, I hope you still believe in your boy…

His bullets found their target just as the bomb was released and they caught not only that explosive egg but the metal nest it was falling from. The explosion spread out before Tracer's eyes, blinding him.

Stars danced before his orbs. Something heavy slammed into him.

Like a dope, he started singing. Stress, among many other things, did that to him.

We hove our ship to with the wind from sou'west, boys
We hove our ship to, deep soundings to take
'Twas forty-five fathoms, with a white sandy bottom
So we squared our main yard and up channel did make

That made Tracer think of Miss Smith's white bottom and he knew then he was delirious. His head hurt and not from Machen's beating. This was something new. He tasted blood and felt wind on his face. He also felt like he was falling.

The young man could hear his radio sputter and someone was asking him something. What was it? Something about falling…

The drone of his Hawk grew louder and louder as he was pressed back in his seat. The salt from the blood in his mouth jangled his nerves a bit and the stars began to clear from his eyes. Tracer shook his head and looked out at his ruined canopy, then noticed the jagged hunk of debris that had stuck itself deep into the headrest right next to his right ear.

Then, Tracer noticed he was falling. Straight down, in fact.

He pulled back on the joy-stick and the P-36 shuddered all over. Tracer could hear and feel the 'plane rivets and plates buck and shake, a sound and a feeling he didn't overly care for, either. How the Hawk had stayed together this long he didn't have a clue.

Up ahead—or was it below?—he saw the airship.

Something didn't make sense to Tracer just then, and it wasn't just that he ached all over and his head felt like several elephants had been using it as a shuttlecock. He should have been falling *away* from the *Silver Cloud*, not towards it.

It was another airship.

Momentarily confused, Tracer's brain finally made the calculations and the realization that this was the enemy's own zeppelin washed over him like cool spring water. Those enemy craft had to have come from somewhere, hadn't they? Sneaky devils, thought Tracer; they had their own airship.

And, best of all, he was right on top of it.

With a booming cry that hurt his own head, Tracer let loose with all that folderol about "shank painters" and "clewgarnets" in that song and then let fly not with tacks and with sheets but with tracers. He spewed bullets like they were going out of style.

He sprayed hot lead smack dab into the center of the enemy's markings and mused over the blow he was striking for all the people who'd cowered under those markings and felt fear. Tracer pumped that gasbag full of bullets and was rewarded soon enough with the knowledge that this ship possessed no "silver lining."

It blew. Boy, did it blow.

As the Zeppelin collapsed in on itself, Tracer glowed from the warmth of knowing that there'd be one less gasbag in the world to bring death and destruction to innocents around the globe. As corny as it sounded, he felt very, very good about striking such a blow.

Now, he just had to make it back alive to tell the others.

His Hawk grumbled and groaned as he leveled out and tried to gain some altitude. He was pretty sure he wasn't going to make it. For one thing, he had no real idea of where he was. He might already be dead, for all he knew.

Guessing that he was, in fact, still quite alive, Tracer ascended. The P-36 had seen much better days and he wondered how mad the captain would be that one of his precious airplanes was now missing a few teeth. Ah well, thought the young pilot; weren't fathers always mad about something?

Feeling delirium once again overtaking him, his anxiety level rose with his 'plane. He had to get back. He didn't want to die hanging out of an airship and he didn't want to die without the chance to boast of his exploits to someone other than himself.

Breaking through the clouds then, he saw the giant airship—and a feeling of *déjà vu* came over him.

Tracer's radio crackled and spat as it came to life in his cockpit. Smiling, though it pained his face, he grabbed up the mouthpiece and sang into it:

Now let ev'ry man drink off his full bump
And let ev'ry man drink off his full glass
We'll drink and be jolly and drown melancholy
And here's to the health of each true-hearted lass

That made him think of the lass that waited for him on the *Silver Cloud*, the enigmatic Miss Smith. Tracer's cheek burned just then from where the brown-haired bonny had slapped him as left to go fight for kith and kin.

He watched as a trapeze lowered from the belly of the great ship and as he positioned the rapidly-failing Hawk to glom onto it, he afforded a part of his brain to thinking about the girl.

A moment of strange clarity came over Tracer, so strange that it frightened him. Several bits of business from the past several hours of his life all lined up in a neat little row and presented themselves for inspection. Here were Miss Smith and Captain Dusk. There were Machen and Crewman Brake. A few things now made sense to him.

Tracer prepared himself for another confrontation.

Back onboard the *Silver Cloud*, Tracer bit the inside of his cheek as crewmen struggled to tear away what was left of the P-36's canopy. Pushing them aside, he threw himself from the 'plane and stalked over to Brake.

"Now, hold on there, mate," said Brake. "We need to have you checked out. You're looking a bit worse for wear!"

Tracer held up a hand to stop the chatter. "I got other things to take care of first," he said grimly. "I need to speak to Dusk."

The crewman narrowed his eyes at the young man, sizing him up. "We just came through a hell of a fight, lad. There'll be time to chat with the captain once we've picked up this mess and—"

Tracer grabbed Brake by his collar and pulled the man closer. "I need to speak to Dusk," he said through gritted teeth. He could taste blood in his mouth again and he wondered what a fright he must look.

"Okay," whispered Brake. "I can see that you do. Let me make the call, eh?"

The young pilot let go of him and stepped back, his usual good-nature eluding him for once. He braced himself for the battle to come.

Once again in the captain's quarters, Tracer Talbot wasn't concerned about catching a glimpse of Dusk. He was only concerned with gaining information he needed.

"You've done us a mighty service, young Tracer," said the captain with a wheeze. "But I can see you're in no mood for congratulations. What may I do for you?"

Tracer steeled his resolve and let go the breath he found he'd been holding in. "You say you weren't aware of our presence before you picked us up, me and Miss Smith. Is that right?"

"Yes, of course," said Dusk. "Our detection system spotted you but too late to warn you off. Why do you ask this again?"

"Following a train of thought," responded Tracer. "This Machen, the crewman who attacked me—Brake said he was new?"

"Yes," said the Captain with a disappointed sigh. "We seek out new crewmembers, but as you may have guessed very covertly and with a high degree of investigation into their backgrounds. Machen came to us with impeccable credentials and, frankly, I thought he'd fit in well. I admit I was wrong about him."

"Yeah," snorted Tracer. "I was wrong about him, too. I just thought he was a creep. Turned out he was a murderous creep."

"I regret that, sir—"

The young man cut him off. "Never mind that. I know he'd built some kind of radio transmitter, right under your noses, and he'd gotten it to work even though it was either unfinished or broken somehow...so where did he get the parts? You have everything onboard needed to build a powerful transmitter?"

"To some extent, yes," said Dusk. "But not completely, no. I was told that what he needed to either complete or repair the device was not a piece of equipment we usually possess in our onboard inventory. Machen would have needed to get that last part from somewhere else."

Tracer could feel the captain's eyes now boring into him, though he couldn't actually see it through the darkness. He was being scrutinized, but he didn't give a damn at the moment.

"You were found out," he told Dusk. "Your position was transmitted to Machen's allies and you almost lost your ship and everyone aboard it. I just destroyed their own airship, so I think the *Silver Cloud*'s safe...for now."

He turned to go. "I have someone else to talk to now, to make sure we're *really* safe. Give me some time, Captain. Time to wrap this up on my own terms. Stay out of it for now, eh?"

Tracer didn't give Dusk a chance to answer. He left the room and stomped off to his next destination.

At Miss Smith's door he paused and throwing propriety to the wind, he entered without knocking. It would be just too bad if she was in the middle of undressing again.

Tracer found the young woman sitting on her bunk, fully clothed and with her eyes shut and hands folded neatly in her lap. Miss Smith looked up with a start, eyes wide and questioning. She saw it was Tracer.

"I hope I haven't caught you at a bad time," he said as he shut the hatch behind him. "You looked…quite at peace just then."

"Oh, Tracer," she squealed and jumped up to hug him. "Thank goodness you—"

"Cut that out," he said sharply, grabbing her wrists. "Maybe save it for later. We've got things to talk about first."

Miss Smith looked up into his eyes, searching them for meaning. Tracer thought he might have spotted some wetness in hers.

The girl took a step back and composed herself. "All right. I was very afraid for you and …"

Tracer cut her off again. "And you were sitting her expecting to die. In fact, I'm betting you were pretty sure you were going to die. Is that right?"

"Of course that thought had occurred to me," she said. "But I had hoped that you and the other pilots would be able to save us from those enemy airplanes…"

Tracer's heart jumped. "See, now, there's another instance when you seem to know more than you should. How is that?"

Miss Smith's eyelashes fluttered and she looked down. "I am not sure what you mean—"

"You know exactly what I mean. A while back you said we were heading north. You didn't say it like it was a guess; you said it like you knew it for a certainty. And just now, you couldn't have known exactly what we were up against out there—incoming airplanes—because you weren't told before you left the hangar."

The girl's eyes widened as she looked at Tracer imploringly. "No, no— they told me as I left! They said that—"

The pilot was beginning to enjoy cutting her off, perhaps a bit too much. "Nope. I know these fellows; they don't talk much. I doubt that they would have spilled the beans to you. You knew what was going on—and you fully expected this airship to be blown out of the sky. With you in it. How self-sacrificing of you, Miss Smith."

She just stared at him for a time and then lowered her eyes. For a long moment she stood there in front of him, not saying a word. Then, she looked back up to him and her hands went to her blouse and fumbled with the top buttons.

"Tracer, I...we could..."

"Save it," he said coldly. "I've already seen it, remember?"

The girl suddenly and swiftly swung her hand to connect with his face but he caught her by the wrist again and twisted it. She let loose a very unladylike oath.

"Yeah," said Tracer. "That was quite a last-minute distraction you cooked up, when you heard me at the door. Could be a record-breaking undressing time, that. But what was it for? Not because of my obvious charms, manly and overwhelming that they are, but maybe to...hide something?"

"Yes," said Miss Smith and produced a nasty-looking pistol to emphasize her agreement. "It was to distract you from what I had laid out on my bunk."

Tracer nodded. "Radio transmitter parts," he said calmly. "The ones you brought to help Machen repair his equipment. So that he could reveal this airship's position to your people."

The muzzle of the gun was placed on Tracer's chest. He felt the cold of its steel through his shirt. Quite a situation he'd gotten himself into—again.

It was Miss Smith's time to smile. "Correct, Mr. Talbot," she cooed as she buttoned up her blouse with her other hand. "Thank you very much for providing me with such able transportation. Though I cannot say much for your ability to fly smoothly. I shall have to report you to the authorities that regulate such things. After you are dead."

"Tell me something, Miss Smith; if Machen couldn't get his transmitter to work and signal where exactly he and the *Silver Cloud* were, how did you find them?"

The young woman sat down on her bunk, all the while keeping the pistol trained on Tracer's heart. She flashed a bit of shapely leg as she did so, which did not go unnoticed by Tracer. Miss Smith took note of where the young man's eyes went and positioned herself so as to show off her legs to full advantage.

"Machen had radioed a general course heading for the ship the last time they had 'come ashore' for supplies. When we lost contact with him, I was sent in that same direction with a rudimentary sense of where he and the ship might be. I hired you to take me up and I hoped that once we were in the air I would spot them and then force you to make contact. It all worked out far, far better than I ever would have imagined, Mr. Talbot. I had thought it would be a tedious mission of trial and error—you are my lucky charm, I guess."

Tracer rolled this around in his brainpan and saw that the pieces of the puzzle were now almost completely in place. He'd been quite a sap all along.

"You came back from your little talk with the captain sooner than I expected," she continued. "Machen had been trying to get to me to get the parts. I had them laid out and then you showed up at my door! Well, what else could I do but provide you with a delicious diversion?"

She twirled her comely legs around and laughed, a pleasant-sounding thing despite the circumstances.

"And when I went off to see the ship, Machen got the parts from you," said Tracer, matter-of-factly. "Why, he was so happy about it he tried to bash my brains in with them!"

Miss Smith stood up and smoothed down her skirts. Her eyes went cold; very, very cold.

"Yes, he did. And you killed him," she said quietly. "He was my lover and now he is dead.

"So, you will be, also."

With a bemused and somewhat chagrinned attitude, Tracer waited for his life to begin flashing in front of him. He looked forward to seeing his father and his mother, his childhood dog Binky and his Anna Lynne. He felt quite appreciative that the human mind, faced with such certain and imminent death, provided this comfort. What a wonder the brain was, he thought.

But nothing happened. There were no images from his life coming in from the left or the right or from down the center aisle. Tracer was confused; wasn't it in writing somewhere he was owed a quick history of his life?

Then, he realized what it meant. He wasn't about to die.

Tracer lunged at Miss Smith and they went down in a tangle on the bunk. He grappled for the pistol, trying to keep it pointing up and not at anything important like his face or his gut. The girl snarled and snapped like a wildcat. She fought like one, too.

He tried to use his superior weight and strength against her but he had to admit that Miss Smith knew a thing or two about keeping a man off of her. The young woman's knees in particular were being used as deadly weapons and the nails on her free hand raked at him. At one point he felt one of her shoes hit him on top of the head and he wondered how that came to pass.

Then, Tracer got his hands on the pistol and with a mighty effort yanked it away from the girl. Before he could bring it to bear on her, she kneed him in the stomach and kicked him off of her with the foot that still wore a high-heeled shoe. It hurt; that and landing on the floor, of course.

A tableau presented itself: Tracer Talbot lying on the floor on his back but holding the gun, and Miss Smith half-sitting up on the bed looking at him with unbridled vehemence.

He pointed the pistol at her and was prepared to put a bullet in her if she lunged for him. Miss Smith's face relaxed and he could see some sense flood back into her noggin. She knew the score.

The young woman's pretty lips curled into a slight smile. It was tinged with sadness.

"I was prepared to die for my country anyway," she said, and pulling up her skirts she removed a tiny pistol from a garter and then blew her brains out.

It happened so fast that Tracer didn't have a chance to even yell out. The smell of gunpowder came to his nostrils and then the unforgettable tang of blood.

He stood up and stepped over to the bunk. His hand trembled and he dropped the gun.

Looking down on Miss Smith's lifeless body he couldn't help but think that despite all the misery she had brought, all the calamity and danger she had wrought, she made a beautiful corpse.

After a few days in the great airship's sickbay, Tracer grew restless and asked to see the captain. An hour later, the telephone by his bed buzzed and he picked it up. It was Captain Dusk.

"You have been through quite a lot, Tracer," said the wheezing, burbling voice. "More than most young men could stand, I'd wager. How do you do it?"

Tracer considered the question. "Well, I suppose it's just that can't stand the thought of never flying again. That gets me through most of my troubles, I suppose. Sorry that it's not much more complicated than that, captain."

Dusk chuckled, a strange sound coming from a strange man. "I hope you will believe me when I tell you that I see and understand at least a small part of that philosophy, my young friend. If I could not, there never would have been an airship like the *Silver Cloud*."

The pilot chuckled a bit himself. "Yes, I see that. She's a thing of beauty, sir. I'm glad to have known her."

"But there's something else on your mind, isn't there?" asked Dusk.

Tracer nodded, forgetting he was talking over the 'phone. "Am I still a prisoner?"

"No," came the reply. "No, I trust that, after all you've done for us, you can keep the secret of the *Silver Cloud* and our mission. You have earned my respect and confidence."

"Thanks," said Tracer, and he really meant it. He'd discovered that he believed in the airship's mission. He'd also discovered a few things about himself, such as not caring very much to go back to the life of an itinerant air courier. Besides, that would be fairly difficult without an airplane.

"There is one more thing, Tracer—I have a gift for you. I hope you will accept it with my and my crew's gratitude."

His heart lifted at the words. "What is it?" he asked.

"I believe Crewman Brake will be there shortly to present it to you. Please have him call me once you have received it. A good day to you."

Brake arrived then and led Tracer through the corridors to a hangar. There, the crewman made a grand gesture at the brand-new P-36A that rested in its carriage before them.

"Not sure how you rate," said Brake, with a grin. "But orders came down from the captain. Its all yours…"

The young man could scarcely believe his luck. For every up there is a down, he thought to himself. For every air pocket there's a good, strong tailwind. He'd make good use of this gift, that he was quite sure of.

Tracer had the crewman ring up the captain again. On the 'phone, he expressed his thanks, giddy with the magnanimity of it.

"Mr. Talbot," said Dusk solemnly. "I wonder if you might consider…

joining our little band. We could use your piloting skills, and, frankly, your youthful exuberance. Though, I'm told, your singing leaves much to be desired."

"Well, Captain," replied Tracer. "I'm…I'm not sure what to say. Can I think on it? I'm used to be a free spirit, you see…though the offer is an appealing one. Give me a bit of airspace to think about it and I promise you a firm answer."

The captain wheezed into the receiver. "Certainly, my boy. I would not care to rush you into an answer, not with such a life-changing question hanging over your head. Please, try out your new airplane, though, I must tell you we are currently far out over the Atlantic Ocean…"

"What?" said the pilot. "Oh, well. Where are you headed, if I may ask?"

"To England," came the reply. "That small nation is being eyed by jackals with too keen of a gleam in their eyes. We are on our way to help shore up their defenses. Our first port-of-call is just outside of Holyhead, in—"

"Wales, yes," said the young man. "I have some distant relatives there. Might be nice to pop in on them."

"It's settled then. I am very glad to have you onboard, Tracer Talbot, at least until you have made your final decision. I hope you will join us—there are dark days ahead and we will need all the stout hearts we can find."

Tracer pondered that; it was a lot to think about. Sadly, not a single song came to his mind to help usher him into the days and weeks to come.

THE END

Zeppelin Story

I knew from the moment I saw the call for "Zeppelin stories" that it would be just the ticket for me. I felt the wind of the propellers in my face and saw the ghostly mass of a gigantic airship in my mind's eye and raised my hand for the assignment.

The lure of Zeppelins must be as strong as that of trains among their aficionados, I think. But, unlike trains, the great airships of the first half of the 20th century are long gone and we have only a few grainy photos to remind us of their magnificent presence—that, and the unfortunate tragedy of the *Hindenburg*. That fateful day is still, I believe, etched into the collective consciousness and unconsciousness of the human race.

So, Airship 27 wanted—hey, cool!—airship stories. The beauty of that was that I could work not with someone else's characters and situations— which is very fun, of course—but with my own. I thought a bit about what I could do with such a story—the sky was the limit, literally—and the opening scene of "Death Seeds the Clouds" popped into my head full-blown.

That's an incredible moment for me as a writer, when imagination takes over and starts painting scenes before your eyes. I will always feel very fortunate when that happens; it makes starting out on a story so easy— and fun. This time around, I saw an airplane flying up through the clouds and into the wake of a massive super-Zeppelin—think the opening shot of the Star Destroyer in *Star Wars* and you'll know where I was I headed.

But wait; who *was* that daring young man in the cockpit of that airplane? By golly, he was a brand-new character! I was pretty sure he was mine and sure enough, he was. Again, the cool thing about this sort of an anthology is the chance to create one's own characters and put them through their paces—personality and peculiarities soon followed as I thought about the man in that cockpit and Tracer Talbot—and his singing —was born. Hooray!

Then, I placed Tracer in his element and brought him to his destiny: the largest airship ever known—or unknown—to mankind. I won't deny the parallels between my story and one of my most favorite tales, *20,000*

Leagues Under the Sea, and hey, neither does Tracer—he even mentions it in "Death Seeds the Clouds." If you also got a Captain Nemo and the Nautilus vibe from it, great; that's what I was after, for the most part. And no, I don't consider myself anywhere near the caliber of the great Jules Verne, but his amazing tale has served to inspire me for almost my entire life.

I really enjoyed envisioning the *Silver Cloud* and peopling it with fun characters for Tracer Talbot to encounter. While Captain Dusk was fully-formed before I even started writing, Crewman Brake came to me during a sequence and demanded he be noticed and named. Who was I to deny him? I think he and Tracer hit it off pretty well and I'm glad my hero had someone around him he could count on for a sympathetic ear. Wouldn't we all?

Another part of the fun—and challenge—of writing this story was the research. Looking into such things as Zeppelins and airplanes of the 1930s and the pros and cons of hydrogen versus helium opened up a whole new world to me, and one I'm glad to have been able to play in.

And as always, for all you completists out there, here are the original chapter titles to "Death Seeds the Clouds," in order: "Brush with Death," "The Captain Speaks," "Tracer Investigates," "A Rude Awakening," "Dogfight!" and "Death Opens the Hatch."

So, hopefully at this point you may have liked Tracer Talbot's first adventure enough to wonder if there might be another one somewhere down the road. That, dear readers, is up to you. If you'd like to catch another ride with our hero, please let me know and Tracer Talbot just might return in "The Secret of Silver Cloud Island."

JIM BEARD—A native Toledoan, Jim Beard was introduced to comic books at an early age by his father, who passed on to him a love for the medium and the pulp characters who preceded it. After decades of reading, collecting and dissecting comics, Jim became a published writer when he sold a story to DC Comics in 2002. Since that time he's written Star Wars and Ghostbusters comic stories and contributed articles and essays to several volumes of comic book history. Recently, he edited a book of essays on the 1966 Batman TV series, GOTHAM CITY 14 MILES. Check it out at www.facebook.com/gothamcity14miles.

Currently, Jim provides regular content for Marvel.com, the official

Marvel Comics website, and is a regular columnist for Toledo Free Press. Future projects include SILVER JOHN, a graphic novel adaptation of Manly Wade Wellman's John the Balladeer for Sequential Pulp Comics/ Dark Horse, a Universal Monsters Chronology for Hasslein Books and a history of 1970s comics for TwoMorrows. And a lot more pulp for Airship 27, of course.

Jim's horribly un-updated blog can be found at www.facebook.com/ thebeardjimbeard, and he can usually be found hanging out on Facebook at www.facebook.com/jsajim.

Airship 27

BY I.A WATSON

The duty sergeant rattled his truncheon on the bars. "Rise an' shine, Finian! You made bail."

Harry Finian forced his matted eyes open and realized he was in the drunk-tank again. His knuckles were bruised bloody. The pounding in his head wasn't all down to whiskey sours; some if it was from the contusions.

Last night gradually tumbled back into his memory. The arm-wrestling with Big Bull Kolowski. The fight that followed. The long mirror behind O'Dwyer's speakeasy bar shattering as Frankie Valetti hit it. Things got a bit confused after that.

A more current concern squeezed into Finian's sore brain. "Bail?"

"Your sister's here for you."

Finian's sister lived in Reno now. She hadn't spoken to him since their mother died. He had a hard time imagining that Myrna would come all the way to Boston to get him out of a 3rd Precinct cell.

The hung-over prisoner dragged himself to his feet, stretched, and followed the duty sergeant out of the lock up to the registration desk. Finian's eyes widened when he saw the girl waiting with the clerk. That sure wasn't Myrna!

"Your fine's paid. O'Dwyer's not pressing charges if you pony up for his mirror," the duty sergeant told Finian. He handed the prisoner his belt and boots. "Try to go a whole week without busting up some place this time, would'ya Harry?"

"I didn't start it."

"You never do." The sergeant took the paperwork docket from the clerk and handed it to the woman. "He's all yours."

She nodded and crooked her finger to indicate that Finian should follow her. He had no problem with that.

Outside was a blustery Boston morning. Finian suppressed a shiver; he was dressed in khaki Army & Navy store pants and a torn white vest, hardly the best outfit for an East Coast November. The woman wore a black knee-length coat that probably cost as much as Finian made in a month at the docks. Her glossy blonde hair was pinned up under a matching black cap.

49

"Okay, sister," Finian said at last. "You ain't Myrna. How is it Ma never mentioned you?"

The girl turned on the steps of the precinct house and held out a gloved hand. "You got me," she confessed. She had a New York accent. "My employer sent me to fetch you. A minor ruse seemed acceptable."

Finian wracked his aching head for all the people who might send gorgeous blondes to pick him out of the drunk-tank and came up blank.

"I'm Verity Castlemere. My employer may have a job offer for you."

"And who's your boss?"

The blonde hesitated. "Your contract would be for some confidential work. My employer would prefer to meet you himself before discussing details."

"Details like who he is?"

"Yes. Will you come with me and see him?"

Finian shrugged. "I'll check with my agent and see when I've got a free slot."

Miss Castlemere didn't seem that amused. "This is a serious opportunity, Mr. Finian. My employer can offer you a lot better than teamster rates hauling crates at the wharfside. Unless you like drinking away your earnings every night and waking up in hoosegow?"[1]

"It's a life."

"Is that what you call it?" She reached into her purse and offered Finian a cigarette. "Look, I came a long way to find you. I had to trawl through half the sleazy bars in Boston before I found which one you decided to smash up last night. I was told you're a smart guy with some special skills, but all I'm seeing is a dumb pug who's forgotten how to bathe. So are you coming with me or not?"

Finian took a long suck at the cigarette. It was well blended, refined, a far cry from the coffin nails he bummed down at the waterfront. Like the girl, it was classy and expensive. He took a moment to decide what his future was going to be. He could stay safe in his dockside self-destruction or he could take a chance.

"Lead on, sis," he said to Verity. "Where are we going?"

Miss Castlemere hailed a cab. "North Station," she told the driver. "Chicago," she told Finian.

---

1 Jail

They travelled the water level route, the long stretch of New York Central Railroad line from Boston to Chicago, on the *20th Century Limited*.[2] Miss Castlemere had reservations in a first class car. Less than an hour after waking in a holding cell, Harry Finian was speeding north and west away from everything he knew.

He leaned back on lush upholstery and went with the flow.

Miss Castlemere opened her bag again and brought out a notebook and an envelope. "While we're travelling, a few preparatories," she told him.

Finian waited for the inevitable questions. He wondered how he was going to explain the dishonorable discharge after two years in military prison this time.

Verity unsealed the packet and laid some photographs on the table between them. "Can you identify these?"

Finian looked at the glossy images, then up at the lady. "Weather pictures?"

"You were a U.S. Navy meteorologist, weren't you?" Verity noted.

"Once." Finian looked down at his dirty fingernails and scabbed knuckles. "Long time back now."

"So can you tell me what these photos are of, or have you completely pickled your brain?"

Finian looked back at the photos. It seemed a lifetime since he'd been a weather-puke for the Service. "Some of these are pretty good. Pretty rare stuff too." He singled out an image of a cloud-shape that was shaded in bands. "If this could be in color you'd see it was like a rainbow," he told Verity. "In fact it's called a fire rainbow, and it's pretty damned rare. You need high altitude cirrus clouds, a sun high up in the sky, and ice crystals. No rain, just ice. Whoever took this was pretty far up."

Miss Castlemere tapped a perfect painted fingernail on another image. "What about this?"

That photo showed thick linked globular clouds louring over a leafless forest. It looked like a puffy white hand was menacing the landscape.

"Mammatus clouds," Finian identified. "It's very uncommon to get clouds in sinking air but that's what these are. Some folks say they mean tornados, but that's old wives' bull."

The blonde made a tiny head motion to indicate that she was mildly

2 *20th Century Limited* was one of the iconic steam trains of the early 20th century, although it refers to a set of engine and rolling stick rather than a particular vehicle. First class passengers alighted and disembarked on red carpets—the common phrase "red carpet treatment" derived from this train—and were treated to a luxury journey in absolute comfort.

impressed. "This one?" she demanded, indicating a picture where a set of glowing cloud-strands twisted like luminous cigarette smoke.

"Mother-of-pearl clouds. Nacreus, if you want their Sunday name. Way above the troposphere, ten miles into the stratosphere, higher than we've ever been. They move real slow and they shine every color you can imagine. You only get them at high latitudes, Alaska and the like."

Verity slid a final photograph out of the envelope. "And what is this, Mr. Finian?"

The ex-weatherman looked at the final image. The dark clouds looked almost like jellyfish, with trailing tentacles spiraling down below them. They formed a strange ring with a perfect clear circle in the middle.

Finian frowned. "This... well, the formation's called Altocumulus Castelanus, castle clouds, 'cause they pile up big towers up top. The weird trailers are called virga. They're made of falling rain drops that evaporated again. You hardly ever see these. But..."

"But what?" Verity prompted. She seemed to be waiting for something.

"But that gap in the middle of them—it's called a punch hole—I've never seen that in a formation of this kind before. A punch-hole's an entirely different phenomenon under different conditions. I don't see how it's possible. It's like this is..."

"Yes?"

"This is an entirely new kind of cloud altogether."

Miss Castlemere picked up the photos and returned them to their packet. "Very good, Mr. Finian. You've just passed my employer's first test."

Finian was about to ask what the second dumb test might be when a pair of men who'd been walking along the corridor stopped at his table. The two of them were identically dressed in crumpled cheap brown suits with derbies perched on close-shaved bullet heads. One of them had his hand inside his jacket on a telltale gun bulge.

"Don't make a fuss," he advised Finian and Verity.

"I'll take another coffee, waiter," Finian told him. "Black as the devil. I've got a pounding hangover."

"Very funny," the goon snarled. He had a slight Germanic accent.

The steward had brought a silver tea tray earlier, with delicate china cups and a two-person coffeepot. Finian slammed his hand down on the tray now and slid it hard across into Brown Derby's crotch. The man folded over. Finian caught the back of his head and slammed it into the tabletop.

Brown Derby Two was taken by surprise. He hadn't expected anything other than a quiet extraction on this genteel train. Instead he found a silver tea tray spinning towards his face as hard as Finian could propel it. It caught him on the nose and sprawled him in the aisle.

Finian rose from his seat. He reached to the first groaning thug and pulled the Red 9 Mauser C96 from its concealed holster. As the second goon staggered to his feet again, groping for his weapon, Finian slammed the butt of the heavy German semi-automatic into his face. Brown Derby Two went down again.

The other first class travelers in the parlor stared open-mouthed. "Damned pushy ticket inspectors should have said please," Finian said to them.

The rear compartment door opened. Another pair of beefy brown-suited men entered the coach.

Finian turned to Verity Castlemere. "Time to go," he announced.

The lady nodded mutely, staring down at the slumped muscle. She stuffed the photo packet back in her shoulder-bag and let Finian drag her forward.

The two new thugs spotted them leaving. One of them shouted something in German; Finian didn't care what. He pushed Verity ahead of him on towards the dining car.

"Who are they?" Miss Castlemere demanded as Finian slammed the connecting door shut behind them and twisted the door-handle off to jam it. "What do they want?"

"You're the mystery gal with the mystery boss, sweetheart," Finian replied. "You tell me."

The dining car was half full. Finian called to the steward behind the bar. "Hey, buddy, there's a bunch of drunk yahoos from third class back there bothering the swells. You might wanna throw 'em off the train."

He didn't wait for a response. He kept Verity moving, right past the diners and into the kitchen car. Behind him he heard the splintering of wood as the jammed door was forced.

He ignored the surprised shout of the diminutive Chinaman in charge of the mobile kitchen and blocked the connecting door again.

"What's your plan exactly, Mr. Finian?" Verity demanded. "Keep running until we run out of train or shoot people with that stolen gun?"

"Stay alive," answered the ex-navy weatherman. "Save your sweet tush too. Move."

The door beyond the kitchen car was sealed. Finian shot the lock out. Kitchen staff dived for cover at the gunfire.

The parcel van was stacked high with mailbags and suitcases. This was the front of the train except the coal tender and the engine. Finian decided this was a good place to make a stand. "Get behind those boxes," he ordered. "And don't make a peep."

Miss Castlemere looked like she might object, then relented and ducked for cover. Finian pressed behind a rack of mailbags on the other side of the doorway.

The first thug kicked open the damaged door and strode in, gun in hand. Finian let him in enough so his partner would be right behind him then toppled the stack of bags over onto both of them. As they fell Finian kicked the gun out of the first goon's fist and planted a solid kick to the kidneys to keep him down. The second man struggled to push the heavy netting sacks away but was too late to avoid a pistol-butt to the temple.

The third man blindsided Finian and knocked him down. This bloody-nosed thug was from the original duo who'd come calling. He'd lost his brown derby and Finian had taken his gun but he was big enough to be a threat anyhow.

Finian rolled and tried to aim the Mauser but the goon was ready for him. He clubbed the stolen weapon aside with a swung mailbag and came in close with fists.

Finian's temper flared. He brought his head up with a sharp jerk and felt it connect with the thug's damaged nose. There was a satisfying crack and the man shouted something obscene in German. Finian followed through with a one-two to the gut before landing a haymaker on that shattered hooter.

He heard Verity gasp. Behind him the first man through the door was on his feet again. He'd armed himself with a fire axe and he closed fast for such a big man.

Finian jumped back from the first wild swing then dived close inside the circle of the weapon's arc. He managed an elbow in the man's teeth but got a savage fist in the eye that sent him sprawling backwards. Finian shook his head to clear his vision and prepared to go in again.

The delay was too great. The goon reached down and retrieved his Mauser. He had Finian right in his sights.

The shot was loud in the confined mail car. Finian expected to be dead. It wasn't the comforting release from a life turned sour he'd expected. Suddenly, for the first time in a long time, he knew he wanted to live.

Blood welled from the thug's mouth and the brown-suited man toppled to the floor.

Miss Castlemere held the smoking gun that had killed him. It was the same firearm Finian had taken off the man he'd downed in the lounge car.

There was more shouting from the kitchen car. Train guards or more goons, Finian wasn't sure.

"We need to be out of here, Mr. Finian," Verity said.

Finian didn't argue. He used the fire axe to jimmy the side door. The express train barreled along at lethal speeds, but up ahead was one of the many viaducts on the water level route. "Can you swim?" he asked the sleek blonde with the Mauser.

She nodded tensely. "You'd better be worth this," she told Finian as she prepared to jump.

Finian hadn't been to the Windy City before. He found Chicago very different from Boston; just as bustling, with crowded streets and a teeming dockland, but more open with big skies. It felt more modern too, with new high buildings jutting across the skyline.

The Buick Eight dropped them off on North Michigan Avenue right outside the Wrigley Building. Miss Castlemere led Finian into the lobby of the massive twin-towered skyscraper. A doorman saluted and a lobby clerk hurried to unlock a private elevator.

"Floor twenty-one," Verity told the liftboy. Finian had just enough time to glimpse the bronze plaque by the entranceway and see that the twenty-first floor was headquarters to Bellerophon Enterprises. He'd never heard of it.

"Don't I get a chance to wash up before I get my job interview?" he asked the blonde woman. He pulled at his collar. They'd purchased dry clothes after climbing out of the Cuyahoga but the car that had arrived for them had travelled all night. Finian had a two-day shadow. Miss Castlemere still managed to look perfect.

"My employer wants to see you before he heads back to Washington," the lady replied. It was the most information about her mysterious boss that she'd given so far.

The smooth elevator car rose through the elegant building until it reached the richly-appointed lobby of Bellerophon Enterprises. Finian still couldn't see any clue as to what those enterprises might be, unless the framed photographs of planes and airships lining the waiting lounge offered some hint.

The receptionist rose and hurried to open the door for Miss Castlemere. "He's in the Board Room, ma'am."

Finian followed Verity past a secretaries' room and an accountants' suite. To one side a long office was filled with drafting tables. Miss Castlemere knocked perfunctorily on the double door at the end of the corridor then went straight in.

A tall middle-aged man with a neat moustache was ticking off three functionaries. He was in shirtsleeves, his ten-dollar shirt rolled up his arms, but he reeked of money.

"I don't want excuses, I want results. You tell the research boys to go back to their benches and find me a solution. Remind them that there's a recession on and they can be replaced easy as you can." He glanced over at Verity and Finian and told the functionaries, "Okay, beat it. I've got important business."

Three harried-looking managers shuffled out of the room, each deferentially greeting Miss Castlemere as he passed. When the last of them closed the door behind him, Verity went over to the mustached man and kissed him on the cheek. "Here he is, Frank."

The name triggered an association with the face. Finian didn't follow politics much but he recognized a man some people were tipping for the next President of the United States four years from now. "Senator Nickelhouse."

The senior shareholder of Bellerophon Enterprises nodded. He wasn't surprised to be known. He spent a good proportion of his considerable income keeping his face on the front pages. "Harry Finian. Thanks for coming." None of the contempt and superiority he'd shown for his three underlings sounded in his voice now. His handshake was firm and honest. "Special thanks for keeping my fiancée out of whatever trouble those criminals on the train had planned."

"Were they caught?" Miss Castlemere asked him.

Nickelhouse shook his head. "Took off the same way you did, honey. Quite a feat with one of 'em at least out for the count after meeting Mr. Finian's fists. Whoever they were they'd got an escape route planned. My guess is they expected to use it to get you and Finian away with them."

Finian felt a strange surge of disappointment as he realized that the beautiful blonde who'd shepherded him from Boston belonged to the rich Senator. *What did you expect*, he chided himself inwardly. *Dames that great always go to palookas like him.*

"Well, I can confirm that Mr. Finian is... inventive and that he doesn't lack nerve," Verity told Nickelhouse. "And he seems to know weather."

Finian shrugged.

The politician gathered up the files he'd been auditing on the board room table and passed them to his fiancée to file. Finian could only read the title of the top folder: *Benny*. He gathered that he wasn't supposed to see even that much yet.

"I'm being a bad host," the Senator said to him. "You've come a long way and you don't know why. Want a drink?"

Finian could have done with a brandy. He'd have settled for a beer. He got fresh-squeezed lemonade. "You're off the sauce if you're working for me," Nickelhouse told him. "I made my name championing prohibition in the mid-west so I can't be seen with hooch in my premises now. Also the reports I got say you're a bit too quick to take offence when you're liquored up."

Finian sipped his juice. "I'm still waiting to hear what kind of job makes you send your fiancée all the way cross country to drag me out of a drunk-tank, Senator."

"Call me Frank. Verity insisted on fetching you herself. She was the one who picked you out for recruitment. Long before she was my fiancée she was my personal secretary. I've learned to trust her judgment and let her do things her way."

"Perhaps you should show Mr. Finian the Gallery Room, Frank?" Verity suggested.

"Good idea. This way, Harry. Can I call you Harry?"

"Most folks just call me Finian. If you're paying me you can call me whatever you like."

The Gallery Room was wood paneled but the walls were nearly covered by 8x12 photographs. Most of them were of clouds. Some meteorological charts and aerial maps completed the ensemble. There were a few bare spots where pictures had been taken down.

Finian looked at the images. They were all of high altitude weather. Each had a identification code scratched on the photographic plate: A17, A25, or A26. Two dozen of them featured the rare castle clouds he'd identified yesterday. Half of those had the weird punch hole in their centre.

"Why are they strange?" challenged Senator Nickelhouse.

"The winds shouldn't work like that. The models for how castellanus clouds form, anything up to 20,000 feet, they need mid-atmospheric instability and a high mid-altitude lapse rate. That's why you get heavy showers and thunderstorms, with flight turbulence and icing. But punch-hole clouds—we called 'em fallstreaks back in the service - they need a stable condition where the water doesn't freeze for some reason even though it's below freezing point. The two phenomena shouldn't be able to happen together."

Nickelhouse exchanged a smug glance with Miss Castlemere. "And you should know, Finian. You literally wrote the book, didn't you?" He pulled a thumbed cardboard-bound volume off a desk and dropped it in the ex-weatherman's arms.

Finian fingered the crude staple-bound service manual. It was like a ghost from the past, something from another life. "How'd you get this? This was classified."

"Frank is on the Defense Appropriations Committee and on Ways and Means," Verity replied. "He works closely with the Joint Chiefs."

Something else about the thick document caught Finian's attention: the publication date. "1932?" he questioned. "This was printed last year?"

"What, you think they tore up all your work when they sent you to the brig?" Nickelhouse asked. "You were the Navy's go-to guy on weird weather back in the day. Your output was so good it's still the current manual now. Some of your prediction models are still classified. Shame they let you go."

Finian tossed the manual back onto the table. "Too bad the court-martial board saw it different."

"You did put a senior officer and two of his staff in the hospital," Miss Castlemere pointed out. "He's never going to walk again. Two years in military prison was letting you off real easy."

"Him still breathing after what he did to that little Mexican girl was letting him off real easy," snarled Finian. He hadn't realized how strongly he still felt on the subject. He ached for a drink.

Nickelhouse had read the official report. The trial transcript was locked in his desk right now. "They couldn't let you off scot-free after that. But they understood the circumstances. They could have given you much worse than you got."

"Captain Kenner got a medical discharge," spat Finian. "But then, his family had old money." *Like yours, Senator,* he didn't need to add.

Nickelhouse was a good politician. He knew when to move the conversation on. "Well, the Navy's loss is my gain. As you can tell, I'm very interested in this particular weather phenomenon and I'm looking to hire an expert who can tell me some more about it. I'm hoping you'll be my go-to guy now."

"The pay's a whole lot more than a Navy lieutenant's salary, Mr. Finian," Miss Castlemere promised.

Finian looked at the weather diagrams pinned beside the photographs. "What about the guys that did these for you?"

"They are no longer with us," said the Senator.

"I looked long and hard to find the right man for this job, Finian," Verity persuaded. "I think it should be you."

"But Krauts with shooters will keep jumping out to try and pop me?" the weatherman noted.

Nickelhouse frowned at that. "We're looking into the incident. I don't like my fiancée being threatened. There were less than half a dozen people knew she was going to Boston to find you, exactly three who were aware of her travel plans on the *20th Century*. My agents will get to the bottom of this."

"And do 'your agents' know why some gunsels are so interested in me or your dame or some damn weather pictures that they'd shoot up a train to get 'em?"

Nickelhouse and Verity exchanged another significant look.

"I can probably tell you," the Senator admitted, "after you've signed on."

"There's a confidentiality clause comes with the job," his fiancée secretary warned.

Finian thought through his options: back to Boston and the bottle and to the hurt-numbing grind that would eventually kill him, or off into the unknown where he'd have to dig up skills and a personality he thought he'd safely buried forever. It was a hard choice. Being drunk two-fisted hellraiser Finian was much easier.

Verity Castlemere took his hand. "Please?" she asked.

Finian didn't even realize he'd signed the papers till he was handing back the fountain pen.

They took Senator Nickelhouse's Cadillac up the I50 to Rockford in Winnebago County, then branched off north just into Stephenson. There were few road signs out here, but Finian guessed they couldn't be far off the Wisconsin border. The sun was setting when the chauffer pulled the sleek black vehicle onto an unmarked farm road and followed a line of windbreak trees out past a chain of cornfields.

The Senator didn't speak to him. Nickelhouse spent the journey rattling off a series of letters to Verity, which she shorthanded down at breakneck speed. Most of the correspondence was about fundraising, confirming Finian's view that politics was mostly about the money. If so then Frank Nickelhouse was a good politician.

Nickelhouse broke off when the car slowed down at a high metal gate. A pair of uniformed security men came out of a watch-house and saluted the vehicle. They hurried to swing aside the barrier so the Senator could drive on.

There was no place sign but the dark blue guard uniforms had Bellerophon Enterprises embroidered onto their breast pockets.

Another turn brought the whole compound into view. Inside the ring of surrounding fields were a vast tarmac and a dozen workshops and buildings of various sizes. Some were clearly aircraft hangers. Three huge brick and tin sheds, each maybe a thousand feet long, dominated the north end of the complex. Their hundred foot high doors were closed. A row of light aircraft were parked on runways to the west.

"This is Bellerophon," Nickelhouse told Finian proudly. "Brooking Field Works. It's a little project I'm running with Uncle Sam."

The airfield at least explained why they might need a weatherman, Finian supposed. A windsock fluttered atop an air control tower. "This is why I had to sign a secrecy form," he guessed.

"Oh, this is just the start of it, Finian. This is the place where the world will change."

The car drove across the tarmac and drew to a halt outside the first big hangar. Men in overalls were already pouring out to greet their employer—telephone poles were strung all over the base. The low sun stretched the men's shadows far off to the east.

A balding man with fierce side-whiskers came forward. He wore a grey lab-coat over a bulging waistcoat. A slide rule and a hammer protruded out of his pocket. He opened the door for the Senator. "Welcome back, Mr. Nickelhouse," he said in a Scots burr.

The Senator didn't bother returning the greeting. "What's the update?" he demanded.

"She's on schedule and close to ready. We need the new stabilizers fitting but all the parts have shipped now. She'll be finished on time."

Nickelhouse got out of the car. Verity and Finian followed.

"Finian, this is McHenry," Miss Castlemere introduced. "Mr. McHenry's the senior engineer on our project. Finian's our new weatherman."

The Scotsman grabbed Finian's hand and pumped it. "Welcome to the madhouse then, laddie," he said. There was some undertone that caught

Finian's attention but he had no time to probe it. Nickelhouse was already striding into the hanger.

Finian followed through the service door to the vast interior. He'd already guessed that a building this size couldn't be for airplanes, but he hadn't expected to see anything like the cat's cradle of frames and pulleys that held the huge construction before him.

McHenry appeared at his shoulder. "Not bad, eh? This is our latest little invention."

Hanging in the scaffolding was a gleaming silver tube, a cylinder with rounded ends. Brushed metal panels were being bolted onto the structure, gradually hiding the fabric bags that filled the interior. A glass and aluminum spine of corridors and cabins hung underneath. Men swarmed over the machine, spot-welding and riveting.

It was the skeleton of an airship.

McHenry took Finian's silence as a cue for more exposition. "Seven hundred and fifty feet long, with duraluminum bulkheads containing fifteen separate cotton gas bags wrapped in three hundred thousand sheets of fish skin with a volume of close to seven million cubic feet. Six Maybeck VL-2 gasoline engines offering a maximum speed of up to ninety miles an hour. With eighteen thousand gallons of fuel in store she'll have a range of ten thousand miles."

"She's big," said Finian.

Miss Castlemere smiled at the weatherman's expression. "Everyone says that. But her size isn't the most impressive thing, is it Mr. McHenry?"

The engineer shook his head. "There's plenty of big ships out there. The Zeppelin company's turning them out over in Germany faster than we can count 'em. The British *R101* was a whisker larger than our girl here before she went down with such losses.[3] But she couldn't do the tricks this lassie will manage."

Nickelhouse came back to the conversation. "The issues with fixed frame airships are all about lift and maneuverability," he lectured. "Our designs include some brilliant innovations by a real genius of a designer—you'll meet him shortly—and allow us to rise vertically and turn much quicker than anything else in the skies."

"Aye," agreed McHenry. "Add in the other wee surprises like the fact she'll carry four little planes for scouting and such-like and a remote

3 On 5th October 1930, the *R101* crashed on its maiden voyage over France, killing 48 of the 54 people aboard including the British Air Minister Lord Thompson. At the time it was the world's largest aircraft, surpassed only by the *Hindenburg* five years later.

"It was the skeleton of an airship."

observation cradle and ye've got something very special indeed." And yet the Scot seemed downcast.

Finian looked along the length of the airship's frame. The main car below was almost complete now. Men were inside the structure fastening in bulkhead walls and covering them with wooden paneling. Gantries led fore and aft to other control stations that serviced ballast mechanisms and engines. The big German motors that propelled the ship forward hung down on strong gimbals that allowed them to turn in all directions.

Amidst all the bustle as workmen swarmed the huge frame maintained a stately majesty, like a queen waiting her moment to rise. It seemed as if the airship was patiently counting the days until she could rule the air.

A painter finished stenciling the vessel's designation on the side of her car: BE-A27. Bellerophon Enterprise's Airship 27.

For the second time in his life, Harry Finian fell in love.

Finian rose from his bunk early the next morning. The clock in the common room said 5:32. He sluiced himself in the sink and pulled on the Bellerophon Enterprises overalls he'd been provided with. He'd brought nothing with him from his rented room back in Boston and regretted nothing he'd left behind. The camp shop had provided the necessaries of life: a shaving kit, a comb, some cheap clothes and underwear, and a carton of cigarettes.

The weatherman looked out across the airfield and the expanse of corn beyond. He stretched, wondering why he felt different. Then he realized he had no hangover. His thoughts were clear. It was the first time he'd woken like that for as long as he could remember.

He grabbed a tin mug of coffee from the pot on the stove and downed it for breakfast. He could have headed over to the mess hut where even this early the cook was frying up bacon and eggs. Instead he jog-trotted over to the big hangar to see the A27 again.

Early as it was, McHenry was there before him; maybe the Scotsman had never been to bed. The engineer was shouting up to the men attaching the hydraulics to the powerful VL-2 engines that turned the aluminum propellers. Evidently they needed some kind of special seal and a grease that didn't freeze up at high altitudes.

McHenry turned and greeted the weatherman with a knowing smile. "I knew you'd be back soon. I've seen that smitten expression on men's faces before when they've seen their first airship."

"I've hired on. I want to earn my keep," Finian covered. "Nobody's told me yet what I actually have to do." Nickelhouse had vanished straight after showing off his toy last night to go answer what seemed like hundreds of administrative questions. Then the politician had driven back to Chicago to catch a connection to Washington. Finian wasn't sure if Verity Castlemere had gone with him.

"What you do?" McHenry chuckled. "They didn't tell you the weather spotter's job on this lady?"

A thrill surged through Finian. He was expected to fly as part of the A27's crew!

McHenry led him up a ladder onto the scaffolding framework then into the main car beneath the gasbags. The long metal spine corridor ran almost the whole length of the rigid 'balloon' structure and contained the various cabins and workspaces of the vessel. Even overnight this section looked much more finished. The walls were all welded in and elegant paneling had been screwed over the frame. Floors were in place and some of them were already covered in carpet or linoleum.

McHenry reeled off a guided tour as he led Finian the length of the carriage. "Stateroom. Captain's cabin. Officer's quarters. Ward room. Radio room. Navigation room. That ladder takes you down to the piloting gondola, the Conn car. Mind that cable." He led on into a wider set of chambers. "Main gallery, a dining mess and lounge salon combined. Those are passenger cabins lining it. Further back is the galley, quartermaster's store, machine shop, engine bays, freight hold, crew quarters, then the service gantries to the tail section."

They moved aft along the underside of the ship. Technicians were installing wire-caged electric lights along the thruway.

The largest space came next. "Hangar," said McHenry.

Finian whistled. The sides of the deck he'd entered actually slid open, making a launching platform for airplanes.

"We use the Curtis F9C Sparrowhawk. They're only twenty feet long with a twenty-five foot wingspan. We can pack four aboard, launched and recovered with a hook and arrow system. The flying trapeze, the pilots call it. Basically we dangle 'em over the side till they catch the slipstream and let 'em go. They have to fly in close formation so we can catch 'em back in again like fish on a line."

"Sounds suicidal," Finian observed.

McHenry chuckled. "You'd have to be mad to fly on this. But the weatherman, he's the craziest bastard of all."

That made no sense to Finian. "Why? What's so dangerous about measuring wind and humidity and pressure?" The jibes of Navy men about a rear-end weather-puke had led to more than one fistfight.

"You're still thinking sea vessels," the engineer said, waggling his finger. "Down this ladder."

The aft gondola was much smaller than the control room where the pilot steered the ship. This wasn't much bigger than a Ford motor car, a glass and aluminum blister below the ship's spine. It currently contained a single chair with leather harness-straps on it. A mass of wiring awaited connection of radio and telephone.

"This is one of our resident genius' innovations," McHenry smirked. "He calls it the weather basket."

Finian looked at a series of levers that made no sense. "There's good all round visibility, I guess," he admitted, looking out of the newly-glazed windows at the underside of the airship. A pair of workmen were hanging in harnesses fitting the searchlights. "Is this where I do weather observations from?" It occurred to the weatherman that windspeed and aerial conditions would be vitally important to an air craft.

"Yes and no," answered McHenry. "You see, one of th' big problems airships have is with clouds. They avoid them if they can, because you can't easily judge altitude in clouds, even with barometer, not fast enough, and because you get pressure ridges and wind systems. But this ship's intended to go through clouds, ye ken."

Finian remembered the room full of pictures of Altocumulus Castellanus and Nickelhouse's curious obsession with the strange punch-hole phenomenon.

"So the idea is that you lower a basket down below the ship, paid out on steel cables, and a man drops out from the cloud cover and takes a look at what's below. A weatherman."

"Wait," Finian demanded. "Are you saying this car here reels down on a piece of string and I dangle under the airship reporting on the weather?"

"I hope you don't get motion sickness, Mr. Finian."

Finian imagined what it would be like, strapped in to that reinforced chair, swinging in the vicious crosswinds under the clouds. "I guess I know now why they hired me. They couldn't get anyone else dumb enough for the job, right?"

"There's not many want to try this again, no."

"Again?" The A-27 wasn't even finished. Then the realization struck Finian. "This is Airship 27. What happened to the other twenty-six?"

Finian was half way through his bacon, eggs and hash browns when he heard someone approach him. "May I join you?" Miss Castlemere asked.

The weatherman gestured at a chair. "It's your fiancée's mess hall," he pointed out.

Verity slid into the seat opposite and laid her tray on the table. She'd picked up a green salad and an orange juice. "How are you settling in, Finian?"

"Well, this morning I heard I was supposed to hang on a wire in a giant yo-yo and tell people if it was raining downside. You didn't mention that in Boston."

"You can see why we have to keep this development secret. This is world-leading stuff we're doing here."

"You didn't mention this was your twenty-seventh go at getting it right, either."

Verity didn't apologize. "We have to do this. The next conflict, the next war, is going to be determined by air power. The Germans know this. That's why they're investing so much in air technology. Their new Chancellor, Herr Hitler, he's a big supporter of it.[4] The British, the French, the Russians, everybody's investigating this stuff. Do you want the USA to be left behind?"

"So this is a government project, some top-secret military scheme?"

Miss Castlemere hesitated a fraction too long. "It was. The Defense Department financed the first models, the A1 through the A19, although most of those never got off the drawing board. When the A20 didn't perform as well as we hoped…"

"You mean when it crashed on takeoff," corrected Finian. He'd talked with McHenry.

"Yes, then, though there was no loss of life that time. But that was when Frank's enemies in government used their influence to cut off military funding for the work. There's a small military air project still happening, but not using the designs and inventions we've pioneered here."

"So all of this, A21 on, it on the Senator's dime?"

"There are some like-minded backers too. You'll meet them when they visit."

---

4 Adolf Hitler became Chancellor of Germany in January 1933. A month later after the Reichstag fire many German liberties were suspended. By April the Gestapo were established. By May the ruling Nazi party had legalized eugenic sterilization. Germany's aggressive new policies and her lead in the military application of airships was not unnoticed by other nations, so interest in developing workable designs to challenge that supremacy intensified.

"Benny?" asked Finian, remembering the file in Nickelhouse's board room.

Verity's eyebrows shot up. "Where did you hear that name?"

"Don't recall. Who is he?"

"Classified. But yes, this project is Frank's money at work. He's a patriot, Finian."

The weatherman bit back a cynical reply about electioneering publicity. Maybe he didn't like Nickelhouse because Nickelhouse had Verity.

"Without government restraints Frank was able to bring Dr. Utter directly onto the project. Edward Utter's that genius we keep talking about. He's eccentric even for a Brit, but that kid solved more design and technical problems in his first day here than our entire team of experts had in a year before that."

"Kid?"

Verity shrugged. "You expect geniuses to be old men with white beards. Utter's no older than me." She smiled. "But you're not going to ask my age, are you, Finian?"

Finian sipped his Navy-style coffee, hot, sweet, black. "There's plenty I'd like to know about you, sweets, but I hear you're already booked."

Miss Castlemere looked at her left hand. There was no engagement ring there. "Frank's career is at a delicate moment. Announcing his betrothal to a nobody from nowhere wouldn't help him get the nomination he's hoping for eighteen months from now."

"But you and he are an item. He's your fiancée."

Verity nodded. "I owe him a lot."

"That's not usually the first thing a girl says when she's talking about the guy she's getting hitched to."

"What I say about Frank isn't your business, Mr. Finian. Your concern, as you just pointed out, is to dangle on a rope and spot which way the wind blows you. That's all."

She left her half-finished meal on the table and walked away.

Miss Castlemere was still formal and distant when she introduced Finian to Dr. Utter later that day.

The man everyone claimed was a genius looked like a spotty teenager to Finian. He wore a white shirt buttoned to the collar but no tie, and his cuffs were held together with bulldog clips rather than cufflinks. His workshop was the neatest, most organized space the weatherman had ever seen.

"You like to be able to find things?" Finian guessed.

"A tidy mind starts with a tidy room," Edward Utter responded. He picked up the file Verity had laid down on a table and placed it on a different table, lined up with the other documents that awaited his attention. "There is finite time in the day. That time has to be carefully apportioned so it is not wasted. Time spent searching for papers, equipment, or materials is time lost. Efficiency in organization equates to efficiency in life."

"Sure," agreed Finian vaguely. He waited until Utter's back was turned then shifted the dossier the scientist had just positioned so it was crooked again.

"I am instructed that you are the new meteorologist for the A27 prototype," Utter went on. "I have reviewed the manual you prepared for Navy extreme weather identification and found it of merit. There is a copy on the third shelf there that you may take with you in which I have corrected the typographical and grammatical errors. You may find some of the marginalia instructional also." He tidied the file again without even realizing he was doing it.

"I wanted you two to meet so you could discuss the fine detail of the weather gondola," Verity explained. "The engineering's already in place, and much improved from the A24 to avoid the accident that, well, that accident, but I thought it might be helpful for you to review the layout of the instruments and so on."

"Makes sense," admitted Finian. "There's some gauges it would be better to have in peripheral vision even while I'm looking out of the windows, and a couple of changes to how the writing table folds out wouldn't hurt."

"I will be happy to review your proposals," replied Utter. "Previous incumbents of your position seemed more concerned about the comfort of their seating harness and the pitch and yaw of the compartment than addressing the technical requirements of their duty post."

"Yeah. Just make sure there's a packet of paper bags I can upchuck into if the chop gets too much and I'm good on that. But from what I saw earlier I think I'll need better window wipers, with manual levers for back-up in case the mechanisms seize. I want a fluid-mounted compass like they have for high seas. I want a mounting for the anemometer that's a miniature of the ones you've put on the engines that can angle it all different ways. And I want a physical hatch on the floor so I can actually open it up and stick my head out if I have to. Please."

To his surprise Utter made quick efficient notes on a pad in his pocket. He tore the sheet out and stabbed it onto a spike docket. "Those seem like reasonable innovations," the scientist judged. "I will schedule some time to discuss the specifications of the equipment and structural modifications with you. Mr. McHenry will also need to be present, Miss Castlemere."

"Oh good," breathed Verity. "Another meeting with you and McHenry in the same room."

Finian took his chance while he was with the scientist. "Since I got you here, Doc, maybe I can ask you something. This isn't the first airship from this production line, not by a long shot. So what went wrong with all the rest?"

Utter looked up. "Different things, of course. It would be ridiculous to repeat the same error twice. Materials failure. A shoddy joint weld. Inclement weather. A failure of the steering coupling on the lateral planes. Sabotage, of course?"

"Sabotage?"

"Airship 24 burned in its hangar," Miss Castlemere explained. "That was when we moved Bellerophon here."

"Airship 20 and Airship 23 may also have been compromised," Dr. Utter noted. "The surviving debris was not suitable for a proper evaluation."

Finian looked at the blueprints for the big sky clipper pinned out across one wall of Utter's workshop. "Just how many of these things have you guys crashed?"

"Airship 27 is the eighth serious prototype ready for launch," the scientist counted. "The early models were mere experiments and cannot be counted. Airship 15 was the first version worthy of the name, first laid down in 1928, completed in 1930."

"That was the one with the structural failure," Miss Castlemere footnoted. "It snapped."

"Airship 16 was cannibalized to make Airship 17," went on Utter. "That one made a successful flight but was broken down to make Airship 18 with better aileron control and a safer fuel containment. Sadly Airship 18 had to make an emergency landing five minutes in flight due to a main joint failure."

"Only one life was lost," Verity hastened to add.

"Yes. The weather gondola was completely crushed," Edward Utter noted. He had no concept of tact. "Airship 19 was scrapped in the hangar when I calculated the limited lift the arrangement of engines those idiots on the design team had specified. Airship 20 corrected that fault but failed on trial when the steering system proved inadequate. I redesigned that piece of folly from scratch myself, I promise you."

"Airships 21 and 22 were each remodeled into their next incarnation as I improved the maneuverability through experiment," the scientist continued. "Airship 23 suffered a ruptured gas sack but managed to land without sparking an explosion. It was redesigned as Airship 24 but was never trialed due to an explosion in the hangar."

Miss Castlemere looked uncomfortable about that one. "That was costly. In life, I mean, not just dollars, though Frank had to relocate everything here. This is where we'd already been building Airships 25 and 26. So we moved the whole operation to Brooking Field."

"And what happened to them?" wondered Finian. He was starting to wonder what kind of suicide program he'd signed on to.

"Airship 25 flew three successful trials," Verity answered. "The photographs of that weird cloud you saw came from one of them. On its fourth mission it crashed. With all hands."

"Crashed?" Finian couldn't see it. "Something like that, with what, fifty, sixty guys on board, that'd have made the papers."

"It's a classified project. Frank has pull. Besides, there wasn't much wreckage. She probably went down over the Great Lakes."

"Mr. McHenry posits that Airship 25 was shot down," Dr. Utter observed. "He believes such fragments as we have retrieved show signs of shellfire."

"What, the Canadians bombed it?" Finian said skeptically.

"That takes us to Airship 26," said Verity. "She tested fine. In many ways she was identical to our current model, although her piloting systems and engine mountings weren't as sophisticated. She checked out fine and passed her maiden flight with a clean bill."

"So what happened?"

"Frank tasked her to investigate those clouds again—the ones with the rings in them? She radioed back that she'd found one and was approaching it. That was the last we heard from her."

"So she crashed as well? There can be all kinds of turbulence under those castle clouds. The trailing virga can…"

"There was no wreckage at all this time," Dr. Utter noted. He seemed offended by the untidiness of the data. "There is no evidence it ever crashed."

"But it hasn't been seen in three months," pointed out Miss Castlemere. "So where did it go?"

"Where did it go?" asked Linden Creed III. The Texas oilman wore a white suit and hooked his thumbs into a big belt-buckle shaped like a steer. He'd had to leave his cigar outside the A27's hangar but he'd kept the Stetson that was such a part of the image he liked to project.

"We don't know, sir," answered Matteson, the dour retired G-Man who was Nickelhouse's head of security at Brooking Field. "The best theory so far is that she was swept into the upper atmosphere, dragged along by some high-altitude airstream, and ditched over the ocean."

Finian thought that very unlikely. Nor did it explain the A26's sudden radio silence, or why it hadn't launched its Sparrowhawk biplanes.

"That's an awfully big thing to just lose, son," Creed told the security chief. "Forty thousand dollars of aircraft just up and vanished. Another forty thousand dollars of aircraft."

"We found traces of the A25," Matteson argued. He couldn't offer any better progress than that. "Senator Nickelhouse will be with us shortly. He'll be able to speak about progress better and answer any technical or financial questions you have."

So Creed was the money too, Finian concluded. He remembered the Texan's name from the letters the Senator had rattled off to Miss Castlemere. Now the oil baron was here to check in on his investment.

"Too many damn problems with this project, I'd say," Creed complained. "Either it's sabotage and there's some guy still working on that there airship who's gonna try again to blow it up or else somebody's using that bullflap to hide the shoddy job they did fitting these balloons out."

Finian could see how much Matteson hated being reminded that he hadn't found enough answers. "Investigations are ongoing," was all the security chief could say.

"And what's this I hear about that little secretary girl who runs round with Nickelhouse getting shot at on a train by some Kraut musclemen? Hell, if that sweet tomato was my personal assistant I wouldn't be sending her off to get chased by goons! I'd be keeping that l'il filly real close an' personal!"

"We've traced the men to a boat waiting offshore. We're checking international shipping schedules to try and figure where they went," Matteson replied. That was news to Finian too.

Creed shook his head. "I don't like it one little bit," he promised. "And you can tell your Senator that..."

"Here's Nickelhouse now," Finian interrupted. He pointed to where the Senator and Miss Castlemere had entered the hangar with McHenry.

"About time," grumbled the Texan. He turned his back on Matteson and Finian and stalked over to the man he's come to meet. "Nickelhouse, you old dog! I guess you know this is the last roll of the dice we money men are gonna give you right? So tell me what you've been throwing my dough at, Senator…"

Finian's days found a new routine. His new role required him to sharpen skills he'd thought he'd never use again, to crack books like he'd done back as a midshipman. Waking sober and opening a textbook came as a novel experience after so long. The weatherman also had to be familiar with the working and procedures of an airship so his meteorological studies were supplemented with lectures and training about the vessel he'd be crewing.

The principles were as rigorous as those for shipboard safety at sea, but different. On an airship lift was life, so every pound was carefully considered before being brought aboard. And flame, not water, was the enemy. A single spark in the wrong place could ignite the hydrogen tanked into the lift body and end everything in a fiery ball. Equipment, procedures, even the soft rubber soles the crew wore aboard the airship were all geared to minimizing the danger.

Finian knew about navigation. He was familiar with longitudes and latitudes and could calculate with sextant and compass. But aboard the A27 there were not only port and starboard but also pitch, yaw, and roll, the mechanics of three-dimensional movement. Steering was not by water pushed against a rudder but by air across ailerons and by turning propellers. The system of communication bells and whistles was adapted from the naval service but still differed from what he'd known before.

Finian threw himself into it. Airship 27 had somehow become his passion, the thing that had been missing from his life ever since Susie had tossed his ring back when that tribunal had sentenced him for his offence. The A27 was a lady who required attention and devotion. He studied and sweated freely because it was for her.

There were other opportunities on base and Finian took them as well. The gym was free and the weatherman hadn't realized how out of shape he'd allowed himself to become. He began each day with a five mile run and worked out till he was topping his best at reps afterwards. As the booze sweated out of his system and his hand steadied he also found the gun range and reacquainted himself with rifle and pistol.

His days were interspersed with meetings. He saw Dr. Utter quite

"There were other opportunities on base…"

often; the eccentric genius seemed to have taken a liking to him. Utter had implemented all of Finian's suggestions and often called the weatherman in to talk though other innovations. Utter had a talent for design but no feel at all for how people might want to use his equipment. Finian's most useful contributions were in sketching out the best layouts for use by men under pressure.

McHenry had a true Scottish temperament, veering from brooding to jolly and back again a dozen times an hour. Finian had time for the man because he took his work so seriously. McHenry had survived the various disasters that had beset previous models and was determined that Airship 27 should be nothing short of perfect. Finian patiently endured hours of tedious rehearsals for his gondola suspension drops because it made McHenry content.

Finian saw Miss Castlemere less, usually only at lunch in the canteen, and then often at a distance. She smiled at him again now, but she kept space between them. He only met Senator Nickelhouse twice; each occasion was to give a brief report before the busy tycoon moved on. He only heard that Lindon Creed III had been at Brooking Field after the tycoon had left again.

Days turned to weeks and the engineers began the final fittings on the airship. Unlike a true military vessel, the specifications for Airship 27 included some touches of luxury. The main lounge was as well appointed as any steamer's ward room with a full-sized bar and a Steinway piano. McHenry shook his head at the weight costs but Nickelhouse had an eye for style. Finian knew that it was these personal touches that would make A27 the queen of the air.

In the evenings Finian played cards with the four air aces who would pilot the Sparrowhawks off the ship. Three of them were ex-military. All had been recruited from flying circuses or show-grounds. Senior amongst them was 'Mac' Machen, who rumor claimed had once flown smuggled hooch from Canada. They were uniformly young, brash, and convinced they would live forever despite the fates of their predecessors. Finian wondered if he'd ever been that naive. They still managed to take money from him at poker though.

Captain Stafford was the experienced Navy Air Corp officer seconded to command the airship. He permanently shifted onto base a few days after Finian's arrival, interviewed the weatherman to satisfy himself of Finian's competence and character, but otherwise stayed out of Finian's hair. When they did meet it was usually when Stafford wanted his officers briefed about some aspect of the gulf stream or the best way to approach or avoid some specific atmospheric condition.

The other officers were likewise Navy veterans. Finian was disappointed to find that he no longer easily fitted with the clean-cut academy graduates. He had nothing against the first officer Thomson or the navigator Oxlen or any of the rest; but he had nothing left in common with them either. The ensigns Harvey, Gilliand, and Bowman seemed little more than boys.

Finian never attempted to leave the base so he didn't join in the objections when all leave was cancelled. A few of the men regularly visited a cat-house in Rockford and kicked up a fuss, but Finian privately agreed with the dour security chief Matteson that in the last few days before flight there were more urgent things to worry about than a few horny guys with Friday night money to spend.

The camp's confinement brought home to everyone that launch day was coming. Scuttlebutt had it that Airship 27 was it; if this model failed then the funding ran out. Certainly the other construction hangars on site were closed up and empty. It was do or die.

Finian asked Miss Castlemere about it one lunchtime when they happened to be next to each other in the serving line.

"There are limits to how many times the project can fail," Verity admitted, "but they're about political credibility more than money. The government's already sore over the loss of the *Akron*. Her sister the *Macon*'s on probation as well now.[5] If Frank is to prove Dr. Utter's design it has to be soon."

Finian detected a tension of urgency in the woman's words that didn't seem entirely accounted for by the imminent development of rival airships. "I get the need to have a product for Nickelhouse to show the brass, and I've heard Lindon Creed's bitching, but I don't get what the big deal about chasing castle clouds is. From what I hear the A25 and A26 were both fine till the Senator sent them hunting his fallstreaks."

Verity slid her eyes elsewhere. "It's just an interesting scientific opportunity, that's all. You know how much we still have to learn about weather systems."

---

5 The *USS Akron*, the ZRS-4, was a helium-filled rigid body Navy airship commissioned in 1929. The largest air vessel built in the USA at the time of her launch in 1931 (only 30ft shorter than the *Hindenberg*), she and her sister ship *USS Macon* had fighter plane launch capacity and innovative "weather stations" or "spy cars" that could be lowered out of cloud. The fictional Airship 27 of our present narrative most closely resembles the technical and layout specifications of these ships. The *Akron* crashed in bad weather on April 3rd 1933 with the loss of 73 lives. The *Macon* crashed in 1935. Both losses were attributed to human error.

"Yeah. The more we learn, the more we don't know."

Still unconvinced, Finian asked Dr. Utter directly what was so urgent about getting Airship 27 up into an Altocumulus Castellanus formation.

"Have you been shown Block 9?" the scientist replied.

Finian checked his mental map of the camp, honed by many sweaty circuits in his morning runs. "One storey brick hut over behind the conn tower?" he checked. "I thought it was just storage."

"If you've not been shown Block 9 then I can't answer your question," Utter said.

With the closure of the gates the social life of the camp became even more intense. The home-made booze got even rougher, the tension fights got more vicious, and the poker games had higher stakes. That was why Finian tossed down his losing hand and walked away from the table while he still had five bucks in his pocket and he hadn't yet wiped the smirk off the flyboys who had the rest of his pay packet.

He bummed a cigarette off one of the ground-crew guys and went outside to cool off.

It was a warm summer's night, clear and bright, and the stars were out. Here away from the city it was almost as good as being at sea for watching the skies. Finian recognized the familiar constellations, watched a shooting star pass across Orion's belt, and puffed at his smoke.

Then he saw the shadows move.

He froze, not sure whether he'd just imagined the ripple in the corner of his eye. Old instincts made him douse his cigarette and draw back into the sheltering cover of the alley beside the mess hall.

He saw movement again, the furtive step of someone not wanting to be spotted.

Finian considered heading back into the mess and sounding the alarm, calling out the men gathered round card table and piano; but if he'd just spotted some drunk sliding off to relieve himself or one of the construction boys creeping to a secret liaison with a pool typist he'd look like a fool. He chose to follow the movement and see some more.

The intruder—if indeed it was an intruder—slipped past the barracks and vehicle pound towards the control tower. Finian followed, hoping one of the guards with dogs would patrol past; none did. The dark shape slid behind the glass-topped observation platform.

Finian hurried after, also slipping from shadow to shadow. When he heard a stealthy step heading back his way he barely had time to press himself into a gap between storage huts

A lithe form rounded the corner and bumped into him. A slash of starlight illuminated the face of Verity Castlemere.

"What are you…?" he began before she pushed a finger to his lips.

"Shh. There's someone there."

Verity felt good in his arms, but she pulled away and poked a head round the corner. "I think there's a burglar," she said.

"I thought it was you," Finian said. "I've been following."

"I glimpsed movement but I wasn't sure. Should we get help?"

"You go. I'll go see what this Joe's up to, whoever he is."

Verity shook her head. "I don't think so, Finian. I'd prefer not to be shot at again but if that mook's got a gun then it's a really dumb idea for you to go after him alone."

Finian remembered the German men who'd tried to get them on the train. "Stay behind me then," he told the blonde. "If you get damaged your fiancée'll dock it from my wages."

He padded round the corner and checked the door of the conn tower. At this time of night it was shut down and locked.

A muffled crack from the far side of the building betrayed a padlock being jimmied.

"Okay, that isn't a moonlight rendezvous," Finian breathed. "That's a break-in."

"We'd better go for help," decided Miss Castlemere. "Together. He might not be alone."

Finian shook his head. "That's Block 9, right? What's in there that's worth stealing?"

Verity shook her head. "Nothing. Nothing I can tell you about. We just need to find Chief Matteson. Come on."

Finian's hands doubled into firsts. "Nah. I've been such a good boy these last few weeks I'd forgotten how much I've missed this." He ran forward, straight for the ajar door to Block 9. If Verity had a problem with it he didn't wait to hear.

It was dark inside the hut. Finian nearly tripped over a large wire box, something like an animal cage. His stumble alerted the intruder, who hurled a heavy set of bolt cutters at him and reached for a pistol.

Finian kicked the cage across the floor. It slammed into the burglar's knees. The man fell backwards with a yelp, knocking open the door whose padlock he'd just snipped.

Finian dived forward, hoping to get to the intruder before the man thought to find his semi-automatic again. He never got there.

Something flew down at the trespasser, flapping bat-like wings that were more than eight feet from tip to tip. Finian couldn't make out the detail in the darkness, but there was a foul musk unlike anything he'd smelled before and a hideous shriek that echoed around what he now recognized to be a giant aviary inside the warehouse.

The intruder screamed as a long pointed beak with serrated edges closed on his arm. Finian heard the bones cracking even before the first blood splashed over the wall.

The burglar had found his weapon. He fired off a couple of rounds—Finian saw the muzzle flashes—but the shots went wild, ricocheting high onto the tin roof. The sharp noise must have disturbed the creature though. It shook the intruder like a bird with a worm then spilled him loose onto the floor, his right arm a wrecked gory mess.

Finian saw the monster for the first time as it unfolded its wings again and came straight at him. Gleaming amber eyes unlike any bird he'd ever seen focused on him. Thick featherless wings beat a heavy rhythm. The weatherman had a brief impression of teeth inside the beak and of talons like knives before his survival instincts cut in and he dived to the floor.

He rolled over the animal cage and tumbled down behind it. He scrambled away, looking for something he could use to fend the creature off. Only when it vanished through the outside door did Finian realize that he'd just been in the way between the monster and freedom.

He dashed to the door. Verity Castlemere was right outside staring at the ungainly shape vanishing into the night sky. "Frank is going to be livid," she said.

The intruder moaned and tried to rise but his injuries were too severe. His arm was almost severed. Finian knew from the way blood was spurting in aortal spasms that there was no saving him.

The weatherman rushed over to try and question the dying man. The burglar wore a black camouflage suit and his face was darkened with soot. He had the same crew-cut stubble as the goons on the train; he might even have been one of them. He muttered something in German that could have been a prayer then stopped moving.

By the time Security Chief Matteson arrived there was nothing to be done.

Finian declined the blanket the guards tried to put around his shoulder but he accepted the slug of scotch that Matteson poured him in defiance of camp rules. He knocked it back in one and slumped onto the security office bench.

"Let me guess," tried Finian. "The guy had no ID, you've never seen him before, and you've no idea who sent him."

"He was too prepared to come with a name tag on," the security chief agreed. "But he didn't come alone. We found where they cut through the wire fence. They had some kind of truck there, so there must have been a driver at least. I'm guessing there was more than one man, given the number of wads of gum I found scattered round."

"So he knew what he was coming for," Finian concluded. "That thing in Block Nine."

"Yep. The Senator's not going to be happy that got out."

He was interrupted by Miss Castlemere returning from the side office where the telephone was kept. "Not happy's an understatement," she confirmed. "Frank's flying out here tonight. He knows how serious this is."

"That'd be because he knows what the hell is going on," Finian complained. "I, on the other hand, nearly got plugged by another Kraut then eaten by some kind of giant bat-bird."

"I'm sorry we didn't tell you about that," Verity apologized, "but it was extremely confidential."

"I nearly got my head bitten off, sweetheart. Your little secrets are going to get me killed."

Dr. Utter's arrival interrupted proceedings again. "I understand you lost the pterosaur," he said. "That is most unfortunate."

Finian thought back to half-remembered museum trips as a kid. "Pterosaur? Like a dinosaur bird?"

"Neither a dinosaur nor a bird," Utter said pedantically. "The term 'dinosaur' denotes a certain group of reptiles with an upright stance of the superorder dinosauria. Pterosaurs are of the class reptilia and the node ornithodera which is quite distinct. It's like mistaking a cow for a dolphin."

"We don't actually know what that was," Verity admitted to Finian. "We assume it was some kind of prehistoric survivor because it looks quite a lot like some of the reconstructions in the natural history museums, but it could be something else entirely."

Utter was not to be stopped. "The term dinosaur is applied very sloppily these days, as a label for a variety of extinct reptiles such as ichthyosaurs, plesiosaurs, and mosasaurs. This is not to say, however…"

"Thanks doc, I get it," Finian cut in. "What I don't get is why whatever-it-is was in that warehouse."

"Well, I guess you'd better know," Verity sighed. "That specimen was captured when it got tangled on some rigging ropes on Airship 25. That crew was able to capture it alive."

"We called him Benny," added Matteson, clearing up one minor mystery.

"And let me guess," reasoned Finian. "They encountered Benny near one of those impossible castle clouds with the holes in 'em that your fiancée's so interested in."

"That's exactly right," confessed the blonde. "That's why we're so keen to find another fallstreak."

"To hunt not-dinosaurs."

Dr. Utter shook his head. "Fascinating as the possibility of an ecology above the clouds might be there are other reasons for our interest in those punch-holes. Airship 26 sent one of its airplanes right through the disc and was in radio contact with it at the time. The pilot reported…"

"Dr. Utter!" Miss Castlemere warned. "Finian isn't cleared for this."

"I guess he's in the in-club now," Matteson noted.

"Its better he understands," argued Utter. "If we want him to operate at maximum efficiency he requires an overview of the mission."

Verity relented. "Fine. Play him the darned recording."

McHenry joined them, hastily dragged from his bed to operate the machinery. They met aboard Airship 27, in the now fully fitted-out radio room. The cabin lit with a green glow as the engineer flicked on a row of power switches to activate the systems.

"This cylinder here records any radio traffic," he explained to Finian. "These soft wax discs hold the sound. That way there's always a record."

"So Airship 26 had one of these going when it sent a Sparrowhawk into the punch-hole," recognized Finian.

"It did, but we do not have access to it," Dr. Utter corrected him. "What we have is the recording of radio commerce between the airship and the ground at the time the airplane was communicating from the weather anomaly."

"You don't have the little wax tube because A26 never got back from that mission," Finian surmised.

McHenry slotted the cylinder into the mechanism and set it spinning.

A crackling voice came from the waxed paper speakers. Finian got a chill as he realized he was hearing a dead man speaking.

"A26 to control tower... Duffy's taken the plane through the turbulence. Cotterill's had to turn back. I think the wind got him. Duffy's saying he's able to go right into the ring..."

"What was the time and date of this?" Finian asked. Altocumulus Castellanus typically formed in the early morning. "What was the altitude?"

"You can read the report later," Matteson suggested. "Listen."

"Duffy's through. He says he's through, we can't see him in this cloud. We're getting a lot of chop, getting bucketed about all over the place. It's like being on a switchback. But Duffy says it's calm in the eye."

"It'd have to be," Finian reasoned. "There has to be some kind of thermal condition that prevents water droplets freezing despite zero temperatures there."

"Duffy says he's above the cloud. It's hazy and purple. He can't see the horizon. Says his instruments are going screwy... Duffy? Calm down. Never mind what your altimeter and plane gauge say. Trust your instincts. Look for which way a pendulum dangles... Duffy?"

"This was the point where they lost contact with the Sparrowhawk," Verity said quietly.

"Captain Akinhouse says we need to get closer to the fallstreak disc," the crackling voice continued. It was harder to hear now, fading in and out amidst wild bursts of static. "We need to re-establish radio contact with.... Try and guide him back in to... some kind of weird... whole thing's rocking now..."

The transmission degenerated into hisses and crackles.

"What happened then?" Finian asked somberly.

"It's not quite finished yet," McHenry told him.

The radio operator had one last message. "...to control, can you...?" There was more background screech, and then his voice came through crystal clear for just a moment. He said, "This is not our sky."

"There you have it," said Verity Castlemere as McHenry flipped off the modified gramophone. "The last words of Airship 26."

"You think it went into that punch-hole, the fallstreak disc?" Finian asked. "But even if it got torn apart by the winds you'd have found some wreckage."

Dr Utter had another explanation. "Unless when they broke up they were somewhere else."

"Such as?"

The scientist admitted bafflement. "Don't know. Somewhere with pterosaurs, perhaps. Somewhere that was not our sky."

Finian had noticed Nickelhouse's car when he'd done his morning laps so he wasn't surprised to be summoned to a meeting later that morning. He took the opportunity to return the mission logs he'd borrowed from Utter the night before.

Senator Nickelhouse had travelled most of the night to get there so he was not his usual well-groomed urbane self. He paced the conference room chain-smoking while he waited for everyone to assemble. Finian helped himself to a coffee and a donut.

Eventually everyone was there. Everyone turned out to be Miss Castlemere, Dr. Utter, McHenry the engineer, Chief Matteson, Captain Stafford and two of his officers, and the senior Sparrowhawk pilot Machen.

Nickelhouse began without preamble. "We had another security breach last night. Someone went after the pterosaur. They knew we had it. They knew where. They had enough information about our security arrangements to avoid patrol routes and guard points. If it hadn't been for the vigilance of Verity and Finian we wouldn't just have lost the specimen but our enemies would have gotten him."

Finian wondered if the Senator had wondered at the coincidence of his fiancée and the weatherman just happening to meet on that starry evening. He wasn't sure it was a good idea to make his rich powerful boss jealous, even for no reason.

"Benny's a loss to us and a loss to science, but there's no use crying over spilled milk," Nickelhouse went on. "You all know by now that we have enemies. We can't prove those guys were German military, but they sure did a good impression of it. Chances are if our opposition know about Benny then they know about the fallstreaks over the Lakes. If they know about the fallstreaks then they know they're in a race to find out what's on the topside of 'em."

"A new frontier," speculated Dr. Utter happily. Finian imagined the scientist dreamed of another world to classify and tidy up.

"Something worth discovering anyway," Nickelhouse qualified. "Something that our government should be chasing up, instead of wasting time on trying to make aircraft carriers fly on helium tanks. But this way at least we get the credit for a discovery that'll change the world."

Finian guessed that it would be Frank Nickelhouse's face on the cover of *Time*.

The Senator continued. "So now everybody here's up to speed on the strange hole clouds and on the unique flying reptile that came through it. What most of you don't know is what happened to BE-A25, so I'll tell you now and I'll tell you straight. Chances are it was shot down."

Captain Stafford wasn't the only one to lean forward but he was the first to speak. "Shot down? How?"

Nickelhouse held his hands out wide, palms down, in a keep-calm gesture. "We dug out more pieces of the fuselage than made it back to the hangar," he admitted.

"It was shell fire," Matteson confirmed. "Air to air fire, I think."

"Air to air?" puzzled Finian. "An airplane. Or—another airship?"

"The latter is more likely given the size of the impact," revealed the security chief. "We think maybe there's a covert airfield somewhere out in Canada, far in the wilds, unknown to the Canadians, and there's a Boche zeppelin staging from it."

"And why haven'ae we been told this before?" demanded McHenry. His accent thickened when he was angry.

"Because confidential information leaks from this base like a sieve," accused the Senator. "I'm not pointing at anyone here, of course, but we do have over three hundred fifty people on site. At least one of them is sending intelligence to the opposition. One of them might even be our saboteur."

"Then they will know that we're only three days off launching the A27," reasoned Captain Stafford.

"Yep," agreed the Senator. "That's why we're looking at a change of plan. I want Airship 27 off the ground tomorrow."

The thump of the gas pumps inflating the ship's airbags was almost deafening but Finian still leaned on the gantry and watched; it was as if Airship 27 was coming to life.

Her generators were running now. A string of lights illuminated her length, casting bright reflections from her silver hull. Technicians hurried with hoists to lift her laterally-mounted weaponry into place. Automatic machine guns were locked into external combat housings fore and aft. From Finian's vantage point he could see into the green-lit command gondola where Stafford and his officers held clipboards as they completed pre-flight checks.

Matteson joined Finian on the platform and watched McHenry scurry past on the hangar floor trailed by a hectoring Dr. Utter. "It's even money which of them will go insane first now," the security chief noted.

"I'll have five bucks on McHenry snapping and doing in Utter with a lug wrench," ventured Finian. The engineer and the scientist had very different work-patterns and methods.

"Could all be for nothing anyhow," shrugged Matteson. "Our boss is good at not mentioning stuff, isn't he?"

"What now?"

"One of my guys overheard Verity Castlemere in the admin office. Seems like the clearances we need from Washington to launch a seven hundred and fifty foot flying bomb haven't yet come through and might not ever. The Senator's enemies seem to have made their play at last."

Finian glanced at the big clock on the hangar wall. "Must be four in the morning in Washington by now. Nobody's going to be in their office issuing flight permits at this time."

"From what Miss Castlemere was saying to Nickelhouse they might not issue one at any time. I think news has broken about the other missing crafts. Nickelhouse and Creed couldn't keep it dark forever. My man heard the Senator instructing Miss C not to say anything about this to anyone—so naturally my guy told me."

Finian frowned. "It's sure looking like a folly, isn't it? I mean, it's the twenty-seventh attempt to get a ship in the air that'll stay there, launched in a last-minute rush so it doesn't get blown up by saboteurs or shot out of the sky by another airship, sent to an uncharted freak weather phenomenon that spits out dinosaur birds."

"But the money's good," Matteson pointed out. "And hey, I don't have to fly in that thing."

Finian pointed to the hangar floor. Senator Nickelhouse himself was making his way over to the entry gantry. His pace was fast and stiff. Miss Castlemere was at his side, carrying a pile of files. "The Senator sure looks like a man who's just been told to tidy his toys away."

The security chief snorted. "You don't want to be near him when he pitches a hissy-fit though. It's not pretty." He pushed back from the rail he'd been leaning on with Finian. "Listen, I'd better get on with my rounds. I've got every guy on staff out there tonight but I'm not exactly feeling safe, you know."

"Sure. Feels like a combat zone, doesn't it, waiting for the shells to drop." He tossed Matteson a mock salute and watched the security chief head off for the rear of the workshop.

Verity and Nickelhouse had vanished inside the airship. Finian saw them again in the gondola, talking earnestly with Captain Stafford. Then Verity pointed through the window at the weatherman and an ensign activated the on-ship intercom. "Mr. Finian and Dr. Utter to the control gondola! Dr. Utter, Mr. Finian to the control gondola please!"

Finian slid down the ladder to the hangar floor and climbed up the temporary scaffolding that provided a way into the glass-sided command deck. Utter appeared from the upper level of the airship, still carrying some piece of electrical equipment whose diodes he was fiddling with.

"There you are!" said Nickelhouse. He seemed tense. "Take a look at these."

The Navy weatherman had no problem at all recognizing Navy weather charts. The date and time-stamps showed they were all from the three occasions when the Senator's airships had encountered the strange punch-hole phenomenon. Another look confirmed that all the events had taken place in the early morning with a falling barometer when cold air was piling from the north, over the vast water-mass of the Great Lakes.

"What can you tell us, Finian?" the Senator challenged.

Finian recounted his observations and added some analysis. "Each time you got one of these things was just before a big storm hit. Each time there was clear air turbulence then particulate ice mist. Your Sparrowhawk jock mentioned a still column right under the fallstreak hole so maybe that's how it stays stable for half an hour at a time. Is that tonight's predictive chart?" He took the last rolled sheet from Verity. "Yeah, you got similar conditions for the morning."

Dr. Utter stirred. "We need to make sure that every camera and hull sensor is properly functioning. I must have data. Data!"

"But this chart models similar conditions to the previous events," Nickelhouse insisted.

"Yeah," agreed Finian. "Of course, there's another factor in those sightings you haven't thought about."

Utter looked up sharply. "What would that be?" he asked. He sounded offended.

"The airships themselves. Now I don't know the physics of it but I'm guessing a great big metal egg passing near ionized clouds interacts with them pretty good, so maybe the thing your Washington boys missed out was the electro-magnetic effect or whatever. I'm not the science whiz, but I know that if you put a plane through a storm you get weird effects— St Elmo's fire, static shocks, foo fighters, all kinds of stuff. And that's something just thirty feet long."

"Finian climbed…the scaffolding…into the…command deck."

"It could be a factor!" admitted Utter. "We need a ring of electromagnetic sensors strung laterally along the hull, attached to some kind of recording needle…"

The Senator stuck to the point. "Thing is, if we send the A27 up there tomorrow morning might we have the same conditions that the A25 and A26 encountered?"

Captain Stafford shifted uncomfortably. "Sir, this will be a maiden shake-down flight. It's not a good idea to…"

"It'll be her last flight if you don't bring back something sensational," the Senator cut him off. "They want to shut the program down, Captain. There'll probably be a courier here by noon."

The Captain was seconded from normal service. "If that's our orders…"

"That's not your orders yet, airman. I'm still in charge here and you're still under my command. I want this ship in the air at first light—first light! And I want you at those co-ordinates where the Washington brain-boxes believe you're most likely to encounter a fallstreak anomaly. Clear?"

"Sir."

The Senator punched a finger towards Finian. "You better get all set in your weather car, mister. You're going to find me a new sky tomorrow."

Finian's reply was drowned out by the base alarm klaxon.

Stafford looked up sharply. "The alert? We have intruders?"

He got his response as the car pool vehicles exploded across the compound.

Finian's first reaction was to reach for a sidearm that wasn't there. His second was to grab up one of the backpack radio harnesses that hung under the flight consoles and strap it on. "Wait here," he told everyone. "Listen in to me on frequency two while I go see what the hell's happening."

Nickelhouse was already on the internal phone to the radio room. "Comms? What the hell's going on out there? Get me the main office. Get me Matteson!"

Finian shot Verity a cheeky wink and jumped out of the gondola. He slid down the ladder and landed on the hangar floor amidst confused crew and technicians.

"What the blazes is it now?" demanded McHenry. "Sounds like the whole damn place is blowing."

Finian thought about the hydrogen gas tower beside the hangar and didn't feel happy. "Get your boys together and keep 'em where you can see 'em," he called to the chief engineer. "I'm taking a look."

Half a dozen workmen were already clustered round the door, peering out into the darkness to where the car pool was a blaze of wrecked autos. A few of Matteson's guards ran towards it but the flames were too intense. The fire trucks were burning.

Finian grabbed the big radio microphone and flicked the switch to transmit. "Finian to command car. Looks like something blew up the parking lot. Over."

It was Nickelhouse who replied. Either the Senator had climbed up to the radio room or more likely he'd had the comms operator patch the signal down to the control gondola. "Can you see any sign of intruders, over?"

A second blast rocked Brooking Field. Finian winced as the admin building detonated. The walls bellied out and collapsed as if a giant had stamped on them. The weatherman knew that there had been people in there.

But more, he glimpsed how it had been destroyed. Reflected in the plume of flame as the building went up he saw the unmistakable metal gleam of a flight frame above it in the sky: an unlit airship.

"It's a ship!" he called through the radio. "It's a goddamned airship, dropping Mills bombs or something. It's like a war out here. It is a war!"

The power went out across the base. Someone else, maybe Matteson, had worked out that a lit-up airfield was too easy to target.

"Finian, they've come to destroy the A27," Nickelhouse called through Finian's earphones. "We've got to get her in the air now. Over."

"Is that even possible? Over."

"Utter says yes. But you need to get the hangar doors open for us. We're trapped in here. Open the doors, Finian. Over."

Finian thought he detected a movement above. The lights might be out but the camp was still lit by the blazing buildings. The zeppelin or whatever it was moved to another attack position.

"You guys," he called to the shocked workers huddled by the service door, "Help me. Get these gates open. Now!"

The men leaned in with him to push back the massive folding doors that formed the whole front of the hangar. Without power it was very hard.

Airship 27 floated on her tethers. As Finian watched, her running lights flicked out so as to conceal her better, but he glimpsed crewmen swarming down to cast off the heavy steel hawsers that pinned her now she was filled with hydrogen.

"Faster!" Finian called to the men pushing the bay doors open.

He heard the whine of a small plane engine. For a moment he hoped that Machen and the other pilots had got to their Sparrowhawks and had taken to the air to defend the base. Then the rapid fire of machine gun shots sprayed across the tarmac beside him. A man screamed and fell, bloody.

The plane banked over the hangar and veered off to take another pass.

"Keep at it!" Finian shouted at the other men. One was wounded and another fled. Three joined him to fold back the hangar door further.

Another blast! This one took out the side of the A25 hangar, furthest of the three great airship sheds. Hundred-foot doors like the ones Finian struggled with now flew out across the landing field. The outer walls of the far hangar teetered then collapsed.

There was another burst of firing. The weatherman flinched but this time it was Matteson and a pair of his security men carrying a Gatling gun between them, feeding it a chain of bullets to try and deter whatever was flying down to finish them.

One door was open. It jammed on the last fold but Finian hoped it would be enough. He pressed his helpers to put their backs to the other door.

There was more gunshot. This time it was up in the air. Finian could see the sharp rapid firing flashes of a plane-mounted weapon. A Sparrowhawk's .3 inch Browning machine guns were at work. At least one of the base's biplanes was in the air.

Behind him the temporary scaffolding crashed down as the airship moved. It was as if she was coming to life, shrugging off her restraints. The thrumming of her Maybeck VL-2 engines was almost deafening inside the hangar but they had not yet been put in gear to turn the great fans that would propel the vehicle forwards.

"Hurry up!" Nickelhouse called unnecessarily in Finian's headphones.

The enemy plane had given the Sparrowhawk the slip for now, or perhaps there was more than one bogey in the sky. Finian grabbed the nearest overalled worker and dragged him behind the door as a new spray of gunfire burst across the threshold. Another man screamed and fell, clutching his guts.

There was no way to get the door open in time. The rest of the men ran.

"Finian!" came the call over his headset; except this time it was the urgent tones of Verity Castlemere. The carnage at the threshold must be clearly visible from the control gondola.

"I'm on it, babe!" he called back.

The other massive door was half-folded back but required far more muscle than one man alone could muster under fire. Finian looked at the frontage of the airship hangar by the red hellfire light of burning buildings. He had to find a way.

His eyes alighted on Nickelhouse's Cadillac V-16. The sleek black roadster hadn't been parked in the pool with the other vehicles; Senator's privilege. It stood just to the side of the hanger itself, waiting to convey its owner to wherever Nickelhouse decided to visit next. The chauffer had fled, leaving the driver's door ajar.

Finian raced over and found the self-starter. The engine thrummed to life. Finian backed the car away and brought it round to the hangar door.

"This ain't going to help the paintwork," he said out loud as he shunted the nose of the expensive car into the edge of the door. In the lowest gear he pushed the vehicle forward, folding back the gate as he went.

He heard the return of the fighter plane before he saw it. The line of flak came right at the Cadillac. Finian rolled out of the driver's seat just before it was shredded with gunshot. Bullets tore the hood up, sending a spray of steam from the perforated radiator. The overhead-valve 452-cubic-inch V-16 engine spluttered and died.

Another explosion was nearer than the last. Flame played out over the hangar's corrugated steel roof. It took the breathless Finian a moment to realize that the fighter plane that had just tried to kill him had been splashed itself. Its flaming shell rolled across the top of the hangar and fell onto the turf behind.

Somewhere above, Mac Machen celebrated with a victory roll.

Triumph was short lived. The airship above flicked on all its searchlights, flooding the base with bright rays that picked out every man and building below. Finian saw Matteson again, dragging one of his team towards cover. He saw the dark objects spiraling down onto the tarmac around the security chief. When the grenades detonated Matteson was flung high like a rag doll before falling like a broken puppet.

"Is it open?" came Verity's urgent voice over the radio. "Finian, is the door open enough? Over."

"I dunno," replied the weatherman, "but that's as far as it's getting. If you're going to try it, try it now."

The enemy zeppelin twisted as the winds shifted and pushed it out of position. The brilliance of the arc lights made it hard for Finian to make out detail. He could barely see that machine-guns much like those mounted along the A27 were all turned to attack the Sparrowhawks.

Behind him the last service gantries crashed down as Airship 27 brushed them away. Finian ducked as the vast silver bulk hovering less than six feet from the concrete ghosted towards the door at minimum speed, no more than a fast walking pace.

"Is it clear, Finian? Over." It was Nickelhouse's voice back on the line.

"Not a chance, Senator," called back the weatherman. "You got a flamin' huge zeppelin up there armed for bear and maybe a couple of enemy biplanes as well. We've got at least one friendly up in the sky but that's it. Over."

The airship kept emerging from the hangar. It was hard to judge if it could stop now; the ship seemed to have a life of its own. It pushed aside Nickelhouse's damaged Cadillac as if it wasn't there.

Finian recognized the shape of the weather car, one of the two lowest points of the craft. Under it was the hatch he'd insisted be added for his observations. It took him a moment to unbatten the trapdoor but he was able to slither aboard as the aircraft left the hangar.

He wasn't a moment too soon. As soon as she was beyond the door the A-27 engaged her propellers on vertical lift. That hundred and ninety thousand pounds of useful load lifted six and a half million cubic feet of metal and machinery almost vertically, maneuvered by those innovative gimbals and gears designed by Edward Utter that Washington had failed to appreciate. The ground vanished beneath Finian at an alarming rate.

He hauled himself in and secured the hatch then dropped into his station chair. "Finian to command car. I'm on board. Over."

There was no reply. Everybody was busy.

From his position beneath the main fuselage in the glass undercar Finian could see the full extent of the devastation on the ground. The flames from the admin building had spread to one of the barracks blocks. Even as he watched the gas pumps near the car pool went up in a bright fiery ball.

Worst of all were the dozens of bodies strewn across the tarmac. The attacking zeppelin had mowed men down without hesitation.

A27 jinked hard to the side. The motion reminded Finian to buckle into his seat, but before he could he saw the missile heading at his station from the other vessel. The 4.6 inch hydropneumatic shell looked to be coming straight at him, but skimmed a few feet shy of the weather gondola and slammed into the hangar below.

The high explosive projectile detonated right where Airship 27 had been berthed, filling the building with lethal shrapnel and a bloom of flame. The remaining windows blew out. The construction crew who'd elected not to scramble aboard the airship were torn to shreds.

The explosion must have ruptured the unstowed hydrogen hoses as well. The bright flash of the field gun's fragmentation shell was nothing compared to the inferno as the hydrogen tanks detonated.

Flame and noise bellied out towards the rising A27. Finian seemed to see it all in slow motion, his adrenaline-soaked brain absorbing every detail to give him a chance to survive. He saw the massive hangar knocked over like a pile of child's play bricks. The crumpled remnant of the Senator's Caddy spun off as if kicked by a giant. The hellfire-red bloom of expanding burning gas welled out in a searing bubble up towards the airship.

For a brief moment the mercury tubes on Finian's weather station soared from 50 degrees to beyond 200. The flames licked the underside of the vessel, engulfing the carriage and washing across the fireproofed outer framing over the hydrogen bags.

The aluminum of the weather gondola became searing hot. Rubber window seals blistered and bubbled. The car was swallowed in inferno.

Then the fireball dispersed.

Finian peered up at the rigid structure to see if the hull had been penetrated. He saw the dark silhouettes of crewman climbing out along the exposed gantries to douse the minor fires where lubricating grease had been ignited. Clearly the precautions of Utter's design and McHenry's implementation had worked; Finian was still alive.

The A27 banked the other way. The enemy airship came into Finian's field of view. He saw Airship 27's M2 Browning machine guns swivel towards the marauder and begin to spit a lethal stream of .50 bullets.

The enemy backed off beyond the machine guns' practical range. Finian wondered if that was to allow another shot with whatever field gun they'd got mounted on the enemy zeppelin but it soon became apparent that the other ship had no taste for combat with an airborne craft in its weight class. The marauder's searchlights winked out and it vanished into the darkness.

"Finian to command car. The bad guys just bugged out. Over."

"Command car to Finian. Get in here. Over," replied Miss Castlemere.

Below them the airfield burned.

Finian's route to the command car took him forward through the saloon lounge. It was full of shocked overalled construction workers wondering what had hit them. A couple of men were being treated from the first aid kits for glass cuts and abrasions. McHenry stood behind the bar, using its long counter to lay out a series of production blueprints. The engineer was giving hasty orders to the crew he had on hand to shore up and repair the flame-scorched airship.

Finian passed the radio room and map room and rappelled down the ladder to the control gondola. It was cold here; it took the weatherman a moment to notice the two bullet holes in the windshield glass.

Stafford himself was at the helm. First Lieutenant Thompson had charts spread on the map table and was at work with compasses and grease pen, calculating a course. A pair of bridge officers watched the other instruments and answered the internal telephone as duty stations reported in with damage and readiness reports.

Nickelhouse was beside the Captain. Dr. Utter was huddled in a corner muttering to himself; the eccentric scientist didn't take well to changes in routine.

"Finian," the Senator recognized. "Good work on the bay doors. Saved our bacon there."

"What's our play now?" Finian wondered. "Fly to Chicago and alert the air corp that we've got a hostile in our sky? If that thing was German it was an act of war."

"It was unlikely to be the German government behind this," noted Nickelhouse. "Any more than the US government is the final backer of Airship 27."

"It's still an armed assault on US soil," Captain Stafford said, outraged at the attack, appalled by the loss of life. "We have to radio it in and get backup."

"And be ordered to stand down?" the Senator snorted. "I don't think so."

The officer on the comms line looked up. "Three Sparrowhawks are ready to come aboard, sir," he called to Stafford. "Or they can fly to the landing strip at Rockford."

"Bring them in," ordered Nickelhouse.

Captain Stafford nodded. "Get the crews ready and deploy the skyhook. Thompson, take the conn. Steady as she goes."

"I have the conn, sir. Steady as she goes," his first officer agreed.

It seemed to Finian that the Senator had no intention of landing the airship. "You're not still planning on still chasing that cloud are you?" he asked.

"After the opposition went to such trouble to keep us from it? You bet I am," Nickelhouse replied.

Miss Castlemere climbed down into the car. Her blonde hair was unbound and wild. Finian thought she looked wonderful. "I've got the register of who's aboard," she reported.

"Tell us," her fiancée instructed.

Verity consulted her clipboard. "We have around, half the actual planned crew, that's twenty-three ordinary airmen and eight officers, including the radio operator, navigator, gunnery sergeant, and senior flight deck commander. And our weather expert." Verity shot Finian a warm smile. "We're taking on board three of the four Sparrowhawks and their pilots. We're short a medical officer, a purser, a chief steward, and the chief engineer. What we do have is Mr. McHenry and thirty-two of his construction team, Dr. Utter, and Miss Dennison, a typist from the secretarial pool who doesn't want to explain what she was doing in an aft cupboard with Mac Machen at the time the assault began."

Finian snorted.

Verity's face sobered. "We lost a lost of people on the ground though. A whole lot if the only survivors are aboard the A27."

"What the hell happened?" demanded Stafford. "I thought Matteson was on top of security. We were on alert!"

"Who could have expected a damned airship assault?" Finian defended the dead security chief. "Anyway, Jack Matteson went down trying to pull one of his guys to safety. That's the way to cash in. We all got caught with our pants down—not just Machen in his cupboard—and we're lucky to still be breathing."

"This is unacceptable," said Dr. Utter from the corner. "Completely unacceptable. Unacceptable."

"Then let's make sure these guys didn't die for nothing," said Senator Nickelhouse. "Look, we've got a working airship and McHenry says there's nothing needs fixing or finishing that can't be done in the air. He's even got the specialists aboard to do the job. We've got a good guess at where and when we might find another of those fallstreak holes, but the bad guys might have the same intelligence so we've only got one chance to beat them to it. I know it's a lot to ask boys, but I want us to take the A27 and go there. Okay?"

"We should report in," said Stafford. "We should seek orders."

"We should complain," argued Dr. Utter. "This is quite unacceptable."

Finian folded his arms and grinned. "Let's go for it," he urged. "Come on guys. If nothing else, I'm spoiling to have another encounter with the mooks who shot up our buddies and tried to deep six us all. And if there does happen to be some big scientific breakthrough up there, well hey, I can live with fame and fortune."

Verity Castlemere shook her head at his bravado, but she was smiling.

It was Verity who brought Finian a vacuum flask two hours later as the weatherman sat at his station in the rear gondola preparing for his work. He took the warm container with thanks. "I don't suppose this is Malt Scotch?"

"Hot cocoa," Miss Castlemere said apologetically. "But I did mix it up myself."

Finian secured the flask with one of the elastic loops designed to keep things falling when the compartment rocked.

"I notice we haven't landed yet to let the non-volunteers off," the weatherman said.

"Frank talked to everybody and they all agreed to stay aboard. I think it was the offer of a hundred bucks each that did it mostly."

"I know I can use that. Mac cleared me out at poker. Again. What about you dames though?"

"I'm all signed up and I think Miss Dennison's enjoying the attention in the wardroom," Verity revealed. "But Frank relented enough to break radio silence and alert emergency services to the situation at Brooking Field. There might have been survivors needing medical attention. That was what decided him."

"But we're still off hunting pterosaurs."

"Yes. Again. Only difference this time is that I hitched a ride."

That bugged Finian. "We could set down and let off you and Machen's squeeze and still chase clouds."

"Captain Stafford's worried about lift. We weren't fully fuelled when we had to leave and we didn't quite fill our hydrogen tanks either. It's apparently best that we stay in the sky."

Finian's instruments put them at around 5,000 feet, passing through wispy cumulostratus, heading west by northwest at around thirty-two miles per hour. The occasional light below betrayed a town or farmstead but no detail was visible in the darkness.

"I'm surprised the Senator's staying aboard," Finian admitted.

"Frank's got plenty of faults, but lack of guts isn't one of them."

"He's got to have something to get a dame like you."

"Apart from good looks, breeding, culture, wealth, power, and charm?" Verity asked.

"Yeah. And you once said you owed him."

The blonde looked away. "I was… in a tough spot once and he helped me out. That's when I first worked for him. The rest came later."

"How long have you known him?"

"What is this, a quiz? I've been with Bellerophon Enterprises for four years, since almost the start. I've dated Frank for two years. We got engaged last fall but we kept it quiet because I'm not really an ideal show-prize wife. I really don't want to talk about Frank. Okay?"

The weatherman reached for his flask and poured himself a cocoa toddy. "So what did you want to talk about, sweetheart?"

Verity shrugged. "Anything. I'm stuck on a ship full of guys who escaped a fiery death. We're heading to a cloudy rendezvous that the last two ships never got home from. I guess I'm feeling kind of homesick, or shell-shocked, or, heck, I dunno… I just wanted to hear someone talk."

Finian nodded. Verity was admirably calm for someone who'd been within two feet of a bullet earlier that night. "You know, it was only when things started blowing up that it all clicked for me."

The blonde's brow furrowed. "I don't get you."

"You saw what I was like when you found me. I'd screwed my life up. Maybe I did the right thing then got hammered for it, maybe not. But what came after, that was all my doing. I was a mess, in the gutter, headed for the morgue."

"From the smell I thought you were already dead, Finian."

"Yeah. Then you brought me to the base. I sobered up, I got back in shape, I had a job and a purpose again. I wanted to see Airship 27 fly."

Miss Castlemere gestured around. "And you have."

"Yeah. But when the lead started raining, when things started blowing up and Joes started dying, that's when I knew where I wanted to be. Here. And now. I feel like I earned it this time. Another chance."

Whatever Verity might have replied to that she didn't get the chance. An electric bell rang on Finian's console. "You'd better get outta here now, toots," he advised her, "unless you wanna be dropped out of the clouds with me."

"Maybe next time," the blonde grinned. "Catch ya on the flip-side, sailor."

Finian waited until she'd gone, strapped in, and thumbed the electric buzzer to signal he was good to go.

Electric motors whined and steel hawsers began to unreel from four heavy cable-spools. Finian pulled the large lever that disengaged the weather car locking clamps from the main undercarriage.

For a moment the glass gondola free fell before the steel cables took the strain and it was jerked to a sharp halt. The car rocked wildly as the side-winds buffeted it.

"Finian, this is McHenry," came a worried Scots voice over the intercom. "How's it going?"

"Finian here. It's a bit choppy. Glad I brought some puke bags."

"Ye're in the most experimental bit of the boat. It's been almost completely redesigned since the A26."

"Do I want to know why?"

"Not at this moment, no."

The night clouds outside the windows betrayed no clue about movement. Finian's stomach told him he was descending. It was like being in a fast elevator except the car was also swinging from side to side.

"I'm switching the lights on," Finian reported. He snapped down the row of switches that activated the battery-powered spotlights around the car's belly; the reflection glare from the cloud band was blinding so he hastily doused most of them again.

The reels above paid out cable, lowering him at a foot per second.

"Is it too shaky?" McHenry asked worriedly. Tests on the similar 'spy basket' on the USS Akron hadn't got further than lowering sandbags instead of men before being abandoned.

"It's no picnic but I've had worse. Keep it up."

Finian's instruments told him he was now two hundred yards below the main frame of Airship 27, near the end of his tethers. He was dangling on four high-tensile cables, attached to the mother-ship by an umbilical of phone wires and a power feed. He was about to make more checks when the car dropped below cloud cover and he could see terrain below.

"Hey, I'm out! Tell Stafford and Thomson to keep her steady and this might actually work!"

"You're below cloud and nae dead?" McHenry answered over the speaker. "I owe Utter a sawbuck."

The car was still flapping laterally, blowing like a sheet in the wind. Finian wondered if more ballast or some lead weights in the base of the aluminum structure might help. For now he just gritted his teeth, ignored the chop, and concentrated on the weather instrumentation.

"Okay, it's 4:57 am, thirty-one minutes before sun-up. I'm deploying the spotlights to try and see ground conditions and landmarks. We're heading on a bearing of eleven-point-four degrees west of north at a speed of forty-one and a half knots. Wind's hard to gauge while I'm rocking like a swing but let's say seven knots south by south west. That'll put our track at around… hell, someone else can do the sums who's not trying to hold down his breakfast."

"Finian, its Stafford here. You're doing just fine. We can do the math. Can you see any landmarks?"

"Too hard by night, but by day I'd have a pretty good view. I think there's a major body of water to port."

"That'll be the lakes. Your instruments and observations confirm our calculations. We're heading to the likely site for those castle clouds with the holes in 'em."

"That's peachy, command car. Any chance this bait can get reeled in any time soon, only I'm struggling to keep my cookies down here?"

"That'll be a good test for the new weather gondola assembly," McHenry judged. "Let's see if we can pull him back in, shall we?"

Finian hoped it was the Scotsman's dour sense of humor. He wasn't certain.

The cables began to wind around their drums again. Finian's car jerked and tilted thirty degrees sideward. If he'd not been strapped down he'd have been spilled to the floor.

"Little slower, A27!" he called urgently.

The winching back seemed to take much longer than the drop. The night clouds enveloped Finian again, cutting off all sense of the outside. Only the whine of the motors and the disturbing tension squeals of steel fiber cables under stress gave any indication of progress.

At last, seventeen minutes by Finian's dashboard clock since the retrieval had begun, he heard the metallic scraping that told of men with long poles guiding the weather car back to its moorings. Then the ready lights winked on above the docking lever and Finian was able to lock home the connecting bolts and slump back exhausted.

There was no rest for the wicked. Finian barely had time for a much-needed visit to the head before he was expected in the stateroom for a conference. The elegant front-most compartment of the ship, above the command gondola, was twenty-two feet wide and thirty-three feet long. The forward wall was glazed to show the sky beyond. Angled windows at forty-five degrees to the floor allowed views of the ground below.

The A27 had dropped below the clouds to 4,000 feet. The first rays of dawn were simmering over the horizon, glinting off the waters of Lake Michigan.

The stateroom had an expensive antique table, French-polished to perfection. The paneled oak walls carried gilt-framed pictures of the earlier BE-A series aircraft, and a series of smaller portraits of Bellerophon Industries investors. Senator Nickelhouse, Dr. Utter, McHenry, Miss Castlemere, Captain Machen, and Captain Stafford were all assembled.

"The man of the hour," said Nickelhouse as Finian entered. He gestured to Verity to pour Finian a coffee. The brew-pot was Navy-style, with a wide flat bottom that slotted into a specially-designed tray let into the centre of the table. The glass mugs were wide and well balanced with cork bottoms.

Finian was more impressed that the blonde remembered he took his java black. "Thanks," he said.

Dr Utter seemed to have recovered somewhat from his earlier dismay. "How was the weather basket?" he asked with keen academic interest.

"It'll go down swell at Coney Island," Finian replied. "Could use some better heaters, though. It gets cold down there under the clouds."

Utter took him seriously and made a note.

The weather projections the Senator had displayed before were now laid across the stateroom. "We're approaching the area where the weather service modeled the fallstreak phenomenon occurring, and the maximal time for it to manifest," he summarized. "So this is our last chance to confer."

"What's our mission?" Machen asked. "Say we find one of these things, what're we supposed to do?"

"You go in," insisted the Senator. "You fly in and you tell us what's there."

"You need to give us whatever instrument readings you get from the pack I've designed for the Sparrowhawks," Utter instructed. "Make copious notes."

"While flying through heavy turbulence?" scorned McHenry. "And what happens when th' radio fails like it did last time? What are we doing different from what got the A26 lost wi' all hands?"

"I've redesigned several key..." began Utter.

"There's a few things we could do," interrupted Finian. "First off, we need to stay clear of those virga. See those shafts of cloud that come out of the castle formation like roots? Those trailing columns are rain that gets re-trapped as it falls, caught between layers of moist and dry air. You'll get

"You'll fly in and you tell us what's there."

lots of turbulence. Keep out of them. Go under then up between."

"Sounds good," agreed Machen. "What else?"

"Take a wingman. You've still got three planes aboard, right? So we position the A27 as directly under the punch hole as possible and hold it stable in the eye of the storm. You send one Sparrowhawk up to the lip of the ring where he can stay in direct line-of-sight contact with the airship—use semaphore lights if the radio gives out. The other two planes head through the hole together so they've each got a spotter. Standard doctrine, really."

"That seems pretty sensible," Stafford agreed.

"There's more. From what we could hear from that recording of the last mission, there's maybe some kind of condition above the punch hole that messes with instrumentation and distorts visibility. So you have to keep a visual fix on the hole itself. That's your route out, whatever turbulence there might be on the other side. Do not, for any reason, lose line-of-sight to the plane patrolling the entrance."

"We'll need spotters on the top of the airship, up on the rigid frame, on the top service walkway," McHenry suggested. "We can roll out some cable and rig a field telephone so they can report."

"Use cameras to record everything," insisted Utter. "That way if you die we could still recover useful data."

"You need to limit the time you spend in there," Finian went on to Machen. "Nobody's seen one of these things before so we don't know about thermal inversions, clear air disturbance, humidity bursts—all kinds of stuff that could take an aircraft out. So you go in, take the doc's pictures, make what observations you can, and then you head back out."

"Wait," objected Nickelhouse. "What you say is useful, Finian, but it's not enough. We need solid evidence of an ecological system beyond the fallstreak. There's a new world up there. We need to verify it."

Verity laid a hand on her fiancée's sleeve. "Men have died, Frank. More might die. What we're doing is risky enough."

The Senator stifled whatever rebuttal he was about to make. "Let's see what we can see," he said. "Right, I want everyone at their stations. Finian, if McHenry's rigging an observation point up top I want you at it. This is our last chance at this, men, so don't screw up."

"And don't die," added Finian, practically.

Airship 27 banked to starboard, twisting almost on her own axis to minimize wind shear. Her maneuverability even in difficult conditions was far greater than a fixed-wing aircraft. Inside the vessel crewmen ran to stations and the engineers and fitters took up the positions McHenry had designated to them. Even the adventurous Miss Dennison was usefully occupied in the radio room making shorthand records of transmissions.

The ship swayed a little as she met the turbulence beneath the castle clouds. Captain Stafford's preferred way in would have been to rise above the formation and search for the fallstreak hole that way, but so far none of the unusual combination punch holes had been located from above. Instead the A-27 battled the unpredictable crosswinds and micro-hailstorms as she tried to avoid the trailing virga beneath the cloudbank.

"All stations call in," demanded Lieutenant Thompson. In due order, engineering then the men on each fan turbine checked their readiness. Auxiliaries maintaining the control fins sounded off. The crew manning the observation stations reported in, including Ensign Harvey subbing for Finian in the rear gondola. Damage control teams one and two were ready to go. The launch crew by the Sparrowhawk 'flying trapezes' were in place, and Machen and his men were already in their cockpits.

Finian called in as his turn came round, shouting into his radio mike over the loud wind noise there at the very top of the canopy. He and a crewman called Burton were lashed to the fuselage where they had the best possible upwards view, but it also meant they were taking the brunt of the below-zero weather.

"Finian up top here. Nothing to report yet."

Miss Castlemere was co-ordinating the communications. "Take care, sailor," she told him. "Don't fall off."

Burton tried to stop his teeth chattering and made a crude observation about what part of him was likely to fall off first.

The A27 jinked again. Finian got the best view anyone had ever seen of the bizarre trailing refrozen clouds that looked like giant creepers growing from the white base of the main altocumulus bank. The complicated wind-patterns twisted the dangling trailers so they moved like tentacles. It wasn't hard to imagine the entire cloud as some living creature twisting jellyfish tendrils down to crush its prey.

"The compass is getting jittery," the navigation officer reported. That had been a prelude to the A26's encounter. "It's spinning like crazy!"

"Big storms can do that sometimes," the experienced Captain Stafford told him. "Keep her steady, helm."

Finian wiped crusted frost off his goggles and maintained his watch. "Conn, take us fifteen points starboard," he advised, seeking to avoid collision with one of the refreezing virga.

"This is Dr. Utter, speaking over the radio," cut in the English tones of the ship's resident genius. "There's something anomalous about these compass variations. They seem to be following some kind of pattern. Also the interference in radio communication has a regular cycle worthy of additional study."

A heavy gust spun the massive A27 on its axis, tilting it twenty degrees to port as it turned. Helm struggled to compensate but the ship continued to spiral until it broke out of the white mist into a patch of clear air.

And right there above them was the calm azure ring where the clouds had rolled round to open a clear gap in their centre.

"Conn, its right above us!" Finian shouted. "We got it!"

Airship 27 righted herself in the calmer column beneath the punch hole. "Say again," came back Verity's voice. "Confirm, Finian."

"We got it, kid! That's a definite fallstreak phenomenon about a thousand feet above us. If Nickelhouse wants to throw fighters through there he's never going to have a better chance than now!"

"Conn to hangar bay. Prepare to drop Sparrowhawks!" came Captain Stafford's cultured Annapolis tones. "Launch at will."

Finian was on exactly the wrong side of the ship to see the skyhook dropping the tiny aircraft from the belly of the craft. He contented himself with wrestling a bulky camera from the field box strapped to the fuselage and getting a couple of new plates of the punch-hole cloud formation. He wished he could capture the weird blue color of the bizarre phenomenon.

Then a shadow moved over the A27's outer framing. Looming out of the clouds less than a couple of hundred feet above came the dark metal airship that Finian had last glimpsed shooting up the airfield at Bellerophon Industries.

"Crap!" he swore. "Conn, we have a bogey above and sixty to starboard! It's the goddamned ship that blew us to hell last night! And it's closing."

Even then, as two million tons of death loomed over them, Finian couldn't help but notice how much like the A27 their enemy looked. The proportions were the same, right down to the distinctive fore and aft gondolas hanging beneath the gasbag. The main differences were in color—the enemy ship's outer skin was darker, with a black Germanic cross stenciled across it—and the heavy field gun dangling under its mid-section.

That field gun swiveled round and oriented on Airship 27.

"Conn, they're gonna shoot! Take us starboard and spin us counter-clockwise on axis! Now!"

A27 moved excruciatingly slowly in Finian's perception. The enemy craft passed above, fully emerging from the wall of cloud into the calm space beneath the cloud ring. The weatherman could see the gunner and his mates strapped into chairs behind the modified Russian M1931 field artillery as it oriented on him.

"They're firing!" Finian warned.

He saw the smoke emerging from the weapon and watched the whole enemy ship recoil from the blast. The thirty foot long corps gun could usually put out three shells a minute with an experienced ground crew; now Finian understood why each airborne shot took much longer to align.

The 4.8" shell shot towards A27 with lethal intent. The airship's maneuverability saved her as she keeled to almost forty-five degrees starboard and spun on her tail. The missile passed her envelope by mere feet and vanished into the cloud.

"Machen, are you in the air yet?" Captain Stafford asked over the radio link.

"Negative, Conn. That last maneuver of ours tangled the sky-hook. I'm dangling like a Christmas tree ornament and about as much good! We can't launch!"

The enemy zeppelin positioned itself steady again to take another shell-shot.

"Conn, that gun of theirs is slung underneath them," Finian called out. "If we're at their height they won't be able to target us!"

Nobody acknowledged Finian's warning but the A27 began to rise. The weatherman suspected a hastily ballast evacuation.

The field gun fired again but the angle was wrong. This time the shell passed harmlessly below Airship 27.

The enemy ship maneuvered as well. Too late Finian understood what they were intending. "Conn, they're bringing their machine guns to bear. Head…"

The rattle of rapid fire was loud and clear in the uncanny still air below the fallstreak. Finian saw the shots hit A27's tail assembly, shredding the upper fin and ailerons. By some miracle the gasbag was missed. A second chatter of noise must have been the A27's own Brownings returning fire.

Both ships were rising now, each seeking altitude over the other for a tactical advantage. Finian saw the gap in the clouds draw nearer and nearer above, the blurred purple-blue sky above casting a weird light over the embattled airship.

"Finian to Conn. If we're not careful we'll pass through the punch-hole's horizon," he warned.

Nobody responded. The A27 jinked aside again and there was another exchange of fire. The weatherman thought some of the shots might have gone into the hard frame of the enemy ship but he wasn't sure. The other ship misjudged its maneuver; its tail vanished into the turbulent clouds outside the still air column and was twisted sideways.

The punch hole loomed ever nearer above. Finian had no idea what conditions might be there. "We're right below the cloud gap, guys!" he shouted into his mike. "We have to drop now or we'll go through."

"Vertical controls are out," came back Stafford's tense reply. "They've shot up the flaps!"

Finian could see the shredded framework lifting up and down but there wasn't enough left of the covering to have an effect. One of the rear propellers had died as well.

A27 shook and spun as she passed through the ring of the cloud gap. The whole ship turned on her axis twice as she was pulled up into the punch hole. Bright sprays of St Elmo's fire played over the metal frame of the lift body. The catwalks sparked.

Finian's radio went dead.

"What's going on?" Burton screamed beside him.

New air currents caught the vessel, banking her hard to port up and away from the cloud hole. One by one the A27's remaining turbines spluttered and fell silent.

The ship was tilted so acutely that Finian could glimpse the fallstreak gap beneath them. The clouds that edged the disc were spinning faster than before, sucking in more vapor as they rotated. As the weatherman watched the hole collapsed and was swallowed up by the castle cloud.

A moment later Airship 27 crashed through one of the tall upward-jutting vapor pillars that gave altocumulus castellanus its name and visibility went to zero.

It took Finian and Burton fifteen minutes to grope their way along the ice-slicked exterior of the ship to reach an access door to the interior frame that surrounded the gas-sacks. The men couldn't feel their extremities by the time they dropped onto the metal-mesh walkway.

To Finian's surprise the steel and aluminum balcony was warm to the touch. The weatherman remembered the strange lightning that had played along it at the fallstreak horizon.

From there the men took access ladders and found their way back down into the long corridor that ran the full length of the vessel's underside. Other crew were heading the opposite way. Finian nodded to a fur-clad McHenry on his way to inspect the tail section.

Finian strode through the main lounge on his way to the stateroom. A steward handed him a metal mug of hot onion soup. Finian was surprised to recognize the short-order cook from the base's mess hut.

Nickelhouse, Verity, and Captain Stafford were conferring in the wood-paneled stateroom. Utter was there too, but he sat cross-legged on the floor scribbling on a series of notepads that he kept rearranging into different orders.

"Well," Finian noted as he tossed his frost-rimed fur gloves onto the polished table, "you sure found your anomaly, Senator."

"That I did," frowned Frank Nickelhouse. He didn't seem too happy about it.

"We finally got a good look at that vessel assaulting the ship," Captain Stafford explained. "Looks like it was built to the exact same blueprints as us."

"The A25 blueprints, I'd say," interjected Utter. "The modified housings on the stern attitude controls were not present, nor the improved couplings on the propeller gimbals. And of course, someone has butchered in an underslung field weapon with no regard for weight distribution or substructure stress ratios."

"You're saying some spy got the plans and they built a ship that can do what this one can," Finian summarized. "That's some espionage."

The Senator nodded, furious. "Creed was right! They've been one step ahead of us all along, stealing our research then applying it, hunting the fallstreak holes, sabotaging our own efforts at the cost of many lives."

"But we still got here first," noted Miss Castlemere. "I mean, here we are, right, up above the clouds?"

Stafford looked uncomfortable.

"What?" asked Finian. He was missing something.

The Captain passed a clipboard to him. Finian recognized one of his own weather condition charts, filled out in the handwriting of the ensign who'd been subbing for him in the weather car. He frowned. "This bozo's got it wrong."

"You can check it for yourself, of course, but two different men have made the same observations," Nickelhouse said.

Finian looked down the sheet. "So according to the glass we're at sea level, not 16,000 feet plus. And there's no steady magnetic field."

"Also we no longer have any radio contact with the ground," added Stafford. "We're not getting anything, even background chatter. We're checking the receivers."

"Okay, that's weird. But maybe that electric field or whatever it was that we flashed through screwed up our instruments. De-gaussed the compasses, wrecked the radio doohickeys, somehow fritzed the altimeters?"

"That's the most sensible explanation," agreed the Senator.

"They're saying it'll be a while before we can land," Miss Castlemere told Finian. "The control surfaces were shredded in that attack. Mr. McHenry reckons it'll take five or six hours to patch them. And all the generators fused, so they'll need fixing too."

"Even without being fully fuelled we have gas enough to stay aloft for three days," Stafford assured her.

"The electric-magnetic phenomenon was fascinating," admitted Utter, still cross-legged on the carpet. "There's something about that which I am missing." He went back to his scribbling.

Finian looked through the big forward windows. The airship was drifting out of the cloud tower. He operated the manual windshield wipers to scrape away the ice and peered out at the purple haze beyond.

"Like that lost pilot said. No horizon. No sun. No land. A constant carpet of cloud beneath us."

Nickelhouse joined him to peer out at the lurid gloom. "You're the weatherman, Finian. Advise us."

Finian rubbed his chilled fingers. "Okay then," he sighed. "Drop me down in the weather car to take a look-see."

Finian hadn't realized how silent the powerless ship had become until McHenry spun up the motors on the cable-reeling apparatus to pay out the line on the weather gondola. Finian released the clamps and survived the short free-fall before he was jerked to a halt by the suspension wires.

"Take it slowly, boys," he said through his hard-wired telephone. "If we really are somehow at sea level I don't want to get wet."

"Thought you were a seaman," Verity Castlemere teased him at the other end of the line.

The weather car descended into the cloudbank. Finian's visibility went to zero. Flicking on the capsule's external lights just increased the reflection glare so he switched them off again.

"Okay, this is a bit screwy," he reported as he watched his instruments. "I've been going down for a minute or so now and I'm not detecting any pressure change. The barometer should be reflecting my descent. It's not."

"Perhaps the magnetic effect Dr. Utter was talking about?" suggested Verity.

"A barometer's just a thin copper case that's sensitive to air pressure. It's only mechanical, the crudest sort of machine at that. Hardly any moving parts. And all the instruments say the same."

"How is that possible?"

"It's not. But I'm getting a slight temperature rise here. It was around minus twenty Fahrenheit. Now it's up to around zero.[6]"

"Are you getting swung all over the place again?"

"Nope. It's pretty calm down here. It's like descending through a snowbank. Kind of pretty in a chilly numbing way. If I find Santa I'll bring you back a present."

"You're assuming I've been a good girl, Finian."

The weatherman snorted. "Bad girls get presents too. Plenty of 'em."

He was chuckling when the object hit his window.

"What th...!"

"Finian?"

Something else rattled off the gondola's windshield. For a moment Finian thought he'd hit a pigeon. The third thing to slam into the glass changed his mind.

The creature was like nothing the weatherman had ever seen. It was closest to a squid the size of Finian's hand, with suckers on its tentacles protruding from a mouth-like opening. The cups adhered to the window this time, allowing Finian a good view of the bizarre entity.

"Finian, what is it? Are you okay?"

Another pair of the squid-creatures fastened to the gondola.

"I've got company down here. Some kind of critter. No idea what. It's got tentacles and some kind of huge bulge that might be... a gas bag? Something to let it fly?"

More of the swarm latched on to the glass around the sealed gondola cabin.

"Did you say creatures?" Verity asked.

A larger version of the same entity slammed so hard into the side of the

6 Roughly −30 degrees centigrade to −20.

vehicle that the weather car rocked.

"Okay, pull me up!" Finian called out. "Now!"

The next attack broke one of the panes. A pair of the monster's tentacles flapped through the gap.

"Right now!" shouted Finian. He unstrapped himself from his chair and reached for his toolkit.

The creature began to ooze itself through the broken pane, squeezing bonelessly through the narrow gash.

Finian found a screwdriver and plunged it into the creature. The thing exploded in a pungent black ooze and died with a high-pitched screech.

The other entities on the windows went wild, flailing and hammering away. Another couple of panes starred, beginning to splinter.

The gondola rocked again as an even larger tentacle-thing latched on below.

The car rose unsteadily, swaying from side to side.

A huge feeler, longer than the fifteen-foot weather car, loomed out of the thick cloud and groped blindly. Whatever it was attached to was far more massive than anything Finian has seen so far.

The weather car broke out of the cloudbank. The adhering creatures dropped away. If it hadn't been for the sad burst specimen oozing down through the shattered pane the whole thing might have been a nightmare.

Finian docked the gondola and went to report to the Senator that descending through the cloud carpet might not be a smart thing to do.

When Finian ventured into the dining hall later there were plenty of crewman eager to hear from him. All were aware of the bizarre weather condition in which the vessel now found itself trapped. Most had now heard about the guy who'd got the hanger doors open so the A27 could escape. Some had even seen the bizarre squid-creature that Utter was dissecting in the workshop.

Finian wanted a plate of ham and eggs, a hot coffee (in the absence of a cool beer) and a long sleep.

Machen came to his rescue. "Cut the fellah some slack, boys," the pilot advised the curious crewmen and ground staff that might otherwise have mobbed the weatherman. "He's had a tough day even by our standards."

Finian didn't object when Machen jumped the mess queue and returned with a heaped plate for him.

"Thanks," the weatherman said, tucking in.

Machen stood guard while Finian ate, fending off would-be

interviewers. Now that the major repairs were underway and Airship 27's flight condition was stable many of the crew had been rotated to R and R; the dining hall lounge was crowded, as was the crew mess behind it.

"Everything that's happened today and the biggest thing folks are bitching about is we didn't get time to load the coffee supplies," snorted Machen. "Enjoy your java, Finian, 'cause that stuff is strictly rationed now."

Finian sipped the hot drink gratefully. His body was starting to ache from the exertion but at least he could feel his fingertips again. "I heard you and the boys went out for a looksee as well," he noted.

Machen nodded. "Once we'd untangled the kite strings we did a fly-round above the cloudbank. Not too far, only line of sight, which isn't more than a mile in this haze."

"What were conditions like?"

"Pretty mild except for pockets of turbulence that were probably some kind of thermal updraft. Hard to say, really. I've never seen conditions like these before. No wonder that missing pilot radioed back that these weren't our skies."

The dull purple blur was visible through the downward-looking lounge windows. "I hear the doc thinks we're in remarkably fresh air, without the usual pollution from chimney stacks and the like. And that it's rich in oxygen, which makes it more likely that a stray spark will blow us all to hell."

"Assuming that's not where we are now," the pilot joked.

Finian looked around the crowded room. "How are the men taking it, being lost above the clouds? Most of them signed on for a short trip. Some of them never signed on at all."

Machen winced. "Yeah, I don't know whether I should feel guilty for dragging little Beth Dennison into this or grateful I had her in that store cupboard with me so she didn't get blown to pieces when the girls barracks went up."

Finian looked at the crowded table where the secretary sat, the centre of attention. "I'd say she's doing okay."

"I guess so. I guess so far folks haven't done the engineering math."

Finian had. "Three days fuel to run the motors. An incomplete hydrogen intake that'll gradually seep out dropping us into those carnivorous clouds."

"McHenry was the first to say it. That raider airship blew the A25 to bits but this is probably what happened to the A26. She flew through a hole and couldn't get back. Then she died."

"Maybe. But we don't know how far this weird weather condition extends. Could be we're a hundred yards off flying out of it and finding ourselves over New York in time for a Broadway show."

"Yeah, we could catch Tamara Drasin singing *Smoke Gets In My Eyes*,[7] or this fog could go on forever." Machen drained his own coffee cup and placed it upside-down on the table. "We could be trapped in another place. This could really be another space, another time, another world."

Finian hadn't chalked the pilot down as a romantic. "Don't be so quick to think we know all about our own world, chum. We still don't really understand how clouds form, how the tides affect weather patterns, why the gulf stream runs, when storms and hurricanes will start up. We know more about the moon than we do about the depths of the seas."

"You sound like you're glad you're here."

Finian realized that he was. "If Miss Castlemere hadn't dragged me out of hoosegow and pulled me onto the A27 then this morning I'd have been waking up in the drunk tank again with a pounding headache and some guy's teeth stuck in my knuckles. I'd be staggering off to haul crates for a buck fifty a day so I could drink myself blind on rotgut tonight." He stared out at the purple blur. "This is better than that."

"It's an adventure, I guess," admitted Machen.

"Yeah. I owe Verity Castlemere."

"She's a hot tomato," agreed the pilot, and nodded his head to indicate that Finian should look around.

Miss Castlemere was there in the lounge. She stood by the piano as some crewmember began to pick out a tune. She leaned back and gathered up the audience with a look.

And she sang:

"Ain't robbed no train, ain't done no hangin' crime.
Ain't robbed no train, ain't done no hangin' crime.
Just a slave to the Blues, grievin' 'bout that man of mine."

Verity's singing voice was rich and throaty, and filled with old hurt. The whole room fell quiet. The lady could sing the blues.

"Blues, please tell me, do I have to die a slave?
Blues, please tell me, do I have to die a slave?
Do you hear me pleadin', you're gonna send me to my grave?"

Machen looked across at Finian with raised eyebrows as if to say: "Did you know she could do this?"

---

7 The big Broadway hit of 1933 was *Roberta*, starring exotic songstress Tamara and her wildly-popular number *Smoke Gets In My Eyes*.

"Verity's singing voice was rich and throaty…"

Finian shook his head, distracted. There was no saxophone, no horn, no smoky speakeasy in some New Orleans backstreet, but Finian could taste the cheap booze, smell the coffin nails and sawdust. And either Verity Castlemere was the best actress in the world or she was a woman in pain.

If I could break these chains an' let my worried heart go free.
Oh, if I could only break these chains an' let my worried heart go free!
But it's too late now. The Blues have made a slave of me.
Too late now… the Blues have made a slave of me."[8]

There was a moment's silence as the blonde finished and lowered her head, then the room went wild. The tensions that had been building in this strange situation evaporated for a while as the whole room fell in love with Verity Castlemere. Finian wondered if that was what Nickelhouse had sent her to do.

The piano struck up *Camptown Races* and Verity sang that too, but she didn't show her soul again.

Finian was woken from a troubled sleep by one of the junior ratings. "Captain's compliments sir and could you please get to the weather car immediately? He needs your opinion."

Finian rolled out of his bunk in the officer's wardroom. Machen snored in the bed opposite and another of the pilots was enjoying some much-needed shuteye, but there was evidently no rest for the wicked. "What's happening?" Finian asked.

It was obvious as soon as he got to a section of the airship with windows. The purple haze had turned an angry dark grey to starboard. Occasional flashes suggested a lightning storm approaching.

Finian slithered down the hatch and dropped into the rear gondola. Someone had patched up the broken pane where the creature had smashed through. The other cracks were held with duct tape. He relieved Ensign Harvey, dropped into his chair, and swung it around to check the instrumentation.

"Finian, are you there?" Stafford asked over the speaker.

"Yeah, I'm at station. We've got a falling glass, although that technically

---

8 Verity was singing *Slave to the Blues*, originally composed and performed by the legendary blues goddess Ma Rainey. The song is now in the public domain and readers are encouraged to track down a copy of Ma Rainey's remarkable performance, which also features the talents of Louis Armstrong, Fletcher Henderson, Buster Bailey, Joe Smith, Coleman Hawkins, ragtime guitarist Blind Blake and hokum-blues duo Georgia Tom and Tampa Red.

puts us about twenty feet underwater, but temperature's rising. Crosswinds and updrafts are shifting those castle cloud columns and you do not want to get slammed by one of them."

"And that smudge to starboard, it's a storm?"

"Bastard of a storm, closing at about twenty-five knots. Can you outrun it?"

"We'll try. Keep an eye on it and stay on the line."

"Wilco. Finian out."

The A27 tilted as the newly-fixed tail-flaps and the revived propellers turned the vessel. The storm was now behind the ship, but still closing.

Finian checked the dashboard clock. It was 21:30, which explained why the luminescence of the purple haze was diminishing. His other instruments didn't seem to make any sense though.

The A27 veered again. Finian watched her maneuver round one of the piled cloudbanks that gave castle clouds their name. Flying through those turbulent stacks was always dangerous, but the entities Finian had discovered in the dense moisture had magnified their threat even more.

The storm was near enough to see details now, a seething mass of black twisting cloud that rose higher than Finian could perceive, discharging forked bolts down in to the thick cloud carpet below. Luminescent trailers joined the two vapor masses together. The metal lattice around the airship glowed with St Elmo's fire.

Finian saw what was ahead almost as soon as the forward spotter, but that man called it in first. "There! Six points to port by ten below lateral! Something's moving!"

Finian pulled out field binoculars from their safety case and focused them on the blobs that were barely in his field of view. It was not, as he'd first feared, the enemy zeppelin reappearing to finish the job. This was something else.

A dozen or more shapes resolved themselves into what the weatherman at first took to be hot air balloons. A closer inspection revealed that they had long cilia descending from them. Finian remembered some of the weird South Seas jellyfish he'd seen; except they had been four inches long, not seventy feet.

He didn't need to advise Captain Stafford to change course. The aerial life forms had so far showed no interest in the airship but that was no guarantee of future amity.

"Has anybody at all got the first idea what the hell those things are?" Captain Stafford sounded rattled.

Finian stayed with his area of expertise. "If you keep this course to avoid them the storm'll take you on the starboard lee," he advised. That wouldn't be good. It would hit the A27 on her broad side and could push her right over.

"What do you recommend, Mr. Finian?"

"Well, since we can't drive through that herd of whatever those things are and the stormfront's gonna impact if we do anything else, I'd say turn into it and keep our nose pointing at its teeth—and hope it doesn't get bitten off."

Stafford considered this. "Can we survive that tempest, Finian?"

"No idea, cap'n," the weatherman admitted. It was the captain's call.

Stafford must have decided to follow Finian's advice. Airship 27 banked again, this time back towards the brooding black roil that was closing too fast to starboard.

"All hands, this is the captain. All hands to quarters. Secure for storm. Batten down. This is going to be a teeth-rattler, so hang on!"

Finian really hoped they'd made a good job of fixing the glazing in his weather gondola.

The first lightning bolt arced through the ship. The charge wasn't earthed so it passed harmlessly through the hull, doing nothing worse than setting the useless compasses spinning again and causing the speaker systems to make obscene raspberry screeches; except that a single spark in the wrong place would ignite the highly flammable sacks of hydrogen that kept the A27 aloft. The first fire control crews would know about the problem was when they woke up in heaven or hell.

The winds slammed into the ship, keeling her to port, trying to twist her on her side. The turbine motors screeched as they were redlined to turn the propellers that held the ship aligned with the storm. Finian wondered just how good McHenry's emergency repairs to the control fins had been; he guessed he was going to find out.

A simultaneous pair of lighting strikes crossed and seared through the airship's metal exoskeleton. Finian knew in theory that this framework formed a protective Faraday cage around the vulnerable flammable sacks within it. He also knew that aluminum melted at twelve-twenty degrees and that lightning-heated joints could exceed that.

Ghostly blue fire danced over the metal frame of the weather car. The wind lashed in, causing the whole gondola to shudder and grind against its restraining bolts.

A wall of sleet followed on. It pelted onto the toughened glass like bullets, deafening inside the closed compartment. Finian flicked on the windshield wipers to try and keep some visibility but it was a losing battle. He imagined the thick crust of ice that must be forming on the critical hinge-joints of the control planes, of the men who'd be out in this tempest on the gantries trying to keep the big engines turning.

The whole ship juddered as if it had been struck. Another lightning strike blew out a couple of the big arc spots on the ship's underside. The other external lights failed then flickered on again. The ship began to turn cross-side to the wind.

"Keep facing the edge!" Finian called urgently, but the phone was dead. "Conn?"

He was about to curse the lightning for frying the wiring when the next flash lit up the front of the ship. He saw the control gondola and he saw the *thing* attached to it, one of the huge balloon-jellyfish creatures now latched onto the prow of the A27. By design or accident it had crashed into the front of the vessel and was wrapped around the control car; and nobody there was responding.

Then he realized that in storm conditions all the other windows were shuttered. It was possible that nobody else on the ship *knew*.

Finian ignored the bucking of the airship and unstrapped his seatbelt. It took him two attempts to climb the ladder up into the main spine. He raced into the dining hall lounge where Verity Castlemere had enchanted the crew just hours earlier. She was there again, this time supervising medical care for a couple of crewmen who looked like they'd been badly burned.

"I need help at the control gondola!" Finian shouted without stopping.

He faced forward, past the radio room and workshop. McHenry was in the tiny tool shop. "With me now!" Finian roared and kept moving.

The door to the stateroom opened and Senator Nickelhouse looked out. "What's going on?" he demanded. Dr Utter peered over his shoulder with wide worried eyes.

"Some problem in the Conn," answered Verity; Finian hadn't even realized she'd followed him.

A weapons locker stood at the top of the ladder down to the forward gondola. Finian wrenched it open and grabbed a shotgun, then tossed another over to Nickelhouse.

"What's happening?" McHenry demanded. "We're not getting any rudder commands."

"Huge gasbag tentacle thing attached to the front of the ship!" Finian summarized before dropping through the hatch to the control car below.

The gondola was wrecked. The windshield was shattered, its reinforced struts twisted like putty. Three torso-thick tentacles lashed around the cabin. One of them was wrapped around the dangling corpse of First Lieutenant Thompson. The two other watch officers were shattered bloody smears on the floor. Oxlen's head was paste. Of Captain Stafford there was no sign at all.

The winds knocked Finian off his feet as soon as he dropped. That saved his life. The twitching tentacle that lashed at him passed over his head and shattered a side window.

An absurd part of the weatherman wondered how the tentacles could tell he was there. The more practical part of Harry Finian brought the M1917 Enfield up to his shoulder and emptied the full six-round magazine of .30-06 bullets into the writhing slimy mass.

The shots cut through the fibrous muscle and almost severed the questing tentacle. Finian pushed his back against the cabin wall and reloaded.

The other tentacles oriented on him. Thompson's shattered body was discarded. Finian emptied his weapon again at the first of the incoming creepers. He had no time to reload before the second got him so he clubbed at it with his rifle-butt.

The snaking length shook off the blows and reached out for the weatherman. Another magazine of bullets from the top of the ladder deterred it, making it recoil away.

Finian looked up for Nickelhouse, but it was Verity who dropped to the gondola floor and broke open her Enfield to reload.

"Thanks," Finian said. The wind whipped the sound away but Miss Castlemere flashed him a wild smile that made his heart do cartwheels. Her hair sprayed out behind her in the gale like a battle goddess riding the storm.

The tentacles came again but this time both Finian and Verity were ready. They fired in unison, aiming so their shots not only shredded the giant feelers but went into the great wall of organic matter that pressed up to the front of the gondola. The creature's screech was audible even above the tempest.

Nickelhouse climbed down to join them in plugging more rounds into the pulsating mass. Nobody else dared the fight.

With a last howl the creature broke away from the front of the airship— or perhaps fell away as its strength failed it—and was swept off into the cloud bank a mere sixty feet below.

"We did it!" Nickelhouse gasped, staring after the bizarre monster.

Finian knew that wasn't the case. Airship 27 was beam on to the storm and was creaking all along her frame as the tensions tested the workmanship of the bracing supports. She was being shaken to pieces.

"Get McHenry down here!" he screamed over the tempest.

Verity nodded and dragged herself back up the ladder to call for the engineer.

Finian looked at the control column and instrument panels. Many of the navigation instruments were smashed. The radio and telephone equipment was a total loss. The steering yoke was buckled and had somehow come uncoupled from the gearing it directed.

Nickelhouse was still staring down after the fallen creature. He gasped as it rose again from the carpet of cloud. "It's coming back!"

But the monster faltered. Through the glazed floor-plates of the gondola it was clear to see that the monster trying to rise from the mists was covered in the fist-and-arm-sized creatures that Finian had encountered. They swarmed over it like ants, more crawling up and latching on every second. The giant writhed and struggled but then vanished under a seething layer of the smaller predators. The whole mass fell back in to the clouds and did not reappear.

Nickelhouse swore.

"No time for that!" Finian called. "If we don't get altitude we'll be down there in that cloud with it. Get aloft and tell 'em to ditch whatever ballast we've got. All of it! There's no other way."

The Senator got a grip of himself, nodded, and shinned up to deliver the order. Almost at once McHenry scurried down, chivvied along by Miss Castlemere.

The engineer saw the wreck of the control car and cursed. Finian just pointed at the couplings. "Fix it!" he demanded.

McHenry had brought a toolbox. That was as well, since the lockers containing the emergency tools in the control gondola were hammered flat. The Scotsman got to work as quickly as he could, unbolting the bent section of the hydraulic housing and plumbing in a makeshift replacement.

The winds knocked into the A27, tilting her to forty-five degrees. Finian caught Verity as she tumbled and held her in his arms.

She kissed him.

"Got it!" shouted McHenry, oblivious to their embrace. "It'll drive like a pig but try it th' now!"

Finian reluctantly pushed the blonde aside and heaved at the column.

There was an unpleasant grinding sound but the ailerons shifted. At the same moment the ballast tanks were opened. The ship surged upwards as tons of water were released into the storm.

"Help me!" Finian told Verity. She joined him in forcing the levers into place to turn the shimmying airship back into the storm. The A27 was reluctant to comply.

"Come on, you dizzy, maddening, wonderful, lethal beauty!" Finian called out. He wasn't sure whether he meant the A27 or the blonde who strained next to him. "Come on!"

The prow turned into the wind and the ship regained its axis.

They were going to live for a few hours more.

Morning was marked only by the bruise-colored haze turning to a sicker shade of violet. The azure hue of yesterday's flight was absent.

Finian had handed the watch over to Machen and a very junior ensign at midnight. He was woken as he'd instructed at 7 a.m. He grimaced at the cocoa he was handed in lieu of coffee.

"The Senator's in the stateroom," the steward told him.

Finian dragged on his flight suit, the only dry clothes he'd still got, and made his way to see Nickelhouse. The Senator was in conference with McHenry and Utter. As always Miss Castlemere was sat near by, watching and listening.

"Finian," the Senator greeted him as he entered. "Sleep well?"

"Like a dead man," the weatherman answered. "So what's our situation?"

McHenry looked so exhausted that Finian felt guilty for taking bunk time. The engineer's dark eye-circles made him look like an anemic panda. "Ah've shored up the steering controls and we're refitting the gondola as best we can. Whatever other repairs we can make we're doing. But we're out o' ballast and we lost a gasbag last night, so we're getting short on lift. And I'm pretty much out of spares to keep the engines running."

Finian winced. "No sign of another punch-hole in the clouds then?"

"Nope," said the Senator. "And we've got two more days in the air tops."

Dr. Utter looked up from the notebook he was scribbling in. "I don't think we're going to find such a hole," he suggested. "I don't believe they are a natural phenomenon."

That was new information to Nickelhouse. "What do you mean?" he demanded.

Utter tapped his calculations. "Well, I've been going over the data on the conditions we encountered just prior to entering the fallstreak aperture. You'll recall that an early phenomenon was radio interference?"

"Storms can often affect radio waves," Finian noted.

"Ah yes. But we recorded this interference on wax cylinders so I've been able to play it back. There was a pattern. A regular pattern."

"Does that matter?" asked Verity.

"It does. Because it suggests that somebody was sending out very powerful radio signals, or at least electro-magnetic signals, on a very precise frequency, very near to the phenomenon."

Finian thought about that. "We speculated that the proximity of a big metal object might interact with the clouds to open this phenomenon. What if that was only part of it? What if it needs a precise place, where rare altocumulus castellanus form over water, and a dense metal mass, *and* a magnetic signal as well?"

Utter nodded approvingly. "I've only done the tentative mathematics on the limited data available, of course, but as a hypothesis it meets all the required criteria. I would need rather more sampling and a comprehensive set of field experiments to be able to firm up my conclusions, of course, starting with…"

"Hold it," interrupted the Senator. "You're saying these special fallstreaks appeared because somebody out there zapped them open?"

Finian was ahead of him. "What if that Boche zeppelin had the kit aboard to do it? They had to invade our airspace because that's the only location it'd work. And then the BE-A's started poking around. Our ships found the fallstreaks because the bad guys had just opened them."

McHenry frowned. "I still want tae know how it is they could put a replica of our design into the air. Seems to me like all the Senator's money has just gone on giving our enemies the best designed ship possible for making these punch-hole things."

Nickelhouse didn't like hearing that. "The BA-E plans are top secret. If they got out then somebody in Washington's looking at life in a federal jail."

"I'm more concerned right now with how to get back so the Senator can play detective and find whodunit," Finian pointed out. "If the doc's right then we're not going to discover a fallstreak outta here because they don't exist naturally. Can we whip up some gizmo to make one?"

Dr. Utter considered it. "I doubt we have the components aboard. All my equipment was in my laboratory." His face twitched as he recalled his lab was now a burned out shell under a different sky. "Even with the transmission equipment I would not be able to calculate the exact waveforms without many months of modeling and testing."

"So we're screwed!" spat McHenry. "I didn'ae sign up for this, Nickelhouse."

"Watch your tone," the Senator warned the engineer.

"Or what?" snapped McHenry. "Ye'll fire me?"

Verity intervened. "We're all tense and tired, boys. It's been an eventful couple of days. We're mourning our dead and we're worried about our futures. But we've made an astonishing discovery too, something truly amazing." She gestured to the livid purple sky in which Airship 27 hung. "Now our only chance of survival is to keep working together like we have so far. We're going to need everyone. Especially you, Mr. McHenry and you Dr. Utter."

Her words quieted the exhausted angry Scotsman and calmed the twitchy scientist.

"Mr. McHenry, why don't you go get some sleep while there's a no immediate crisis?" the girl continued. "Your excellent crew is well-trained and knows what to do now you've instructed them. Dr. Utter can continue assessing his theory about the radio transmission and maybe he'll come up with some clever idea about how to open a fallstreak hole for us after all."

Dr. Utter was more than content to continue working on his latest theory.

"Frank, you need someone to be in charge of the airship now. We've lost Captain Stafford and his bridge officers. I suggest that Finian takes over."

"Me?" the weatherman said, appalled.

"Can you suggest anyone better?" Verity challenged him.

So Finian left the stateroom with the burden of Airship 27 on his shoulders and Miss Castlemere's eyes upon his back.

The day passed and night fell again around the A27. As the shipboard lights came on Finian sat in the officer's wardroom completing a laborious entry into the ship's log.

They had survived their second day in the purple haze. Repairs were continuing, albeit slower now that every component had to be improvised from what spares remained. McHenry finding a bottle of whiskey somewhere and downing it all before supper had not helped matters. He'd been carried to his bunk before someone punched him out for it.

Finian could have used a slug of that booze. He'd been on the go all day, checking the vital equipment of the airship and the crew who manned it. Even more than the loss of two men to the storm, Captain Stafford's death with his entire command crew had shown the lost airmen how much danger they faced so far from home. Morale hung by a thread.

Finian looked down over the scrawl he'd added beneath Stafford's neat script. He'd recorded the change of course at 11.17 to avoid a grazing shoal of the floating jellyfish creatures, and another at 13.49. The topmost lookout had reported a sighting at 17.02 that might have been a pterosaur like the one the A25 had found, but the report was unconfirmed.

The weatherman rubbed his eyes while he thought. He'd only had a brief impression of the bat-winged reptilian in Block 9 but it had definitely had limbs, legs with sharp talons. That meant that in its natural habitat it had somewhere to land; somewhere out there must be a safe place to moor. But where?

Finian turned to the weather charts. There seemed to be a prevailing wind here, a gulf stream of sorts that inclined them in a single direction— Finian had arbitrarily designated it west for ease of calculation. If it resembled the trade winds in the regular skies of Earth then it would curl round major landmasses and there would be even fiercer currents higher up; yet the turbulent castle clouds seemed to move on other vectors too. There might also be entirely different winds below the thick vapor banks.

There was a knock on the wardroom door and Miss Castlemere let herself in. "I brought you more inventory reports. I was afraid you wouldn't have enough paperwork."

Finian accepted the lists of food and medical supplies and added them to the pile on his left. "How's Ensign Bowman?" he asked.

Verity's face fell. "He's not going to last the night," she admitted. "His burns are too severe. We don't have the equipment to treat him, even if we had a doctor."

The junior officer had been caught in the backflash when one of the generators had blown out during a lightning strike. His death would be the tenth since the ill-fated encounter with the enemy zeppelin and the transit through the fallstreak.

"No chaplain either," Finian said. He'd stumbled through the services for Captain Stafford and his comrades earlier in the day.

Verity sat beside him. "Are you mad at me for getting you a promotion?"

"I find it hard to stay mad looking into those smoky-blue peepers," he admitted. "At least you're shafting me to my face."

Miss Castlemere had read Finian's file. "Your girl dropped you when you were court-martialed and she married while you were in the brig," she recalled.

"Yeah. A lot of people I thought were on my side turned out not to be. A bunch of them kicked me when I was down. After a while that gets to a man."

Verity nodded. "Nobody's what they seem."

"That include you?" Finian challenged. "You're engaged to a US Senator. That kiss in the command gondola wasn't regulation."

The blonde smiled ruefully. "It sure wasn't. Sorry, Harry. It just kind of happened. Do you mind?"

"I'm not the guy who steals another guy's dame."

"I'm not a dame who gets stolen."

Finian put down his pen. "So what's the story with you and Nickelhouse? The real skinny. Why hasn't your engagement to a potential nominee for the highest office been splashed across the front page coast to coast?"

Verity smiled ruefully. "Public relations. Till Frank gets the nomination I'm a liability, a gold-digger from nowhere. Once he's named then I'm an asset, a photogenic doll who'll look great in the newsreels, a romance story to win the hearts of America."

"You sure don't sound happy for a gal who might make First Lady."

Miss Castlemere shook her head. "It won't happen. Frank's hasn't got what it takes to win the White House from FDR.[9] Not quite. And he'll blame me." She smiled at herself. "That's assuming we were somehow able to get out of this mess and back on the campaign trail. Maybe fate's punishing us for all the other men we sent off into the sky to die hunting this place?"

"Say you got home, though, and the Senator was able to show off a whole new frontier for human exploration, wouldn't that be a winning ticket?"

"Frank thinks so. But…"

"But?"

"But we won't get home, will we?"

There was a matter-of-fact acceptance in Verity's voice, the tones of a woman who'd learned that nothing ever turned out good for her. Finian wondered who had taught her that and broken her heart.

"It's gonna be tough, sweetheart," he admitted, "but you've done tough before, I think. According to McHenry we've got about another day's lift

---

9 Franklin Delano Roosevelt was sworn into office as 32nd President of the United States on 4th March 1933 and went on to become the longest serving Chief Executive in US history.

"*I'm not a dame who gets stolen.*"

and push. After that we're going down one way or another. So tomorrow afternoon, if we've not found a clever way out of this jam, I'm gonna batten the hatches and drop us through the clouds and count on those tentacle-things not being able to breach our hull."

"Will that work?"

"Dunno, but it's the best we've got. If you know any good prayers you might wanna dust them off."

Verity's eyes were moist in the subdued wardroom lighting. "I don't trust in God, Finian. And I learned long since not to trust people. I sure don't trust myself—I always let myself down. I only trust…"

"What? What do you trust?"

The blonde got up abruptly and walked to the door.

"You," she said, just before she left.

Finian was roused twice in the night. He'd ordered a call if the watch spotted anything unusual. The first awakening was because of lights down and behind to larboard; by the time Finian got to the weather gondola the illuminations had gone. The later alarm was when something huge and dark rustled past above the airship. Finian elected not to train the spotlights on it and attract attention.

Machen woke him next morning with a precious mug of coffee. "Rise and shine, boss. We're all waiting for you to pull our fat out of the fire."

"Thanks, Mac," the weatherman said ironically. "Sure you don't wanna steer this bucket?"

"I'm far too irresponsible. I'd be flying the A27 loop-the-loop to impress Beverly. Better you take the Conn."

Finian wondered what he might end up doing to impress Miss Castlemere.

The officers' wardroom phone rang. Finian had bunked there; he hadn't felt up to moving his things into Stafford's private cabin. He lifted the mouthpiece and held the earpiece to his head. "Finian here."

"Sir, it's the Conn," said the nervous Ensign Harvey, now the ranking officer in the forward gondola, "We've got something weird ahead five degrees port."

"A little more description, kid."

"Something in the clouds below."

"A break? A hole?"

"Something else. It's… I don't know."

"I'm on my way." Finian pulled his suspenders up and re-buttoned his shirt. "C'mon Mac. There's weird out there."

Machen moaned. "I knew it was a bad idea bringing you coffee." He trailed after Finian towards the control car.

The weatherman picked up Dr. Utter en route. By the time he got to the gondola Senator Nickelhouse was already there, peering out through binoculars.

Harvey handed another pair of field glasses to Finian and pointed. "There, sir."

Even without enhancement it was clear that there was a disturbance in the clouds. Something grey-white and rounded protruded from the cover.

"Is that a ship?" Machen asked. "How far away is that?"

"Half a mile easy," Finian judged. "And massive. It dwarfs the A27. That's an island. It could be solid land."

"We could tether!" realized Nickelhouse. "We could set down." He'd also done the hydrogen and fuel math.

"Not yet," Finian cautioned. "Mac, you and a wingman go take a look-see. Are the Sparrowhawk radios working?"

"They're fine at short range," the pilot captain answered. "It's just the rest of the world we can't pick up."

"I want a full radio check before you drop. Keep an open line, Mac. Get out there; see what the hell that thing is, then get home."

Mac shot the weatherman a sloppy salute. "Aye aye, admiral!" He climbed out of the gondola before Finian could formulate a response.

"Mr. Harvey, can you hold us steady at this distance?"

The ensign looked stricken. "I'll... I'll try sir. But it's difficult to judge."

Dr. Utter took his turn with the binoculars. "Look at the turbulence patterns. That object is moving."

Finian kicked himself for not seeing it himself. The grey lens was drifting with the prevailing wind. "Keep us in step with it then, Mr. Harvey. We need more than ever to know what that thing is."

Machen and his wingman flew in formation towards the shallow dome. Their Sparrowhawks seemed absurdly small in the vast purple sky, dwarfed by the lofty towers of piled vapor and the rolling white cloud carpet below, insignificant next to the huge swell of whatever pushed through from beneath the canopy. Finian thought it symbolic of how out of their scale the men of Airship 27 truly were in this new sky.

He kept his doubts to himself as Machen reported in. "SH1 to A27," came the pilot's voice over the makeshift replacement speaker McHenry had rigged. "We're approaching the hill, over."

"Okay Mac. See what you can see, over," Finian responded.

"Ask him if there's any place to tether an airship," Senator Nickelhouse instructed. Finian ignored him.

"We're over the target now," Machen went on. "It's dappled, like mould on cheese? Looks kind of soft. I'm dropping lower."

"Can they land on it?" wondered Dr. Utter hopefully. "Could they bring a sample?"

"Take it carefully, Mac, over," Finian said through the radio.

"I'm thirty feet above now. Looks solid, looks stable. I reckon a man could stand on that. And it's huge. This thing must be quarter of a mile from rim to rim."

"Ask him to check the edges," Utter urged. Finian relayed the request.

"It just tapers down into the cloud," Mac reported. "Could be like an iceberg, with most of it under the surface."

"But can we land?" Nickelhouse insisted. "Tell him to try it, Finian."

Finian pushed back his annoyance at the Senator's rank-pulling and back-seat driving. "Mac, could you try setting down? Just you. Keep your wingman aloft. Over."

"Guess I'm game to try, Finian. Can't have you hogging all the hero-glory, can we? I'm going in now. Over."

Finian forced himself not to reply with any be-careful platitude. Instead he kept his glasses pointed at the distant speck as it wheeled round for a landing approach on the grey dome.

The tiny Sparrowhawk came in low and bounced once, twice, then ran along the surface.

"Conn, this stuff's squelchy. Kind of like landing on a hot water bottle. You want I should get out and take a stroll?"

Finian considered this. "No. Stay where you are, keep your engine running. We're coming to you."

"We're mooring then?" Nickelhouse asked.

"I'm going down there to check," Finian said. "Before we attach the A27 to that thing I'll get lowered in the weather car. I can drop down a rope ladder through the floor hatch and climb to the surface. We need to check this thing very carefully before we risk the whole ship."

"That makes sense," admitted the Senator. "I'll come with you."

Finian shrugged. "Back-up makes sense too. But it's always a bumpy ride dropping in the weather car. The two of us'll get pretty knocked about."

"Three," said Dr. Utter suddenly. "I must have samples. I want to go."

"Call it four," said Verity Castlemere, shinning down into the gondola. "I'll pack a picnic."

Finian was still trying to figure how Verity had got her way about being in the landing party when the restraining bolts swung free and the weather car dropped to swing on its steel hawsers. The winding engines whined and the gondola inched down towards the grey surface below. A sobered and chastised Malcolm McHenry watched from the Conn in temporary charge of the A27.

The airship held station directly over the centre of the wide grey mass, somewhat sheltered by the bulk of the dome from the usual thermals and crosswinds of the purple sky; or else the weight of the extra people aboard kept the weather car from swaying quite so much. The gondola's occupants were still relieved when Finian called a halt to the descent twenty feet above the puffy floor and unrolled a ladder for the last drop.

"I go first," said the weatherman. "Any trouble and you just haul yourselves out of there, see?

Nickelhouse checked his rifle. "Got it," he agreed. Miss Castlemere's expression seemed to say otherwise.

Finian waited until the car was as steady as it was going to be then climbed down the ladder. The ground was squashy not muddy, like an unburst blister. An unpleasant dust with a pungent musk rose wherever the weatherman trod.

"It's solid all right," Finian confirmed Machen's earlier diagnosis. "Hey, Mac, we're down!"

The pilot was listening in over the radio. He'd kept his distance from the landing operation. Now he waved from his cockpit and began to taxi for takeoff. He and his wingman intended to quarter the floating island at low altitude.

Nickelhouse climbed down after Finian. He slipped on the penultimate rung and dropped heavily onto the spongy mass. It undulated unpleasantly beneath his boots.

"What the hell is this place?" the Senator wondered. He had a box camera round his neck and hurried to get an exposure.

Dr. Utter came down next, clearly unfamiliar with chain ladders, possibly with ladders in general. He managed to get himself tangled in the rigging and Finian had to help him free before the scientist choked himself.

Utter lost all interest in his own difficult descent as soon as he touched the surface. "Look at this!" he gasped, fondling the ground. "I think it's organic!"

"Organic?" Finian echoed. "Like in living? This is a creature?"

"Or a plant," Utter considered. "A vast simple lifeform traversing the cloud bank, straining it for those small tentacled creatures you encountered earlier much as a whale collects plankton from the ocean. Perhaps."

"But this is vast, far bigger than a whale," objected Nickelhouse. "This must be the largest creature that ever lived!"

Finian wondered if these were what the pterosaurs lived and bred upon; or maybe there were even bigger things out there in this strange sky, things that preyed upon even these wide grey living islands?

Verity dropped down gracefully beside the weatherman. "This is different," she admitted.

Nickelhouse took a few paces on the springy membrane as if that would afford a better view of the vast whole. "If this is a living creature then it presumably contains organic resources?" the Senator asked Utter. "Oil? Ivory? Water, at least?"

"The most useful to us now would be hydrogen," calculated the scientist. "I doubt we could fraction down any natural oils to produce usable diesel but this thing must stay aloft somehow. If it's a giant gas bag, as with that jellyfish predator that attacked the control gondola, then we may be able to siphon off much needed hydrogen for our own reserves."

"What if it's helium?" objected Miss Castlemere.

"We could improvise."

"Yeah, could we take a moment before we start digging into the quarter-mile-wide monster?" suggested Finian. "We're making a whole lot of assumptions, one of which is that this thing's not hostile, another that it can't fight back. Right now we just need to know if we can safely tether to it overnight and rest the engines. If so then tomorrow I say we drop the weather gondola over the side of this thing and see what's down there. If it's keeping those tentacle suckers at bay then this might be the best spot to try flying through the cloud layer."

Nickelhouse considered this. "Very well. Let's see if we can't find something more solid to hammer holding posts into."

"And some place where I can get some samples," added Utter, holding up the field kit he'd brought.

Finian reported back to McHenry and checked in with Mac. The pilots had discovered a darker area over to one side that Utter posited might be a muscle knot. The landing party of four headed in that direction on foot.

It was strange walking over that quaggy membrane. Finian found himself imagining the pungent white dust as dandruff and himself as a flea crawling over a bald giant's head. He wondered if the others found it as strange and alien.

He sneaked a glance at the exploration party. Nickelhouse was looking around like a man who'd discovered a new continent. His face was a mask of pride and ambition. Verity was tense, unsure how to behave in this unique environment, unwilling to back down now she'd committed herself. Utter was rapt, observing everything, his lips moving to some internal monologue.

The suddenly the scientist dropped to his knees. "Look!"

The Senator and Verity peered over his shoulder but didn't understand.

Utter traced his finger along the dull metallic veins that were more prominent there than elsewhere on the pulpy surface. "Here," he insisted "This webbing!" He dug down through the skin with a knife to expose some of the tracery. "If this is what I think it is…"

"Metal?" hazarded Nickelhouse.

"Not just any metal. At least three kinds, I think. I'd have to test it but at first glance I'd say cadmium, chromium and… maybe vanadium? That's chrome anyhow. I need samples…"

"I don't get it," Verity admitted. "So this thing has a metal epidermis?"

"A rare metals epidermis, honey," Nickelhouse corrected her. "Back home chromium's used for all kinds of industrial stuff. It sells for more than silver. Cadmium's rarer still. They use that for batteries and plating and the like. I don't know about the other stuff."

"Vanadium mixes with steel and toughens it. The Ford production line uses it," Utter supplied. "All three of these elements are very useful."

"And expensive," the Senator noted happily. "Can you imagine the reclamation value of something this huge? It's like finding a gold mine."

"If only it wasn't a living creature that we need to camp out on," Verity brought him down to Earth. "Leave your bank book out of this for a moment, Frank."

Nickelhouse's face darkened. "Mind your place, Verity," he warned.

The blonde flinched. "Sorry, Frank," she said quietly. Finian didn't like it.

"The ramifications of this lifeform—if indeed it is a lifeform—are immense," Utter continued oblivious to anything but his discovery. "A whole new taxonomy, with implications for the entire fields of biology, electro-chemistry, botany… It will require intensive study, a joint effort of many disciplines to…"

The Senator cut him short. "Finian, you wanted to check this thing out. You've checked it. Now bring the A27 in, get it moored, let McHenry do whatever he needs to get her back in the best condition possible. Once we're tethered we can send down more guys and get some proper samples to prove to the folks back home that we've discovered a treasure trove and to stake Bellerophon's claim. But first get the ship landed."

Finian didn't want to agree with Nickelhouse just then on principle. "Finian to Mac, how's the search coming along? Over."

"Hey, admiral! There's a few big holes round the edges just before it rounds down into the mists but I can't see what they are from the air. Could be elephant-sized rabbit holes for all I can tell. Otherwise what you see is what you get. Over."

"Okay. Head back to the airship, Mac. Beth Dennison will be missing you. Over."

"I doubt Beth'll stay lonely long, Finian. Mac over and... what the hell?"

Finian heard the surprise in the pilot's voice. He tried to see the pair of Sparrowhawks through the ever-present haze. He thought he could spot a vague silhouette far over to the edge of the grey platform but he wasn't sure. "Mac? You okay? Over."

Machen's voice came back garbled and hasty. "We're under fire! Fighter planes! Four, I think. We're... Namson's hit! He's going down!"

Now Finian saw it; the sudden burst of flame over towards the distant rim as a Sparrowhawk crashed onto the dusty surface was unmistakable.

Nickelhouse couldn't hear what was going on in Finian's earphones. He only saw the weatherman's face change. "What is it?" the Senator demanded.

Verity pointed upwards. "There!" she cried.

The looming silhouette of a dark zeppelin faded out of the haze.

"Back to the weather car!" Finian shouted. "Now! Run!" He grabbed Utter from the ground and pulled him on. "C'mon doc. Run!"

Nickelhouse couldn't believe it. "Where did they come from? How did they find us?"

Finian had an answer. "There's a prevailing current up here. We've used it. Anyone else would too. And we've been chattering on radio thinking nobody was listening in."

Machen still was. "Mac to Finian. Namson's dead. I'm trying to shake these bogies but there's four of them." Another flash lit the distant ground. "Three of them," the pilot amended with a grim satisfaction. "I'm gonna have to bug out!"

"Do what you have to, Mac. Finian out. McHenry, are you still receiving us?"

"Aye," came the worried tones of the Scots engineer.

"Well so might the bad guys be, so watch what you say," Finian warned. "Be ready to pull off the minute we get back."

Miss Castlemere looked over her shoulder at the approaching zeppelin. "We're not going to make it back before that thing's within firing range of Airship 27. They've got to go now!"

"Not till we're aboard," insisted the Senator, seizing the mike from Finian. "Run faster! McHenry, hold your position."

The enemy airship moved over the rim of the island, twisting so it presented its narrow prow to any A27 counterattack. The big field gun slung underneath cranked into a firing position.

"I'm sorry," McHenry said over the radio. "I didn'ae sign up for this. I'm not dying for ye, Senator."

"I said no!" insisted Nickelhouse. "No!"

Dr. Utter stopped pelting forward and stared, his eyes wide. "The A27 is lifting off!"

Finian watched as the airship rose, the weather car still swaying beneath it. The dangling ladder no longer touched the ground; soon it was high in the air.

"They left us!" gasped Frank Nickelhouse in outraged disbelief. "They left me!"

"What else could they do?" Finian reasoned. "If they don't move they're sitting ducks."

"But I ordered them!" the Senator insisted. "Malcolm McHenry is fired!"

Verity Castlemere stood with her hands on her knees, panting. "I'll be sure to send him a memo when I get back to the office," she said acidly.

Utter was watching the dark zeppelin chase off the A27. "That underslung gun is very badly mounted," he commented with a professional disdain.

Finian retrieved the microphone from the Senator. "Finian to Mac, are you receiving, over?"

There was no reply.

"Well, if you can hear me, Mac, get back to the A27 in your own time. Take command."

"Tell him to bring her back for us," ordered Nickelhouse.

"Do whatever you think best to get the crew out of here," Finian instructed the pilot. "McHenry, if you're still listening, I don't blame you.

You've got plenty of guys counting on you. Take good care of 'em. Over and out."

The A27 receded into the purple haze. The grey and black airship took station over the grey mass.

Then it drifted down to land.

"Keep moving!" called Finian. He chivvied the landing party along. Verity was mostly able to keep up, but the Senator was out of condition and Dr. Utter was worse. The scientist would have been more content to sit down and list all the reasons the situation was unacceptable than to pelt across the dusty gelid landscape away from the enemy airship.

"We need... a moment..." gasped Nickelhouse.

"We ain't got a moment," Finian told him. "We've got to find those holes Mac saw from the air, over at the rim. If they're caves or something like it, big enough to hide out in, we've got a chance."

"They could be pressure release holes," Utter speculated. "Or breathing tubes, or cloacal vents."

"Oh joy!" winced Miss Castlemere.

"Just move!" Finian said. "Anyone remember what that ship did to the guys on the tarmac at Brooking Field?"

They staggered further towards the far edge of the dome. The black zeppelin ghosted after them.

"We're not going to make it!" panted Nickelhouse. He unslung his rifle and turned to aim.

Finian knocked it away. "Don't be a dummy. They got machine guns and a better range. You start a firefight they'll win it. Just run!"

"I'm a U.S. senator!"

"You'll be a dead U.S. senator if you don't move!"

The four fugitives continued across the disturbingly yielding landscape. When they found one of the tubes Machen had seen they almost fell into it.

"Watch it!" Finian yelled, grabbing Verity before she toppled down the shaft.

Nickelhouse stared down the almost vertical hole. It was four yards wide, ribbed and slimy, with no evident bottom. "Great! What are we supposed to do now, you dumbass sailor?" he snarled at Finian.

The weatherman was disappointed too, but he was low on options. "Maybe was can climb down?" he speculated. "Maybe..."

It was too late. The airship was almost overhead. Finian could see the gunners aiming their Browning at the fugitives; from this range they couldn't miss. It seemed odd to him that a German warship would have an American-made arsenal.

The airship's speakers crackled into life. "Crew of the A27, place yo' weapons on the ground an' raise your hands."

Finian blinked. The voice didn't sound German. It sounded like Panhandle American.

Dr. Utter looked alarmed. "I don't have a weapon," he whispered to Finian. "What do I do?"

"Just put your hands up, doc. Looks like they want us alive."

"They must know who I am," Nickelhouse said. "Leave the talking to me." He laid his rifle down and held his hands up to shoulder height.

Finian and Miss Castlemere downed their rifles too. Finian didn't yet reveal the Magnum he'd concealed under his insulated flight suit. He couldn't easily reach it anyhow.

It took a long while for the airship to tether. Ladders were dropped from the ship's spine; the vessel didn't have a functioning weather car, although there was a rear gondola with an observer in it. Airmen made the perilous descent on the twisting chain ladders and lashed them to the surface. Other crew descended to drive in heavy mooring posts and to receive and attach steel cables that would hold the ship in place. Only then were those clever turbines twisted to drift the ship downwards where it could be locked into place.

"That is a very inefficient way of doing it," sniffed Dr. Utter. "Every change to my design had compromised the effectiveness of the craft."

Finian reckoned that the ship was only loosely bound so it could take off quickly in case the A27 decided on a counterattack; he didn't rate the chance as significant.

At last the armed men on the ground moved the hundred yards or so to the vent hole where Finian and the other stood. The prisoners were patted down—Finian's concealed weapon was found and confiscated—then held where they were for a while longer.

"Do you know who I am?" Senator Nickelhouse raged at them. "Do you know how much trouble you're in?" He turned to the others. "Does anyone know how to say 'I'm a rich and important man' in German?"

"I don't think they're German," said Finian. "American sidearms, American khakis and kit, American wristwatches. These guys were kitted out in the U.S. of A."

"Look at the side of their zeppelin," argued the Senator. "There's a big German cross on it."

"Great way to make us think it's the Krauts," the weatherman considered. "Same thing sending those German goons after us before."

"What are you suggesting?"

Just then the answer came into view. Now a more secure fixed ladder was in place, Lindon Creed III descended from the airship.

The Texas millionaire enjoyed his moment of triumph as he strutted over to the captives, sucking a big Havana cigar. "Well now, who'd have thought we'd be meeting heah like this?" he asked.

"Creed?" Nickelhouse seemed more than happy to supply the other side of the dialogue the oil baron expected. "What the hell are you up to here?"

The man in the white suit gestured up to the zeppelin. "Like my airship? I figured I might as well build myself one while I was funding all of your efforts. 'Cause, I didn't sabotage mine."

"You!" the Senator hissed. "But how did you get the blueprints?"

"Money talks, and so do people who need it," Creed smirked. "Like the radio operator on the A17 who picked up the natural electro-magnetic fluctuations on that first proto-fallstreak they photographed. Like the guys at the universities you paid to analyze the data but who sold me the full results while fobbing you off with trivialities. Like the Swedish mathematician who worked out for me how to use radio signals to catalyze the punch holes into doorways to somewhere else."

"That's amazing!" enthused Utter. "How did he model the waveform calculations to take into account the..."

"You can ask him yourself, Dr. Utter. He's aboard the *Creed-Bird One* right now."

Finian glanced up at the looming airship. "The *Creed-Bird One*? Really?"

"I still don't understand how you learned so much," the Senator growled at the smirking tycoon. "You knew about the pterosaur, about us recruiting Finian, about base security, about our changed launch schedule."

Creed preened again. "That's because I had an inside man—or woman." He held out his hand to Verity Castlemere. "Come to daddy, sugar."

Pale and silent, the sleek blonde moved over to Lindon Creed and took his arm.

"Verity!" gasped Nickelhouse, stricken.

"What?" mocked Creed. "You can loan her out for favors from your political allies because she owes you for keeping her sister from the gas chamber but you never thought she might have been loaned to you in the first place? Who do you think arranged for her to work at Bellerophon so you'd notice her? Who do you think set up the deal you made with the

Governor to save poor li'l Caroline's life?"

Verity looked down, away, anywhere but at Finian. She bit her lip and blinked back tears.

"I knew you hoped to be a big shot one day, Nickelhouse," the Texas tycoon sneered. "At first I thought it'd just be good to have another U.S. Senator in my grip. You're hardly the first I've got the goods on. Later when you started the BE-A program I figured there was money to be made in pirating your designs. When it all came together with the fallstreak phenomenon I saw even before you did how much wealth and power that discovery could bring a man. So here we are."

Finian understood now why Miss Castlemere had been out prowling on the night the intruder went for the pterosaur. She hadn't been stalking the burglar; she'd been keeping watch for him.

Nickelhouse had nothing to say. He seemed to crumple. He looked at his fiancée once, then looked away.

Creed snorted. "Look, Verity, your Senator's gonna cry."

The blonde showed a momentary flash of her former fire. "Leave him be, Lindon. You've won."

"And you've forgotten your place, you two-bit whore," the Texan warned. "'S gonna be my pleasure to remind you of it."

Finian took a step forward. "You're a real big man when you're insulting a girl, Creed. Care to come out from behind your goons' guns and try squaring up to me?"

The Texan seemed to notice the weatherman for the first time. "Oh, you're the drunk, right? I don't need you no more." He turned to his guards. "Take the Senator and the brainbox back to the ship. Verity, go with 'em and wait for me in my cabin." Then he pointed at Finian. "You can shoot him."

"No," said Miss Castlemere. "Don't!"

She met Finian's gaze for the first time since her betrayal was revealed. She was crying.

"Don't?" frowned Creed. "You don't tell me…"

The blonde pulled a snub-nosed pistol he hadn't known she'd been carrying and fired it at Finian three times.

The weatherman folded over and fell backwards into the vent hole.

"That guy turned me down," Verity said to Lindon Creed.

"The blonde…fired..at Finian three times."

The *Creed-Bird One* loaded its prisoners aboard, cast off, and glided away into the maroon mist. Night was falling across that other sky.

Thirty feet down the strange duct Finian held on to a ribbed ledge, chilled fingers scrabbling to keep their hold. He was alive.

He wondered why. At that range there was no way Miss Castlemere could have missed him—unless she'd chosen to. But Verity was a traitor, a spy all along, planted on Nickelhouse to chain him to Creed. So why had she stepped in when the Texan's thugs were about to shoot?

The word 'chain' pitched up a strange association in Finian's mind: Verity Castlemere in the A27's lounge bar singing to the crew.

Oh, if I could only break these chains an' let my worried heart go free!
But it's too late now. The Blues have made a slave of me.

Finian's arms were going numb. The cold was clamping down. He knew he had to ignore the pain and climb the vent again while his strength lasted. If he didn't move he'd die.

He painfully hauled himself onto the next ridge. When the shots had come at him he'd instinctively jumped backwards, some part of him calculating his survival chances dropping into the unknown shaft were better than those of taking three slugs in the chest or head. He'd managed to stop his fall before he'd gone too far. It had cost him bloody fingers and more cuts and bruises than he wanted to think about. But the bullets should still have got him.

Ain't robbed no train, ain't done no hangin' crime.
Just a slave to the Blues, grievin' 'bout that man of mine.

Creed had mentioned some things about the woman, Finian remembered. What was that about a sister? Verity had evaded saying why she owed her fiancée. A girl trying to rescue her sibling from death row might do just about anything. Finian wasn't too sorry that she'd turned on Nickelhouse; from the sound of it he'd used her no better than Creed.

"I'm trying to find excuses for a dame who just tried to plug me," Finian said out loud, his breath steaming in the freezing air. He forced his aching limbs to pull him up to the next ridge.

"No," he argued with himself. "I'm trying to find excuses for a dame who could have plugged me but shot wide. That gal didn't try to kill me— she saved my life! But why?"

Another moment with Verity flashed back to him. *What do you trust?* he'd asked her. And she'd said: *You.*

Finian's numbed fingers slipped. He scrabbled for purchase. The narrow ledge under his boot crumbled away, dropping grey crusted carapace down into the unfathomable depths of the vent. For a moment the weatherman teetered over the shaft; then he managed a desperate swing to catch another purchase on the half-ridge three feet below.

"I'm shutting down," he said out loud. His mind was as foggy as the purple skies at the top of the shaft. If he didn't vocalize his thoughts they wouldn't come. "I need to keep going."

The bitter, mocking part of Harry Finian that had grown louder during his trial, after he was jilted, when his friends turned on him, during long nights in solitary, sneered at his words. He was in sub-zero temperatures in an alien duct with no way home, as abandoned as he would ever be. It wasn't a question of whether he was going to die; only how.

Verity had kissed him. He remembered her in his arms as Airship 27 had lurched and that sudden contact of lips on lips. It hadn't lasted long. Why did he remember it like a lifetime?

The mocking part of Finian was shocked to realize that the weatherman had climbed another two ridges on the memory of Miss Castlemere's kiss.

Finian thought about Verity and about the A27. In his cold-addled, pain-wracked mind they blurred together, beautiful and dangerous adventures, both battered and in trouble; both things he loved.

Blues, please tell me, do I have to die a slave?

Do you hear me pleadin', you're gonna send me to my grave?

Verity Castlemere had been begging for his help all along and he'd never seen it. She wasn't a traitor. She was a prisoner.

Finian was twenty feet from the top of the shaft. He recalled that a man at the bottom of a well saw the stars even in daytime because of the linear nature of light. He wondered why all he saw was a dark purple smear. He wondered if there even were stars to see beyond the disturbing haze.

"Your mind's wandering, bozo! Climb. People are counting on you."

He forced himself to keep lifting his heavy arms, forced himself to come back after every stumble and misstep.

He tried to figure out what he could do at the top. His first jumbled plan was to hail a taxi; that was how badly his mind was drifting. More realistically he thought about radioing the A27; except that Creed's men had taken the radio when they'd carried off Nickelhouse, Utter, and Verity. Finian could only build a signal fire if he burned his clothes.

"Just get up top and do the next planning then," he growled at himself. "C'mon Finian. Don't be a quitter. Don't be a loser. Don't prove everybody right!"

He tried to think of Verity again, but her image faded from his mind.

He tried to think of anything.

He realized he'd stopped climbing. His ice-rimed body wasn't moving at all. He forced himself to shift, and it was only then that he realized he'd run out of vent to climb. He was clinging to the lip of the shaft, shivering.

Finian cajoled his protesting muscles to stand him up and he looked around.

Full night had come, the endless haze turned almost black. The temperature had dropped beyond the ability of the weatherman's thermals to protect him. Worse, a thick shroud of mist was creeping over the grey pitted surface of the floating dome. The island was slowly sinking down into the clouds.

Finian remembered the things that hunted those vapors. He hoped the cold got him first.

An annoying buzzing sound kept him from going to sleep. He forced himself to turn and look.

A Sparrowhawk fighter plane was taxiing to land, heading towards him. Machen in the cockpit held up a hand in greeting.

Finian staggered over to where the biplane stopped.

"You're one lucky sonofabitch!" Mac told the weatherman. "I'm damn near scotch fuel. I told myself if I didn't find you guys this pass I'd have to head back alone to the A27." He looked around. "Where are the others?"

"The bad guys took 'em," Finian supplied. "And by bad guys I mean that Texas slicker in the white suit and cowboy boots. Creed. He's the one running that black zeppelin."

Machen's eyebrows raised. "How did you escape?"

"Verity helped me." He pressed his mittened hands onto the Sparrowhawk's warm engine cowling. "I don't suppose you happen to know where Airship 27 is, do you Mac?"

"Not exactly," admitted the pilot, "but I could always ask them. A27, this is SH1 calling in. I'm ready to come home, over."

Finian's frozen lips cracked into a grin. "I definitely owe you a drink later on," he told Mac.

"I'll remember that, admiral," Machen cautioned. "Now strap yourself to a wing. We're going home."

Finian stood in the ship's lounge and addressed the ship's company. Machen flanked him. McHenry stood at the bar, still ashamed of himself for taking the A27 and running. The crew perched where they could and waited to hear what trial they would face next.

"I think I know what happened to the A26 now," their acting captain said. "She tumbled through a fallstreak hole like we did. If she wasn't ripped apart by the storms or the giant floating monsters or the carnivorous clouds then that black zeppelin followed her and blew her to pieces. That's why the *Creed-Bird One* came after us too, by the way. They wanted the Senator, Miss Castlemere, and Dr. Utter, but they expected to put the rest of us out of commission for good."

"Lindon Creed!" marveled McHenry. "I hate th' idea of that big-mouth getting the last laugh on us."

"Yeah well, it's not over yet," Finian replied. "Sure, he's got who he wants. He can leave the rest of us to die as we run out of hydrogen gas or motor fuel while he uses his gizmo that opens fallstreaks and sails on back to Texas. But he can only do that when the castle clouds are properly formed and the conditions are right for punch-holes."

Mac looked up from his cocoa. "And when would that be?" he wondered, suddenly interested.

"Early mornings," the weatherman answered. "And only early mornings, unless there's other factors we don't know about. But say I'm right—say that black zeppelin can't get out of here until maybe six hundred hours—then that gives us a chance to catch up with them."

"And then what?" McHenry asked. "They outgun us, they're not damaged, and they have a full crew."

"But we've got moxie," argued Mac.

"Yeah, we've a couple of other things too," Finian told them. "Remember, Creed's ship is based on the A25. Our baby's got a few refinements since then. We're gonna need 'em."

"The propeller gimbals and the redesigned weather car?" McHenry puzzled.

"We also have the cover of darkness and one crackerjack weather-puke who can calculate wind vectors," Finian went on. He grinned wolfishly. "I'll take all comers who wanna bet we can't catch up with Creed's bucket before they can escape in the morning."

The weatherman's confidence was catching. His wager got no takers.

Finian clapped his hands. "Right then. You know your stuff. Go do it. We need this lady purring like a kitten before we go to round three with that black zeppelin. Get your assignments from McHenry and Mac. Reports go to Ensign Harvey at the Conn."

Beth Dennison raised her hand. "But what are you going to do when you catch that airship?" she asked.

Finian held up three fingers. "I'm gonna rescue Miss Castlemere and the others. I'm gonna beat Creed like a redheaded stepchild on a Saturday night. And then I'm gonna steal that fallstreak-opening gizmo so we can get back home. Any other questions?"

Airship 27 cranked up her engines and pushed faster through the gulf stream that swept them along. Finian checked in with Ensign Harvey. The junior officer was diligently keeping watch in the restored command gondola.

"I'll say this for leaving a self-preserving engineer in charge of the boat, he does fix up the mess nicely," Finian noted.

"Yes sir!" answered the nervous ensign.

"At ease, pal. It's Ned, isn't it? Folks generally just call me Finian. Folks who like me, anyhow."

"Yes sir—I mean, Finian." Harvey wasn't long out of academy, another loaner from the navy. He'd logged more flight hours since the A27's hasty departure than in the rest of his career combined. He handed the field glasses to his acting C.O. and pointed out of the patched windshield. "It's that way, si—Finian."

The weatherman focused the binoculars. Sure enough, the sighting he'd been called to observe was another of the cloud-travelling domes. This one was slightly smaller than the first but seemed otherwise identical.

"Should we go in?" Harvey asked tentatively.

"Nope," Finian replied. "We're hunting bad guys. No time for detours. Keep her steady, helm."

They left the living island behind. It sank back into the cloud carpet.

Finian checked the log, talked to the helmsman and comms station operators, and ordered a minor course adjustment where the prevailing winds seemed to shift slightly to starboard.

"This is a race now," he explained to the men who hadn't been able to attend his conference. "I'm gambling that Creed's zeppelin will take the route of least resistance, following this airflow. Saves fuel and keeps 'em away from the castle cloud towers if they're alert. They only need to stay in the air till morning then they're scot-free. We've got to catch 'em before that."

Harvey nodded. He didn't really understand but he was willing to do what he was told.

"So note that big thing in the log, Ned, and keep us moving."

"Yes s—Finian."

"You can call me sir if you want to, kid."

Finian spread out the large wind vector charts he'd sketched. He was studying them when McHenry returned to the Conn to make more repairs to the communications station. A makeshift lash-up that barely served offended the engineer's pride. When he saw Finian he looked stricken.

"Relax, McHenry. I'm not gonna punch you out," Finian promised the Scotsman. "You did the right thing. I told you that."

The engineer rubbed his sweating balding head. "It doesn'ae feel like the right thing."

"We're here, aren't we? Between you keeping the ship alive and Verity Castlemere keeping me alive and a bit of heroic grandstanding from Mac Machen we're still in the ball game."

"I suppose."

"And now it's time to step up to the plate, buddy. I was about to call for you anyhow."

McHenry looked cautious. Finian noticed the engineer's hand trembled slightly. He wondered when the man had last slept.

Finian showed McHenry his charts. "These are my best projections of the weather systems up here. I've tried to get all the data I've taken since the fallstreak onto these models. There's a characteristic airflow above the cloud base, and we're seeing that, but the way the castle formations shift tells me there's other winds at other levels above and below. See?"

McHenry could read blueprints in his sleep - he virtually was—but the strange wind vector diagrams meant nothing to him.

Finian still went on, beckoning Harvey to listen in too. "First off these altocumulus castellanus formations are much bigger than anything that's ever been recorded. We must have travelled a couple of thousand miles in the time we've been here but we've never seen a break. That changes the whole airflow thing. Second, there seems to be no significant change in air pressure by altitude here. But we do get thermal variances. Lastly, I think there's probably a different wind pattern below those clouds than here above 'em, interacting with their movement."

McHenry looked at the scribbled calculations on the penciled charts. They seemed to be force vector determinations. "Why are you showing me this?" he asked.

Finian swapped out one drawing for another. "Because that's the layer we're in now. We're moving along at around ninety miles an hour, our best speed. But the enemy's going to be doing that as well. They're built a lot like the A27 so they can get that kind of ride out of their ship too, right?"

"Aye," agreed McHenry sourly.

Finian tapped the new diagram. "But on top of the cloud towers there's a whole new air pattern. Different currents. Chicane streams, maybe. Above these endless castle clouds, who knows what we'll find?"

"You do?" asked Harvey hopefully.

"I can take a best guess," the weatherman said. "I think there's a fast-moving airstream that's piling those clouds and informing this current we're following. I think we could get higher and hop on it like a tramcar racing downtown."

McHenry looked at the gauges he'd just reinstalled and at the latest report chart from the gasbag inspections. "I don't know that we've got the lift, Finian. We've lost one hydrogen compartment—non-explosively, thank the Lord—and we were shy of full pressure when we had to run from Brooking Field. We'll be lucky to keep a level altitude for more than another twelve hours, let alone climb."

"You already had us ditch all the ballast," Harvey added apologetically.

"You said the A27 had improvements over the A25 design they stole," Finian argued with McHenry. "You said this ship had vertical lift because of how we could angle those gimbals and change the propeller directions."

"Aye, that'd help. We could ha'e done it two days ago, maybe."

Finian shook his head. "We gotta do it now, McHenry. It's got to happen. If we've ditched all the ballast then ditch all the other stuff you can that's weighing us down. Every pounds counts on an airship. You taught me that on day one I was at base. So get me a lighter ship, buddy. I need that lift, one last time."

McHenry's hairy eyebrows met together as he thought. "The piano?" he asked hopefully.

"We'll get another one back home," Finian said. "All those extras that you fought with Nickelhouse about, the bar, the fancy furniture, the works, lose it. And launch the last two Sparrowhawks and have 'em fly alongside. That'll lighten the load. Just get me that altitude."

The engineer was starting to see possibilities. "It might be possible. It might be just possible. But I make no promises."

"Get to it, McHenry. We need to go up."

Airship 27 was in chaos. Technicians were stripping out the facilities they'd installed over the weeks of fitting that had just ended. As Finian made his way to the Sparrowhawk hangar he saw men breaking down the metal-framed bunk beds in the wardroom. The furniture and even the bar counter had already gone from the main lounge.

Machen was supervising a clean-up of the launch deck, arbitrating what could be cast overboard and what constituted essential equipment that couldn't be spared. "You sure know how to wreck a guy's evening," the senior pilot greeted Finian.

"My shoulder's screaming at me, I've got a bitch of a sore head, and there's no booze or coffee left on this bucket," the weatherman replied. "I'm feeling foul and I decided to spread it around."

"Is it working?" Mac wondered. "Not spreading your bad night around, I can tell you that's working just fine. I mean are we actually getting lift?"

"Some. Not enough."

"So are we gonna be able to jump up to this theoretical airstream of yours or not?"

Finian shrugged. "I've got another idea."

The pilot gestured at his biplane. "Want me to head upstairs and take a look-see? Put a finger up and test the wind?"

"I won't risk it, Mac. Above the castles there might be very different conditions, gale force conditions. I don't want you swept away not able to find your way back. It'll be bad enough when you're flying escort on the A27. I'm not sending you on your own."

"I'm all for not dying," approved Machen. "So what's your idea?"

He and Finian had to move aside as a large workbench was manhandled towards the hangar doors. "There are some fierce updrafts around those tower formations," Finian explained. "It's risky but they might give us the boost up we need to get our altitude."

"You want to fly us into one of those clouds you've been saying to avoid for the last three days?"

"Pretty much." The weatherman gestured round the stripped-out hangar deck. "On the bright side there's less to batten down."

"I'm so glad they made you the boss, admiral," Mac replied snarkily. "I'd hate to die in some conventional, unmemorable way. Your scheme's *so* much better for that."

"You doing okay?" Finian asked Ned Harvey. The junior officer was now the senior ranker aboard ship. The gunnery specialist and the flight deck sergeant might have years more experience but the young ensign was their commander. "I guess you didn't count on this when you were seconded to Bellerophon Enterprises."

"I did not," Harvey admitted. "I didn't even know what I was being sent off to. Classified, they told me, a U.S. Senator's pet project. Good for my career jacket. I should have guessed when I heard Bellerophon."

"Why?" Finian wasn't up on classical myth.

"In legend Bellerophon was the hero who tamed the winged horse Pegasus and mastered the skies. I guess that's why Senator Nickelhouse called his company that."

"Makes sense now you say it, kid."

Harvey hesitated. "But… I don't know if the Senator did his research properly."

"How so?"

The ensign dropped his voice as if he was being disloyal. "Bellerophon was a pretty big hero. Rescued a princess, saved a country, all that stuff. But in the end he decided to ride his winged horse all the way to Mount Olympus, right up to the home of the gods. It was too much. Zeus, king of the gods, he sent a horsefly, a tiny thing, to bite Pegasus' flank. She bucked and Bellerophon fell off and dropped to his death. Great big hero, killed by such a trivial thing when he over-reached himself."

"Yeah, that is a bad choice for a name," Finian admitted.

Harvey swallowed. "Do you think that's what we've done, Finian? Flown too high, trespassed somewhere we're not supposed to go? Will we get killed by some tiny thing going wrong in this hostile sky?"

Finian shook his head. "Nah. You can take myths too far." The boy still needed reassuring, so the weatherman went on. "You know the difference between a classy dame and a cheap floozy? The classy dame leaves with the guy that brung her. She won't wander off with some other swell that catches her eye. She's loyal and true. Treat her right and she'll always see you home." He gestured round him. "Airship 27, she's pure class. A real lady from top to tail. She's not some dumb horse that'll kick you off 'cause she got stung. She's that gutsy dame who'll see you through thick an' thin."

Harvey managed a timid smile. "That's good to know," he admitted.

"You stick by her, son, she'll never let you down," Finian promised. Then he wondered if anyone had ever stuck by Verity Castlemere to find out if it was true about her.

"Verity?" said Bethany Dennison in answer to Finian's question. "She was an okay gal, I guess. Didn't put on airs because she'd hooked a Senator."

Finian didn't like talking about Miss Castlemere in the past tense, but he went on. "How well known was her relationship with Frank Nickelhouse?"

"Open secret," answered the pool secretary. "All the girls knew. We hoped it might stop the Senator's wandering hands, but it didn't. Good luck to her, I say." Beth sniffed. "I wouldn't go out with some mook who cheated on me and beat on me no matter how rich he was."

"Nickelhouse hit her?"

"The Senator's got a temper. Mostly he's real nice but... he's a guy. I'd have expected him to think twice with Verity though, after what happened with her sister."

This was new gossip to Finian. "Tell me."

Beth leaned in confidentially. "The way I heard it, the sister's husband was like that, sleeping round and slapping his wife. Then one day this Catherine just couldn't take it no more. Put an icepick right through his eye. That's the story."

Finian recalled what Creed has said to Miss Castlemere. "She got the death penalty."

"They don't like murderesses in Florida. 'Cause, there's some say it wasn't Catherine who did him in. I heard whispers it might have been Verity herself when he came on to her, or when she saw what he'd done to her sister. Anyway, Catherine confessed to it and she was headed for the gas chamber. If it wasn't for some big-shot lawyers from nowhere arguing she was nuts she'd be six feet under now."

"She was pardoned."

"Yeah, but committed. Some New Orleans snake-pit. Senator Nickelhouse used to pay her bills."

"Used to? What happened?"

Beth shrugged. "Dunno. I used to have to send the checks off. About nine months back they stopped."

"What did Verity say about that?"

"I don't think she knew. I wasn't supposed to talk about those payments, and especially not..." The secretary stopped herself.

"Specially not what?" Finian prompted. "Especially not to Verity?"

Beth bit her bottom lip. "Specially not the one to the doc at that private clinic," she whispered. "Looks like Catherine got herself knocked up in the nuthouse and it had to be taken care of."

Finian checked dates with Miss Dennison. Catherine's conviction had been overturned three years ago, just months after Verity had started to work at Bellerophon. Efficient and beautiful Miss Castlemere had quickly risen to become Nickelhouse's personal assistant, presumed mistress, and secret fiancée. Beth called it a pretty smart piece of work.

And it would have been; except that Verity had been doing whatever she must to keep her sister alive. She didn't even know that Catherine was probably dead now. Why would Nickelhouse tell her? Why would Creed?

"She was a tough cookie inside that pretty package," Beth summarized as if giving a eulogy. "She could dazzle men so they never even noticed she was crying."

"All hands to stations," Finian called out. "All stations sound off."

One by one the various operation points of Airship 27 called in their readiness. There was a brief pause as a suspect cable was restrung on the starboard fin, then the vessel was ready.

In the absence of working altimeters it was impossible to tell just how far the A27 had risen, but the cloud carpet below now looked considerably more distant, partially obscured by the omnipresent atmospheric haze. It was as good as they were going to get.

"Okay Mac, take a hike," Finian called through to the hangar deck. By now he was sensitive to the weight shift lurch that meant the harness apparatus had dropped one of the Sparrowhawks into the air. He waited until the second jink and got confirmation of launch.

"Point the A27 upwards," advised Machen flippantly. "Maybe push?"

"Can it or I'll have you tow her," Finian shot back. "Okay helm, go for vertical. Take us up."

"All vertical, aye," confirmed Ensign Harvey.

The whine of the motors intensified. The airship shuddered a little as it bucked the winds and began to climb.

"It's working!" cried Malcolm McHenry.

"Not enough," said Finian. The ship gained height but then remained steady.

"We've thrown off everything but the deck plates," McHenry warned.

"Okay, we've done what we can that way. Time to toss the dice again," Finian judged. "Ned, set course ten degrees port from actual. Aim us at the far edge of that cloud tower."

"At it?" asked the ensign.

"At the edge. There's an updraft there I want to catch."

"The airship…began to climb."

"Ten degrees port," Harvey agreed. The ship turned and swayed.

"All hands brace for rough weather," Finian called over the ship's intercom. "Hold tight, fellahs."

He'd hardly spoken when the A27 lurched, spilling Finian and the whole command car crew off their feet. The airship was buffeted like a child's toy balloon, twisted around and sucked by immense winds.

Finian struggled for his feet and dived for the control yoke. "Propeller planes to forty-five degrees straight!" he shouted across at the comms yeoman. "Tell them!"

While the message was being relayed Finian struggled with the steering controls to bring the ship back to axis. Her prow was spun around into the thick white cloud of the altocumulus tower. The windshield was immediately patterned with fast-forming ice.

"Weather car, can you still see?" Finian called out. "Report and direct!"

There was no time for a response. The ship turned on its side as the air currents dragged it deeper into the column. Finian barely held onto the steering yoke. McHenry, Harvey and the rest were thrown hard against the starboard windows.

The A27 was sucked right into the massive cloud tower. Visibility went to zero but the whole ship spiraled on its axis like a toy boat above a plug hole.

"Propellers to full vertical!" Finian shouted into his communication line. "Acknowledge."

There was no reply. Finian spared a worry for the men who'd been strapped on the exterior of the hull to maintain the heavy motors and vital propellers.

The ship turned with a sickly speed, dizzying those aboard who had managed to regain their feet. The lights flickered.

"This'll snap her apart!" McHenry warned, his voice shrill with panic.

Somewhere at the comms station Mac's urgent calls were still being relayed through the radio room above. "Airship 27! Guys?"

Finian jammed the ailerons to full port to counter the spin. It wasn't enough.

The first tentacle-headed predators slammed onto the glass of the command gondola.

McHenry screamed. His face had been right up against the window where the first hand-sized creature had latched on,

"All hands, secure quarters!" Finian called. "Any crew still outside, abandon your posts. Get under cover right now!"

The ship tilted more as it spun ever faster. Its motion was actually a blessing; it limited the number of predators that could latch on to the whirling vessel.

A speaker feed from the fin service gantry was filled with sudden screams. "Aaaahh! It's got me! It's…!" Then nothing.

"Issue firearms, Ensign Harvey," Finian commanded. "Set a watch for any of those things getting inside. Patrol the inner skin. Go now!"

The pale-faced boy nodded and scrambled up the ladder to the main spine. He somehow made it to the top despite the lurching that was shaking the ship to pieces.

A new influx of the tentacle predators slammed into the gondola. The largest of them began drilling at the glass. A few panes splintered. Finian called after Harvey for him to toss a rifle down.

Airship 27 shifted again. Finian felt the steering yoke go slack. The temporary connections to the control cables had failed, leaving them rudderless.

"McHenry!" he shouted across at the terrified engineer. "Do something!"

The Scotsman crawled across the pitching floor and pulled up the service plate around the control column. The couplings there had sheared again, disconnecting the levers from the cabling.

One of the tentacle-mouthed gas-bags leaped out of the service duct right at McHenry's head.

Finian saw it move. He dived across and caught it like Mickey Cochrane at the World Series.[10] The creature was chilly and slimy in his hands. He squeezed. Its dorsal sac burst with a foul hydrogen odor. He tossed the creature to the floor and ground it to paste beneath his boot.

McHenry had scrabbled away, making tiny whimpering sounds. Finian grabbed him and dragged him back to the couplings. "Fix it!"

A cry from the navigation officer alerted Finian to the next danger. A side window panel shattered and one of the creatures slithered through. Finian shouldered the rifle that Harvey had now dropped into the gondola and released three rounds into the monster.

The hours of practice on the base firing range paid off. Finian's old skill had returned. The creature was blown back out of the car and lost to the swirling vapors.

The airship was pushed to the side again, so sharply that Finian thought she might roll right over. His head hit the side of the car hard enough to

---

10 Gordon Stanley "Mickey" Cochrane was the star catcher of the Philadelphia Athletics in their pennant-winning years 1929-31 and was World Series champion in 1929, 1930 and 1935. He was inducted into the baseball Hall of Fame in 1947.

crack the pane. He blacked out for a moment.

He couldn't have been down for more than a second. When he opened his eyes his stomach was churning like he was in free fall. Blood tricked from his forehead. But the gondola was surrounded by night haze again; the choking clouds of the deadly tower were gone.

The remaining parasites dropped off back into their habitat.

Finian hauled himself up on the conn column and peered outside. The cloud towers were receding beneath him, their puffy tops looking clean and innocent at the increasing distance. The airship was being pushed along sideways by a dangerous gale.

"We did it!" the weatherman shouted out loud. "We're above the towers! And there's an actual fast-air current up here. I was right!"

He quickly sobered. The ailerons and rudder of the airship were uncontrolled, slamming from side to side and pitching the vessel at random.

He grabbed up the shipboard microphone again. "This is Finian. I want whatever crews we've got out there on the manual flap levers. Damage control teams, do your stuff. Get any injured to the main lounge. Weather car, look out for our planes. Radio room, try and call 'em. Everybody keep on your toes. This isn't over yet!"

McHenry made a noise that might have been a growl and might have been a sob.

Harvey scrambled back into the gondola. "We've lost eight men," he reported. "They were outside when we went into the cloud and those things attacked. A dozen more crew with broken bones or concussions from being knocked about in the turbulence." He pointed to Finian's skull where the trickle of blood was running from temple to chin. "You'd better have that seen to as well, sir. Finian."

"Later. Right now we need to get this gal under control before she shakes apart. McHenry?"

"I'm doing my best," snarled the engineer. "Moithering me won't help."

Finian wasn't sure what moithering was but he backed off and let the Scotsman do his job.

Airship 27 was flipped again. This time there were some unpleasant snapping sounds as struts and wire supports gave in the rigid body around the gas sacks. Finian winced.

Everyone's doing their jobs, he assured himself. *Do yours.*

He forced himself to check the flight controls that still worked and confirmed his results with the weather gondola. His suspected high-altitude stream was pushing them along at forty-five knots, force nine on the Beaufort scale, a considerable improvement over the prevailing currents near the cloud carpet. Unfortunately the ride was going to crack them apart.

"I've done it," McHenry announced. "Again." The engineer crawled back from the service duct and took a deep breath.

Finian gestured for Ensign Harvey to take the helm. "Try and bring us steady," he told the young officer.

"Steady, aye. I'll try, anyway."

It wasn't a quick process. The winds on this tier were fiercer and more unpredictable than those below, as violent as the storm-front had been. It took fifteen minutes before the A27 was facing away from the gale, skimming like an arrow in the direction it wanted to take her.

"Not bad work for a web-footed Navy puke," said the radio.

Finian grabbed up the mouthpiece. "Mac!"

"Yeah. We couldn't find any good bars so we decided to head on back to the barn," came back the flyboy's laconic reply. Then more seriously he added, "I thought you were goners when you got sucked into that cloud."

"It wasn't a day at the park," agreed Finian.

"Nah. Listen, we've used a helluva lot of fuel trying to stay alive out here in this hurricane. Any chance of giving us a ride?"

"Affirmative, hotshot. Come on in and we'll see if there's any cocoa mugs we didn't ditch overboard."

Finian realized he was smiling. He hadn't realized how much Mac had grown on him.

He glanced at the dashboard clock: 2:14 am. He sobered. The next part of the plan wasn't going to be much fun at all.

With engines at full they rattled along on the ferocious topwind at speeds exceeding a hundred and forty miles an hour. It was an exhilarating experience—except for Finian in the weather gondola.

Airship 27 was profiting from her altitude to outpace the *Creed-Bird One*—hopefully. But this wasn't a race to some flag or finish line; this was a game of chase. The A27 had to catch the black zeppelin somewhere downstream, and that meant she had to find it.

The thermal layer above the tower clouds was still hazy despite its velocity. There was little chance that a fast-skimming airship at that height would detect Creed's dark zeppelin below. So someone had to drop back down into the tier beneath where a keen observer had at least a hope of spotting the aircraft they hunted.

Finian could hardly ask anyone else to take the unpleasant and hazardous task.

Mac Machen had the Conn. McHenry had ventured onto the outer gantry to inspect the damage to the airframe and do what he could to hold the ship together. Finian hung at the full extension of the steel hawsers, his tiny glass and aluminum bubble jinking in the turbulent juncture layer between the high velocity streams above and the cloud-riddled maze below.

It was a good thing he'd missed supper.

It also meant he was in exactly the wrong place when a frenzied squawk came over the general band of the radio channel. "Conn! Conn! We're under attack!"

Finian wanted to cut in, to find out what was wrong, but he knew that his chatter would be unhelpful during the crisis—whatever it was.

"Who's calling in?" Mac demanded. "Identify yourself!"

"Rear service gantry!" came back the voice. "It's Thompson here! They're diving at us!"

"Thompson, who's attacking you?"

Finian imagined that Mac must have already dispatched someone—Harvey if he was available, the boy had grown up fast in the last twenty-four hours—and was now trying to work out the nature of the threat. Had Creed's biplanes got the drop on the A27 again?

"Monsters!" Thompson screamed. "Bat-things from hell! They're back! They're…" His appeal for help ended in a squeal.

"Mac," Finian called urgently. "We could have found those pterosaur-things!"

"We have," the pilot replied. "I can see them from the control gondola. A whole colony of them by the look of it. They're swarming the ship!"

"Get our guys back inside!"

"Won't work," Machen judged. "We need guys on maintenance watch in this gale. We have to chase these things off. Finian, you've gotta let me take this one. Just hang in there, admiral."

Finian stared up through the thin shallow cloud layer but Airship 27 was no more than a faint blur far above. His car was knocked around by the turbulence and the hawsers holding him in place creaked alarmingly, reminding him that he dangled in an alien sky on four metal threads from a bag of gas being sieged by prehistoric monsters.

The A27's spotlights blazed on to dazzle the pterosaurs.

The weatherman waited as long as he could restrain himself before calling the control gondola again. "This is Finian. What's happening up there?"

"Gilliand here. Captain Machen and Ensign Harvey are up top with rifles fending off those weird birds."

Finian almost corrected the airman's taxonomic identification; Dr. Utter must have rubbed off on him more than he realized. Thought of the missing scientist spurred him to turn his eyes back to his watch as he spoke on the wire. "What happened?"

"Don't really know, sir. Mr. McHenry was outside when those things came out of nowhere, dozens of 'em."

Finian could hear the rattle of machine guns over the telephone. Mac had obviously got the gunnery master to unship the Thompsons. "Was McHenry hurt?" The weatherman couldn't imagine keeping the ship aloft without the mercurial Scotsman.

"Sorry sir, no word yet from any of them."

Finian ground his teeth. The weather car bucked again as it broke through a new airbank.

He waited.

It was sixteen minutes by his panel clock before somebody called him again. "Ensign Harvey here, sir. Can you hear me?"

Finian was being bounced around like a dice in a cup but there was nothing wrong with his hearing. "Report, Ned."

"We chased them off, sir, and we've set armed watch for any more of them."

Finian didn't like the subdued tone of Harvey's announcement. "But?"

"But Mr. McHenry was mauled, sir. They're treating him in the lounge now. And... we lost Captain Machen."

Two hours later Finian was still numb. It wasn't just the chilling cold of the glass car trailing through the cloud layer, nor the constant tumbling and rocking through the wild air currents; it was the knowledge that he hadn't been there to back up his comrade in the pterosaur fight.

Harvey had seen it all. Mac had led the rescue party to relieve the men pinned down on the tail gantry. They'd chased off the leather-winged brute that was tearing at McHenry with a needle-toothed beak but the other reptiles hadn't wanted to give up such promising food. Machen hadn't even seen the creature that had snatched him over the side until it was too late. When he'd struggled he'd been dropped.

It bothered Finian that the brave pilot would fall through the freezing skies, down into the cloudbank of carnivorous tentacles. Perhaps his descent would be too fast and he would drop through the whole formation into whatever lay below; perhaps Mac Machen would fall forever? It didn't seem right.

He glanced at the chronometer again. 5:09 a.m. It would soon be dawn. The anomalous punch-hole phenomena in the altocumulus castellanus banks would form, excited by a large metallic structure and whatever high frequency broadcast the *Creed-Bird One* had perfected. The enemy ship would escape triumphant, with Dr Utter their captive to perfect a new line of fallstreak-ranging skyships, with Frank Nickelhouse as Creed's blackmailed puppet however high the Senator could rise, with Verity Castlemere bound forever to that cruel Texan who held her chains.

Then Airship 27 would falter and fall and all the bravery of Mac and Stafford and Thompson and Matteson and so many others would be in vain.

"C'mon, baby," Finian said to Airship 27. "Give me a sign. Don't walk out on me like everyone else."

The weather gondola performed a wide lurch that nearly tangled the cables that held it. Finian's sore head smacked hard back onto his chair back.

"Dames!"

It was 5:15 when he first saw the lights.

Finian snapped fully awake, adrenaline spurring his bruised exhausted body to more endurance. He snatched up his binoculars and stared down through the floor-plate window at the pattern of illumination moving below. It was a pale white nimbus around a dark elongated oval silhouette— like an airship with an array of belly searchlights seen from above.

"Finian to Conn! Drop us down out of the fast air. Make sure all our running lights are doused."

"Finian, it's Ensign Harvey. Are you sure? Once we go down out of this stream we'll never climb back up again."

"I'm sure. Do it. Drop ten thousand feet and come around. Is McHenry fit to come to the phone?"

"I'll get him to the radio room. Best not to make him climb a ladder."

"Make it so. Just get down out of the big winds. And warn the ship to radio silence from here on. Phones and speakers only."

"Got it. Aye, sir!"

Finian felt the shift in attitude as the A27 began to drop. He checked the far haze but there was still no telltale lightening of the blurred horizons to warn of day or to betray Airship 27's approach. Even if the zeppelin kept a watch aloft nothing would be visible until it was too late.

"Okay, can you see the zeppelin yet?" Finian checked as he dropped lower into the region between the castle cloud towers.

"Roger that, Finian," enthused Harvey. "It's really them, isn't it?"

"It's really them. Is McHenry listening in yet?"

"I'm here, laddie," said the engineer.

"McHenry, you're in the radio room, right? I want you to set up a listening post for that weird radio interference that Dr. Utter identified. When you catch that it'll tell you a fallstreak's opening. Harvey, that's when you drop this ship through it as fast as you can and no looking back, capeesh?"

"Understood. But..."

"Yeah, we're missing a few things first. And we don't have the hole-opening gizmo yet either. I'm gonna see to that."

McHenry remembered what Finian had said about the technical improvements since the A25 and made an intuitive leap. "Finian, ye're insane!"

"Yeah. Harvey, you're going to use the vertical lift capability to station Airship 27 right above Creed's ship. Then drop me in the weather car so I can board it."

"Sir, you intend to invade the *Creed-Bird One*?"

"How else do we get our people back? I'm counting on them keeping their people off the outer gantries for fear of pterosaurs or giant squid things or whatever. Those glaring lights round the underside will keep anybody in the spine or the gondolas from seeing what's going on up top. I go in, find the prisoners, steal the punch-hole activation gadget, and make my getaway back to the A27. Easy."

"Mr. McHenry's right. You are insane. Sir."

"I'm willing to hear any other plans."

There was a pause. "Good luck," said McHenry.

"Make the descent," said Harry Finian.

It was quite a feat of maneuvering to position the A27 atop the *Creed-Bird One* so that the weather car dangled just above the top service walkway. Finian dropped the chain ladder down and rappelled to the top of the enemy zeppelin. A Navy background was useful for knotting the loose ladder in place to keep it from flailing in the wind.

He picked up the body of the watchman he'd shot at long range from the weather car hatch at long range and tossed him off the zeppelin.

Finian would have liked to tell Harvey and McHenry that he was down but he was maintaining radio silence; he hadn't even brought the backpack radio. He flashed a torch but couldn't know if the control gondola had seen it.

He'd brought his rifle though, plus a pistol inside his fur-lined flight jacket and a bowie knife sheathed at his hip. Finian was expecting trouble.

It helped that he knew the layout of the craft; with a few exceptions it was identical to Airship 27. He slipped down one of the long ladders that curved inside the upper section of the hard outer shell and made it to the main gantry that ran round the belly of the ship. A bored watchman was wasting his time staring out of an observation plate at the thick fog that the big spotlights lit. He didn't look in Finian's direction at all. Finian took him down with his rifle butt.

There was another lookout in a similar position on the far side of the ship. Finian had no worse trouble with him. He avoided the stern section of the walkway though, in case a maintenance crew was observing an uncomfortable freezing vigil on the tail planes.

From the main gantry a caged-in walkway screwed down the underside of the balloon between the struts and cables. This led to the long balcony atop the spine of ship's rooms and down into the workshop bay and hangar deck. Finian expected those would be occupied so instead he slipped along the catwalk and took the less-used forward hatch. That put him on the landing down to the control gondola, the lobby next to the stateroom and captain's cabin.

He hadn't expected it to be guarded. He hadn't expected the bullet-headed thug to recognize him from the *20th Century Limited*.

Fortunately the thug's first instinct was to go for his truncheon. Finian launched himself off the ladder and barreled into the German mercenary, slamming him back into a bulkhead and following through with a tension-releasing haymaker to the goon's chin.

Finian shook his hand as the guard slumped down. Either his knuckles were getting softer or cabbage-eating goons were getting more bone-headed.

He looked around for somewhere to stow the thug. The weapons locker was too small, and stuffed with far more armament than its counterpart on the A27. From the harpoon guns, fragmentation grenades, and heavy-bore shotguns Finian concluded that the *Creed-Bird One* had ventured into the purple skies before.

The obvious hiding place was the captain's cabin. If it was empty it offered secure concealment for the unconscious Kraut. If the captain was there then Finian had a useful prisoner. If Creed had taken the room then things would get even more interesting.

The door was locked. Finian pulled his bowie knife and snapped the latch.

He dragged the goon inside and checked around.

Verity Castlemere looked up at him with surprise. Her lips formed his name but no sound came out.

The weatherman dropped the guard like a sack of potatoes and gazed at the blonde. He spotted the smudges under her eyes where she'd been crying before he noticed she was dressed in a long sheer negligee. He noticed the outfit before he saw the handcuff on her wrist and the long silver chain leading back to the bedpost.

"Hey, sweetheart," he said, "I thought you might like a better offer." A lady always left with the guy who brung her; unless that man turned out to be a swine.

Verity swallowed hard. "I didn't expect I'd see you again, you dumb cluck!"

"What, just 'cause you shot at me and I fell down a deep mysterious hole? Like that's the worst a dame's ever done to me!"

"Because now you know what I am and what I've done," she whispered, and looked away.

Finian strode over, caught her chin, and turned her face to him. "Hey, did you want to be Creed's patsy?"

"No. But I…"

"Did you want to play Mata Hari with Nickelhouse or did you have no choice?"

"I knew what I was getting into. And by then I thought what does it matter?"

Finian fingered the long chain snaking back to the bedpost. "Does Creed always keep you locked up like this? Or does he have other ways to tie you as well?"

"You know about Catherine," Verity realized. "As long as she's incarcerated on Frank's dime and kept from prosecution by Lindon's tame judges they both own me."

"Turns out that Nickelhouse stopped writing checks to that Florida snake pit nine months ago. I don't... I can't say what that means."

The girl's face went bleak for a moment. She wiped her mascara-smeared eyes. "I... kind of knew... When Frank said no more communication with Catherine. I didn't want to believe." Her face twisted in fury. "That sonofabitch... those sonofbitches, they both lied to me, strung me on..." She slumped down on the bed. "I'm the dumbest patsy that ever walked the Earth! I've made myself a whore and a traitor and a murderess."

"Hey, she was your sister." Finian wondered what he would do for shrill-tongued Myrna in Reno. Quite a lot, he surprised himself by answering.

"I didn't know what I spied for Lindon would be used to sabotage the ships. Or that he'd come and shoot up Brooking Field. But I still as-good-as killed Chief Matteson and all those others."

"I'd say the guy who sent in the saboteurs and ordered his zeppelin to shoot up the airfield was the murderer. Look kid, we have to get out of here."

Verity tucked her legs up and hugged her knees. Her chain rattled. "Leave me. This is where I belong. Where I deserve to be."

"And if I think different?"

"Then you're a bigger fool than I am, Harry Finian."

"Then I'm a bigger fool. So do you wanna get out of this place and maybe have a beer with me?"

Miss Castlemere let out a half-laugh half-sob. "That'd be... It's too late, Finian. Much too late."

Finian sat her up. "Hey, this from a girl who's ridden Airship 27? Twenty-seven! Took twenty-six failed attempts to get it right before they got perfection. You gonna give up now just before it might get good? Where's that gal with the moxie to take it on the chin and come back fighting?"

"That gal gets hit an awful lot."

Finian took her hand. "Not when she's with me, kid. Not while I breathe." He smoothed Verity's unbound golden hair. "Now I'm gonna kiss you, and you can tell me 'no' and I'll back away. Or you can kiss me too an' come with me. And this one's all your choice."

Verity Castlemere looked up into Finian's dark eyes. "Go on then," she challenged him. "Find out, I dare you."

Finian kissed her. She kissed him back.

"Right then," he said at last. He brought the bowie knife down on the

"Finian kissed her. She kissed back."

silver bed-chain and hacked Verity free. "Fill me in."

"Frank and Dr. Utter are held under guard in one of the guest cabins. Lindon's probably in the stateroom with his pet Swede egghead, Skjöldebrand, the guy who worked out the fallstreak frequency—plus a whole bunch of muscle."

"Where's the gizmo that makes the holes open?"

"It's controlled in the stateroom too. Why?"

"Later. Right now I want to get your fiancée and Utter out of here."

"Ex-fiancée," Verity assured him. "Frank was very explicit about that when he knew what I'd done to him. We both said things. We both used each other." She looked down again. "You know I'm not proud of it, Finian."

"Hey, you got me out of hoosegow when I'd hit rock bottom. Let me return the favor, okay?" He looked at the scantily clad blonde. "You look real swell like that but you might want a coat. It's a bit chilly out."

Miss Castlemere found a long-coat of Creed's and slipped it on. She had to settle for slippers on her feet. She opened a dresser draw and took out a thick wad of banknotes and a derringer that she stuffed into her pocket.

"How long did Creed have to live?" Finian wondered.

"Just as long as he had my sister," the woman confessed. "Now he doesn't."

"She might be okay. It's a long shot but I'll find out somehow," promised the weatherman.

"Don't make promises to me. Guys do that a lot. They never keep 'em." Verity paused and frowned. "But you came back, Finian. That's a first. How did you even find me?"

"Some idiot left the running lights on and I have a weather gondola."

Miss Castlemere gave him a secret smile. "I convinced the captain that Lindon ordered the rig lit up," she confessed.

"Why?"

She blushed. "Trust," she said. "There's this guy, and I had this stupid, hopeless hope…" She squeezed Finian's arm. "Good things never happen to me—up till now."

"Me either. C'mon."

He kissed her again, because he could. Then they stepped over the sleeping goon and out into the landing. Finian assumed a confident stride leading Miss Castlemere along, as if he belonged there.

They walked right into another guard.

Finian hit out before the goon could call for help, but this guy was faster than he looked. Finian's fist went over the thug's left shoulder and a returning punch caught the weatherman in the gut. He came back with a one-two but the thug got in another box to Finian's ear then closed for a crushing bear hug.

Miss Castlemere pulled the Bowie knife from Finian's hip-sheath and sank it into the thug's side. She angled it upwards into the chest cavity and twisted.

The guard's eyes widened and he fell to the floor. Verity backed away, the bloody knife in her hand, red stains seeping up the sleeves of Creed's overcoat.

Finian took the knife from her. "You saved my bacon, babe. Remember that part." It was the second time Verity Castlemere had saved his life.

"These are the men who blew up Brooking Field," the woman told herself, trying not to shake. "These are the men who bombed the Admin Block and all the girls there. They blew up the barracks where people were sleeping. They gunned down everyone on the tarmac. They don't deserve mercy. They're the enemy."

Finian was still glad that killing bothered her. He dragged the dead man to join the other thug in Creed's cabin. "Does Creed allow the other ranks into his lounge bar?" he asked the blonde.

"Of course not. They're cramped in the crew mess."

That was what Finian needed to know. He entered the big room dragging Verity by the arm. "The boss wants the tootsie in with the prisoners," he told one of the two hulking guards at the door.

It worked just long enough for the weatherman to get close. By the time the thugs worked out that they didn't know this guy or questioned why the girl should be admitted to the locked cabin Finian was on them.

This time he didn't rely on fists. It was two to one and they both outweighed him. He brought his Bowie knife up in one sharp arc, slashing right across the first man's throat, then brought his blade up between the other man's third and fourth ribs. In five seconds both guards were dead.

Miss Castlemere looked on the fallen guards but said nothing. Finian had heard her: these were men who'd devastated the Brooking Field Works and left scores, maybe more than a hundred, dead.

Finian searched the downed men for the keys and opened the cabin. Utter was awake, curled in a corner muttering to himself. Nickelhouse roused as the door creaked.

"Verity!" the Senator snarled; then, "Finian?"

"Time to go," the weatherman said. "Follow me."

"But how did you…?" began Nickelhouse.

Verity Castlemere cut him off. "Frank, the man is saving your goddamned life, so for once just shut the hell up and do what you're told!" She was gentler with the wild-eyed Edward Utter. "We have to go, doc. Come with me."

"This shouldn't be allowed," Utter said faintly, far from reality. "They said I could talk to Dr Skjöldebrand. I left my notes in my laboratory."

Miss Castlemere tucked her head under Utter's armpit and heaved him up. "Help me, Frank."

"I wouldn't help you if you were bleeding to death at my feet," snarled the Senator.

He paused then because Finian's bloody Bowie knife was at his neck. "Help the lady," the weatherman instructed. "Silently."

"This is the little bitch who sold out Bellerophon," Nickelhouse objected. "It was her information that got all those men killed."

"And your ambition that sent the A27 though the fallstreak and lost us everybody since," Finian retorted. "Although I'll share the guilt for that one with you. So yeah, we all got dirty sins. Let's keep 'em locked up till we escape. Now with me and stay close."

"I don't have my samples," fretted Utter.

Finian scouted ahead and led them back along the passageway. Nickelhouse came next, with Verity still leading Utter.

"Does your shining knight know everything you've done, Verity?" the Senator challenged her. "Everything?"

"He knows about Catherine, Frank," the blonde warned her ex-fiancée. "And now so do I. What happened?"

Nickelhouse blanched. "Nobody knew how she got that razor..." he began.

Finian caught Verity's wrist as she reached for the derringer in her pocket. "Old business. You're both A27 team now. We get it right at last, okay?"

The blonde's fingers relaxed. "Okay. But there'll be answers later."

"Okay?" Finian asked the Senator.

Nickelhouse nodded. Revenge could wait for safety.

The argument had brought them to the forward lobby. "Head up top," Finian told them. He passed his rifle to the Senator. "Use the chain ladder into A27's weather car. Wait for me there while I get the fallstreak gizmo."

All three ex-captives looked at him. "Is that what you intend?" Miss Castlemere said. "That won't work."

Dr. Utter supplied the why. "The apparatus is huge. It includes that absurd dish on the forward gantry, a substantial and ill-conceived redesign of the radio room, and a control panel in the stateroom. You can't remove it. It can't be done."

Finian's heart sank. He knew what that meant. "Fine, fine. Then you three head back to the weather car and get back to Airship 27. Tell 'em to listen out for the special broadcast rhythm the doc spotted. Then drop out of this weird sky. I'll get the fallstreak signal going from here."

"You can't stay behind," Miss Castlemere objected. "It'd be suicide."

"It is logical," reasoned Dr. Utter. "Mr. Finian is the best suited to achieve this task for the benefit of all."

Nickelhouse took the weatherman's hand. "You're a brave guy, Harry Finian. I was smart to hire you. Thanks."

"She hired me," Finian replied, nodding to Verity. "Look, I know she's shafted you bad, but from what Creed said you've not exactly been boyfriend of the year to her either. So listen up. I'll stay here and pull your fat out of the fire. You see that Verity walks away free and clear. Right?"

"Very well," agreed the Senator reluctantly. "I'll arrange it. But I don't ever want to hear from Verity Castlemere again."

"You have a deal," agreed the blonde. "Without you and Lindon holding my sister's welfare over my head do you think I'd spend five minutes with either of you?"

"Move," growled Finian. It was clear there were years of bitter tangles that couldn't be unraveled on an airship ladder in the middle of an escape. "Watch out up top."

He watched the scientist, the Senator, and the complicated blonde climb out onto the lower balcony and battened the hatch after them. Then he went to save the day one last time.

Lindon Creed III was in the stateroom with Dr Skjöldebrand when Finian knocked on the door. A guard answered and found one of the weapon locker's heavy-duty double-bore shotguns pressed into his belly.

"Back inside nice and slowly," Finian advised the goon, walking him into the stateroom.

His appearance turned attention away from the charts debate. Creed looked up from his conference with the Swedish scientist and frowned at the weatherman. "How the hell...?"

Finian held up his left hand, the one holding the Mk II 'Deuce' fragmentation hand grenade. "The pin's already out," he smiled.

"Hold your fire!" Creed ordered, unnecessarily.

"Smart move. One fumble and this room looks like the inside of the A27 hangar after you bastards shelled it."

Creed gripped the edge of his desk, trying to figure out his next move. "What do you want? Finian, wasn't it? Ex-Navy guy who wrote that weather manual."

"Guy you tried to kidnap off the Chicago express," Finian agreed. "Something else Verity Castlemere tipped you off about, I'm guessing."

"You're a smart guy, Finian. So tell me what your deal is. You want the girl? Take her, she's yours, she'll do whatever you tell her to. Money? I can give you enough that you'll live in a palace for the rest of your life."

"I don't want your dough, slimeball. And you can't give me Verity. She knows about Catherine. She's not your slave any more."

Creed paled some more. "Then what?"

Finian pointed at the array of controls laid out on the desk. "I just wanna get home, Creed. I don't care about the rest. Spin up your radio gizmo and whistle up a fallstreak so I can get out of this crazy sky."

The Texan's face relaxed a little. "That's it? Hell, son, that's what we were about to do anyway." His wits started to catch up with his shock. "But how did you get aboard?"

"Been aboard ever since you left that grey island," Finian lied. "Miss Castlemere missed when she tried to plug me. I took a dive into that hole, hid just under the rim, caught your trailing ropes as your airship launched, and hid out till now."

"So why show yourself at this point?"

Finian thought fast. "A couple of your goons found me. So I decided to get me some insurance and ask to go home." He waved the grenade. "Take me home, Creed."

The oil tycoon turned to Skjöldebrand. "Open the fallstreak."

The Swedish scientist nodded and leaned over the complicated controls. Diodes lit and an electric hum filled the cabin.

"Ah gotta tell the captain to prepare," Creed told Finian.

"Be careful what you say," the weatherman cautioned.

"Captain Clarke, make ready for a fallstreak aperture. Take us through."

"Aye, sir," came the reply.

The electronic buzz intensified. Finian felt the hairs on the back of his neck begin to stand.

"Do you realize how rich this is going to make me?" Creed asked the weatherman. "How powerful? Nickelhouse expected to make President of the United States on the back of this discovery. Hell, I might still let him now ah've got him by the short hairs. But the man who controls the fallstreak apertures, the man with the fleet of airships that can mine out this new frontier for all its wealth, that man can buy and sell Presidents, buy and sell countries!"

"Even after he murdered an airfield full of people?"

Creed made a dismissive *pah!* "Nickelhouse hushed up losing a whole airship when we splashed his A25. You think there's not enough cash to make Brooking Fields go away? But ah'm thinking that maybe it's a *good* thing if the Germans launched a surprise airship attack on a US installation. Even if nothing can be proved its sure going to convince the Joint Chiefs and the Cabinet that they need a fleet of Creed-made zeppelins to keep our nation strong."

"You've thought out all the angles. Except that Airship 27 can tell what really happened."

"A27? She's lost, son. Lost forever in this purple sky, like the A26 before her. She's no way back and she can't last long. Maybe the same giant squid things that got the A26'll take her too?"

Finian realized that life had no value to the millionaire Texan—except his own. "You're sure a smart guy. Until you meet someone with a hand grenade."

"Ah'm still a smart guy then," Creed replied. "Take him."

Finian had been distracted by the oilman's exposition. Someone had slipped into the room behind him. A huge hand closed over Finian's fist, clamping the grenade trigger tight down. A heavy blow crashed into the back of Finian's skull.

When the starburst had mostly cleared from the weatherman's vision he was pinioned on the floor and the grenade was in the hands of the German mercenary giant who'd blindsided him.

"The Captain's not called Clarke," Creed smirked down at him.

Finian was hauled up to his feet. Two of the thugs pinned his arms so Creed could punch him. The tycoon seemed to enjoy it; he kept it up for quite some time.

"The fallstreak aperture has formed," Skjöldebrand said at last, interrupting his employer's exercise.

"Tell the Conn to drop us through."

The zeppelin vented hydrogen and began to descend.

Creed returned to the battered Finian. "I always win," the tycoon boasted. "Now you're going home through the fallstreak, just like you wanted." He turned to the giant. "Toss him over the side. He's going home the hard way."

Finian spat at the Texan. The bloody wad left a red smear down Creed's spotless white suit.

Creed drew back his fist again; but there was a sharp crack of a gunshot. The man on Finian's left lost his grip on the weatherman's arm and fell over. Finian jerked his head left to avoid the Texan's blow and planted a boot in Creed's gut. He slammed the other goon into the wall.

The gun spit again. The windshield splintered. The cracks spread out in slow motion across the plate glass before the whole window shattered.

The icy gale of the purple void hammered into the room. Finian punted his toecap into the downed guard to keep him that way then dived across at the next man who was fumbling with his sidearm.

Two other men were already bleeding on the floor.

Finian leaped over the cowering Skjöldebrand and hard-tackled the giant. He caught the big man just where football padding would have offered protection and he heard a satisfying crack.

That didn't put the giant down, though. The bruiser grabbed Finian and hoisted him towards the shattered window despite the roaring gale. Finian ruthlessly crammed his fingers into the mercenary's eye-socket. The giant yelled out and dropped him.

Finian followed through with a belly-punch and an uppercut. The wounded thug grunted but reached for him again. Another man came at Finian from the side but fell before he could get a grip; another crack of gunshot!

Finian went in close on the giant, getting his shoulder into the staggering man's gut and heaving. The huge mercenary toppled backwards and tripped over Skjöldebrand, flailed wildly then disappeared through the broken windshield.

More men hammered at the stateroom door. Finian looked across and saw Verity Castlemere locking it, holding the derringer she'd taken from Creed's room.

"I told you to get away!" said Finian.

"First time I ever came back for anyone," the girl told him. "*My* choice."

Gunfire from the lobby splintered the lock the blonde had just turned. Creed staggered to his feet, still clutching his stomach but pointing a .38 at Verity. "In here, now!" the tycoon called his guards.

Finian picked up Skjöldebrand and threw him at the Texan. Creed spun round and fired by reflex, pounding five rounds into the Swedish scientist. "No!" the oilman shouted as the realized what he'd done.

The final bullet from Miss Castlemere's derringer took Creed right in the temple.

She'd bolted the door as well as locking it. More gunfire splintered the latch.

"Let's get out of here!" Finian called. Beyond the window was the swirling ring of tormented cloud that divided the purple haze above from blue morning skies below. The *Creed-Bird One* was descending through the fallstreak phenomenon.

"Where's there to go, sailor?" Verity asked. There was only one door and it wasn't going to hold back a shipful of armed gunsels any longer.

Finian beckoned her. She ran to his arms. He climbed up onto the window frame. "We have to climb onto the gantry above. Think you can do it?"

Verity hitched herself after Finian and scrambled aloft.

The guards burst into the room after them. Finian had retrieved the grenade and left it for them. There was a loud bang and the cabin was plumed with fire.

"Climb!" Finian shouted at the blonde clinging beside him.

It was a hard pull across the battered outer shell of the stateroom. The descent through the fallstreak played havoc with the wind patterns. St Elmo's fire danced across the outer frame. The purple sky didn't want to release its captives. It sucked at them and pushed at them as they struggled across the stateroom roof.

Verity lost her grip. Finian caught her wrist and hauled her back.

The black zeppelin dropped below the cloud circle.

"What happened with the weather car?" Finian shouted to her over the wind.

"Frank ordered McHenry to pull us in. He wouldn't. Said he wouldn't leave you again. Then Frank ordered Ensign Harvey to run the winch and Harvey told him to screw himself. The car's still there!"

Finian doubted that even the maneuvering capability of Airship 27 could match the descent of the zeppelin through a fallstreak circle well enough to keep the weather car lashed to the other vehicle's top; but it was the best he had.

He dragged Verity inside the airship's framing where the structural beams formed an aluminum maze. Some of the crew were already swarming up the midships ladder to cut them off. Finian and Miss Castlemere ran for the cage-stairs up to the middle gallery. Bullets spanged off the metal mesh beside them.

"Those dim-bulbs are really firing shots near the gas bag? Really?" the outraged blonde demanded.

Finian raced the metal steps two at a time. A surprised technician met them halfway up, took a hard cross-hook from Finian, and rolled to the bottom of the staircase. The fugitives gained the middle gantry and raced for the ladder to the top of the envelope.

Guards rushed at them from both sides. Finian pushed Verity before him up as they scrambled for the high walkway. Someone tried to grab his ankle. He kicked down hard. The man screamed as he fell.

They made the upper hatch and shimmied through onto the zeppelin's top. Verity dragged herself hand over hand, her glorious blonde hair streaming in the gale, her coat and negligee billowing. Finian kept close behind, trying to block any firing line the goons below might have on her.

She held the balcony rail and pointed. The weather car was no longer tethered but it still hung tantalizingly close, swaying as the A27 kept pace with the descending black zeppelin.

"I don't believe it!" grinned Finian. "That's my girl!"

From here the weatherman could clearly see Nickelhouse at the floor hatch with a rifle cocked and Utter babbling fast on the telephone link back to the Conn. The whole mass of Airship 27 loomed overhead, unsuspected till just now.

A pair of black-garbed crewmen had beaten Finian and Verity to the top by using the starboard ladder. Finian saw Nickelhouse orient his rifle as the thugs closed on the weatherman. The shots went wide.

Finian had recovered one of the .38 sidearms from the stateroom. He took the approaching men down with neat double-taps and kept racing for the nearest point to the bucking weather car.

Nickelhouse fired again. The shot ricocheted off the aluminum sheeting covering the gasbag. Finian looked behind him to see what new threat the Senator was shooting at.

Only Miss Castlemere was behind him. She staggered and fell, clutching her side.

"Verity!" Finian rushed back to her. Another bullet dented the sheeting beside her.

"Finian!" she gasped as he gathered her in his arms. "Frank knows I can finish him. He can't afford to let me get home."

The shooting stopped for a moment. There was a quarrel going on in the weather gondola. The Senator ended the argument by slamming the butt of his rifle into Dr. Utter's face.

"Come on!" the weatherman told Verity. "I'm getting you out of here." He heaved her over his shoulder in a fireman's left, ignoring the sticky warm wetness that soaked his jacket.

Nickelhouse had dealt with his interruption and took station at the weather car hatch again. His targets were much nearer now. They could even see the regret on the Senator's face.

Finian emptied his .38 through the glass side-panels right into the U.S. Senator. The weather car jinked again and tossed Nickelhouse forward. The wounded man fell headlong through the open hatch. He tumbled down, crashed off the side of the black zeppelin, then vanished into the clear air below.

Guards were approaching on Finian now from both ends of the upper gantry. They had guns and a clear shot that didn't risk the envelope.

The A27's weather car rocked from side to side like a swing. It passed over the *Creed-Bird One*'s top walkway in a pendulum arc. The chain ladder scraped across the duckboards of the upper gantry.

Finian dived as it rolled past. His fingers wrapped round the fifth rung and he let himself be dragged off the black zeppelin to hang under the weather car. Verity Castlemere was still slung over his back.

The world turned topsy-turvy. He was flung about like a doll in the hands of a petulant child. He held on for dear life and tried not to fall.

It wasn't enough. Already his arms ached. He knew his strength was failing. He had to climb.

Verity's weight dragged him. She might be dead already but he wasn't going to leave her. There had to be one guy somewhere who didn't let her down.

Rung by rung, muscles screaming, Finian climbed.

The *Creed-Bird One* swerved away beneath him. The fallstreak hole slammed shut with a sudden rush of cloud but the A27 was already through. Bullets shattered more of the weather car's windows as the black zeppelin brought its machine guns to bear. Utter cringed in one corner, babbling.

The gondola jinked in a different way, almost dislodging Finian. The whir from above told that the hanging car was being reeled in—fast!

Finian gritted his teeth and kept on hauling himself and Verity's dead weight upwards.

Another rattle of gunshots was louder than the last. The A27's guns were returning fire. Airship 27 was descending rapidly, bringing her alongside her enemy.

Something sliced into Finian's leg. He felt a searing pain. In his desperate focus to climb he didn't realize it was a bullet graze. He struggled to make the last few rungs to safety.

"Drop me," Verity said. He hadn't known till then whether she was still even breathing.

"Not gonna happen, babe. We're getting a drink."

"It's going to come out, Finian. What I did. Frank's got a signed confession from me about killing Catherine's swine of a husband. His attorneys will open it now he's dead. It's all going to come out and I'm finished. Save yourself and let me go. I'll drag you to your death."

"You dragged me from my death, Verity. You stuck by me. Now it's my turn." He heaved them another rung up the chain ladder but couldn't go further.

The black zeppelin keeled to the side. At first Finian thought it was bad navigation. Then he realized the marauder was setting up an angle to bring that big field gun onto the A27. Had McHenry realized?

Suddenly the enemy zeppelin got a whole lot closer. Airship 27 was veering in to her, closing to slam into the side of the tilting enemy before it could fire its cannon. The weather gondola was within thirty feet of docking when the two ships impacted. Finian lost his hold on the ladder and actually fell two rungs before his flailing hands closed on a steel grip.

The off-centre *Creed-Bird One* was knocked on her side and lost control, her propellers pushing her in impossible directions. The heavy field gun beneath her unbalanced her just as Utter had said. For a brief moment she was side-on and helpless.

Airship 27's machine guns chattered, each spewing six hundred searing hot .50 BMG rounds per minute at 2,910 feet per second into the enemy envelope.

Finian saw the first red explosion bloom beneath the metal skin of the zeppelin.

He called on his last desperate reserves and dragged himself up the chain ladder. As his strength failed Edward Utter caught hold of him and pulled him in. "They shouldn't have slung that gun there," the battered scientist told him earnestly.

Finian laid Verity on the deck of the weather car then hauled the hatch shut as the *Creed-Bird One* exploded beside them.

The blast caught Airship 27 sideways on, peppering her with hot fragments. All the remaining windows of the weather car starred as it was slapped by the shockwave. One of the steel hawser cables holding it snapped, dangling the gondola at a dangerous angle as it spun.

A score of fires rippled across the A27's hull, each one potential death for the damaged airship. Damage control crews raced to patch up the ailing boat. The motors winding in the gondola died.

The black zeppelin fell away beneath them, burning. More explosions tumbled it over. The last one cracked it in two. It dropped into Lake Superior and sank without trace.

"Dr Skjöldebrand and his equipment were aboard that ship," worried Dr. Utter. "We can't access the fallstreaks without him! This is all most unsatisfactory! Most improper! I'm going to complain."

The weather car speaker crackled into life. "Finian? Is there any chance you're alive in there?"

"Ned? Yeah, I'm here."

"And Senator Nickelhouse, Dr. Utter, Miss Castlemere?"

"Utter's with me, beaten up but okay. The Senator's dead. He fell." Finian looked over at the blonde sprawled out on the floor of his weather car. "And Verity Castlemere didn't make it."

Airship 27 landed at Brooking Fields four days after she had vanished. The site had been cleared, although the skeletal remains of sheds and buildings were testimony to the war-zone it had been. The military had control of the site now. A row of soldiers waited with the medics and engineers as the A27 landed.

An exhausted Finian surrendered his command to a smart USN Admiral and allowed himself to be dragged away for debriefing. It was going to take a long time.

He was surprised by the room-full of brass waiting for him in the temporary base HQ. He hadn't seen so many shoulder stars in five years as a Navy officer combined, including his court-martial.

He was still more surprised to see the mild man in the round glasses sitting ramrod straight behind a desk.

"Son," said President Franklin D. Roosevelt, "tell me what happened."

"Yes sir," agreed Harry Finian, standing to attention. "On two conditions…"

The Boston winter had clamped down but there were still plenty of guys in O'Reilly's speakeasy. Finian bellied up to the counter and looked at his reflection in the new mirror he'd paid for. He didn't recognize the guy staring back.

"Thought you'd skipped town for good," O'Reilly said to him. "What'll you have?"

"Beer. Whiskey chaser. The usual."

"Don't cause no trouble," cautioned the barman.

Finian snorted. He'd been gone five months. It had been as much of a lifetime as the two years in prison or the five years in service. He'd seen to the handover of Airship 27 to her new captain and crew. He'd shaken the hand of the airman who'd command her and heard the apologies that a guy with Finian's record couldn't stay on a military roster.

He'd said his goodbyes. Dr. Utter was happy in his new government lab, trying to recreate Skjöldebrand's work and find a way back to the other sky. McHenry was grousing about the problems of setting up a new hangar to service and maintain the refitted A27. He'd shrugged off as nothing his change of heart in refusing to abandon Finian at the last, but he stood a little taller. Lieutenant Harvey was preparing to ship out as a Conn officer on her official shakedown flight; Finian privately felt the lady had already been tested pretty well.

The weatherman had been there for the topping out ceremony and the A27's official launch. They'd honored the President's promise to him. Now she was the USS A27, and her name was *Verity*.

He'd travelled after that; to visit Machen's parents in Cleveland, to talk to Matteson's wife in Oklahoma, to take flowers to the neglected Florida grave of a girl he'd never met.

And so to Boston, and the beer, and the whiskey. He picked up the glass tankard to surrender.

A delicate hand covered his. "Hey, aren't you going to buy a lady a drink? I was promised one."

Finian didn't turn round. He didn't need to. His flip-flopping heart was way ahead of him. "Guys always let you down," he said.

"Not this one guy. He dragged me out of an exploding zeppelin. He convinced a whole airship crew to pretend I was dead. Then he got me a written pardon from the President of the United States so I could vanish away like I was never there. I heard it was the only thing he asked for after all he did."

"That guy's a dumbass, Verity Castlemere."

"That's the guy I trust, Harry Finian. The only one. Ever." The girl leaned to his ear. Her perfume was from paradise. "He asked me out for a beer.

And said he'd never let me down."

Finian turned round. The classy blonde was always lovely, but now she shone. She was free. She could go anywhere, do anything. But she'd come to save him.

"Ready to fly, babe?" he asked her.

She smoothed a finger across his stubbly cheek. "Find out. I dare you."

Then she was in his arms. The world fell away beneath them as they soared.

THE END

The Romance of the Air

Some forms of transport are inherently romantic: sail boats and steam trains and perhaps horses all stir the mind with ideas of adventure and mystery. Perhaps it's because they are, for the main part, transport from a bygone age. Or perhaps it's because all of them require effort to maintain and are rich with lore. Each of them has a specialist jargon, famous exemplars, limits which can be pushed in heroic endeavor.

Airships are the same. Blossoming at a particular time and place that evokes mental images of crisp black and white newsreels and a world marching towards progress and world war, they capture our imagination.

They were a folly: complicated, dangerous devices that we dreamed would one day become commonplace tools of civilization. They were playgrounds for the rich, famous and beautiful. They were harbingers of a new kind of warfare that defied boundaries and could bring death anywhere. But they were never, ever boring.

When the brief came to write an airship story I knew it had to be a romance story too. And it had to be a romance about continuing to try in the face of all common sense, about persisting past disaster and horror until finally there was triumph. That's the *story* of the airship. That's why people believed in them.

Given an airship, and a date, and a story type, the plot rolled out naturally. An airship needs to fly somewhere. She needs a mission, a new frontier, adversity to overcome, threats to survive. Hence the need to create a world that only an airship could explore, to spin a yarn that wouldn't work as well with any other transport.

Airships pit humans against an element far from our natural habitat. That drive to climb mountains, to fathom ocean depths, to rocket to the moon is a fundamental and noble part of our nature. Airships require heroes, and teams of heroes; our forefathers understood that the highest undertakings required men to band together to conquer challenges that seemed impossible. This story is about our race's indomitable quest to go where reason says they should stay away. Of course we cheer our madmen on!

Apologies to those who feel I've misrepresented the technical detail of airship operation and to any who worry that I've overlooked the real history of the extraordinary airmen who pioneered their field. We authors wrap our stories in broad canvases to pretend verisimilitude, but always our concern is telling the tale not listing the stats. All fiction, of airships or not, is truly set in cloud-cuckooland.

In my head, *Airship 27* played out as a black and white movie, with Bogart as Finian toughing it out with that stoic rough-guy endurance and Bacall as Verity emerging from the shadows with a band of soft light playing over her eyes while the orchestra swelled. Throw in a touch of *King Kong*—Verity and Fay Wray would have a lot to talk about—a bit of Hornblower and Conan Doyle's *Lost World*, stir with just a pinch of Lovecraft and the brew is done.

Airship 27, then, for all its trappings of high adventure, of espionage, of political double dealing, of warfare and monster-fighting, of exploration and discovery, is still really a romance. Men (and women) fell in love with those ships and the dream of where they might fly them. We hold onto our dreams even when all common sense tells us to move on. This is love.

May each of us find, like Finian, that if we dare all then loyalty, courage, and love will make us fly.

I.A. WATSON enjoys telling stories but hates writing paragraphs about himself for pages like this one. He nurses his compulsive writing habits with the help of occasional novels such as his award-nominated *Robin Hood: King of Sherwood*, *Robin Hood: Arrow of Justice*, *Robin Hood: Freedom's Outlaw*, and *Blackthorn - Dynasty of Mars* or by contributing stories to anthologies such as *Sherlock Holmes: Consulting Detective volumes 1-4*, *Sinbad: The New Voyages*, *Grand Central Noir*, *The Spider: Extreme Prejudice*, *Monster Earth*, and *The New Adventures of Richard Knight*. His first non-fiction book, *Where Stories Dwell*, is due out soon. A full list of his publications, free samples, and some complete short stories are available at http://www.chillwater.org.uk/writing/

UP SHIP!

I wish I could tell you when I first saw a photo of an old airship but that memory is lost in history. What I do know is, whatever the circumstances, that singular image imprinted itself on my soul forever. Unlike conventional aircraft with wings and propellers, here was a giant, mighty gas-filled balloon floating through the clouds so smoothly it truly was akin to the poetry of a sailboat as opposed to the driving force of a motorized craft (Yes, I know airships are also propelled through the clouds via mechanical engines, but they still look way cooler than airplanes).

Along the road, aside from still pictures, I began to see film clips of early Zeppelins, whether real or models constructed for movie adventures. Republic Studio, the champs of my favorite serial cliffhangers, often showcased wonderful airships in their weekly melodramas and believe me, I was enthralled by all of them.

Enough so that by the time pal Rob Davis and I had this crazy idea to launch a pulp publishing enterprise, the idea for a company name didn't take all that long to come up with. I'd already been using Airship 27 as my personal e-mail address so it was a logical step to make it the company title. And then Rob went out and designed our logo much to my delight and those of our soon to be Loyal Airmen supporters.

And still, you would think with all this attention to dirigibles etc. we would long ago have launched a series around the theme of airships. You would think. Chuckle. Oh, there was a germ of a thought far in the back of my mind, but somehow there were always other projects and series that would come along to keep it on the back burner. Then, just a short while ago, writer-pal, Frank Schildiner, asked me flat out: "How come an outfit called Airship 27 doesn't have a series about airships?" And of course I didn't have a reasonable answer for him either than, "Well…I always thought one of these days…"

It was the final push required. "One of these days…" had finally arrived. The excuses were no longer valid and the time had come to get this series born. I put out the word to our stable of writers and within a week Jim Beard had offered up a wonderful short action piece that he hopes will be a regular series and the amazing Ian Watson turned in an entire novella that, quite frankly, blew me away. And that was it, volume one was done. Happily, artist Pedro Cruz, signed on next to do the interior illos and

England's own Mike Fyles whipped up a stunning cover based on a scene in Ian's story.

We had issue #1 of AIRSHIP 27—ZEPPELEN TALES ready to launch. Leaving this captain with only one thing left to say….

"UP SHIP!"

Ron Fortier
10/24/2013
Fort Collins, CO
(www.Airship27.com)

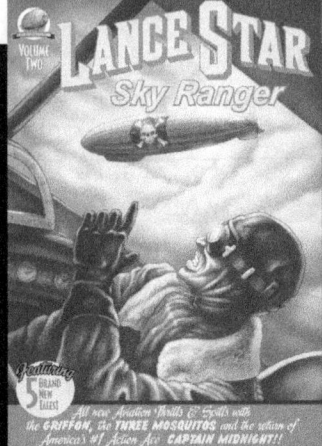

www.ingramcontent.com/pod-product-compliance
Lightning Source LLC
Chambersburg PA
CBHW071239250626
47163CB00001B/250